THE CHRISTMAS DOG SITTERS

LUCY MITCHELL

BLOODHOUND BOOKS

First published in 2024 by Bloodhound Books.

www.bloodhoundbooks.com

Print ISBN: 978-1-917214-52-0

For Sue and Catherine

PROLOGUE
AUGUST

'It's time to get you smiling again, Rachel.' Olivia, her face shiny and sweaty in the oppressive August heat, grinned at me from across the living room.

Olivia and I, plus our two friends, Kate and Connor, were all sat sweltering in vests, shorts and flip-flops. Kate, Olivia and I had strategically positioned ourselves next to the three electric fans dotted around the room and Connor had a cold flannel draped across his face.

'I am smiling,' I replied, holding up the corners of my mouth and at the same time trying to forget about seeing my ex-boyfriend, Sam and his new fiancée kissing on a blanket in the park. The painful image had been seared onto the backs of my eyelids so there was no escape from it.

We had gone to the park to sunbathe. Our trip had been brought to an abrupt halt after I'd caught sight of Sam and Chantelle locked in a passionate embrace. I had seen them together a few times since Sam and I split up. In a cruel twist of fate, Chantelle had recently moved to a flat near me. However, the sightings – up until now – had consisted of them holding hands walking down a street or standing close to each other in a bar. Those sightings I could handle as they were always fully clothed, and I could swiftly turn away.

It was seeing her lying on top of my ex-boyfriend in a skimpy bikini and them both locked in a passionate kiss that sent me over the edge. I don't think they realised I was near them.

Tearful and frustrated, I grabbed my towel, shades and suntan cream. 'I can't sit here; I am going home.' My loyal friends packed up their stuff and came with me.

Olivia shook her head. 'Sam took away your smile last Christmas. You'll be glad to know I've had one of my brainwaves about getting it back.'

In the two years Olivia and I had been flatmates, our friendship had been punctuated with these grand lightbulb moments of hers. Some of her brainwaves were amazing – the surprise holiday to Spain last summer after a friend of hers let us stay in his fancy villa for free; the unplanned girlie road trip to Brighton after I'd been made redundant and the many spa weekends she organised.

Some of her ideas we still laughed about – her dyeing my eyebrows bright orange by mistake; the time we climbed out of a pub toilet window so she could avoid someone she disliked and got stuck whilst she nearly wet herself with laughter; and the pink inflatable boat that got us carried away on a rip tide, leading to a rescue by a handsome lifeguard on a jet ski.

And a few of her suggestions, like the twenty-mile cycle ride for charity, were unforgettable for all the wrong reasons. My body still hadn't forgiven me for that bike ride. I've been a stranger to strenuous exercise since I cancelled my gym membership two years ago. Olivia, a keen cyclist, thought we both only needed a week to train. As the charity bike nightmare was still fresh in my mind (Olivia kept pointing out that I was still walking in an odd manner) my initial reaction to this brainwave was... panic.

'We are supposed to be talking about ideas for my first date with the hot waiter,' Connor said, lifting his cold flannel. On the way back to our flat Connor had revealed the waiter from our favourite Italian restaurant had finally agreed to go on a date with him. I sensed Connor was keen to take my mind off the park sighting; so he'd suggested a brainstorming session on locations for his first date.

'Connor, we will come back to you, I promise,' explained Olivia, before turning her attention back on me. 'A male friend of mine is venturing onto the dating scene.'

I let out a groan that made both Connor and Kate laugh.

Olivia continued. 'He would be perfect for you, Rachel. I'm going to set you up on a blind date.'

Kate, also single, raised her hands. 'Whoa... what's this man like and why does Rachel get first dibs?'

'Blind dates never end well,' interjected Connor, removing his flannel. 'My ex-boyfriend and I met on a blind date and look what happened there – heartbreak and eternal misery for me. The sexy waiter down the road is my glimmer of hope.'

Olivia ignored both Kate and Connor. 'I can't believe I haven't done this sooner. Rachel, you and my friend are a match made in heaven.' She patted the seat next to her. 'Come and watch me message the man of your dreams.'

'You don't have to do this,' I moaned. 'I'm taking a break from men after what happened with Sam.'

We'd been dating for eight months when he revealed on Christmas Eve that he'd been cheating on me. It had been incredibly painful as I'd thought we would be together until we were old and crinkly. I'd also become emotionally attached to his little boy, Rupert. Whenever we picked Rupert up from primary school, he would come racing out with a painting of his dad and me. In Rupert's paintings my long brown hair would always be touching the floor and Sam's dark red hair would always be vibrant orange.

I had been getting ready to travel to Aunty Karen's for Christmas when Sam's car pulled up outside my flat. I'd raced downstairs buzzing with festive excitement thinking he and Rupert had come to exchange gifts. As soon as he got out of the car, I knew something was wrong. My eyes flicked to the woman in the passenger seat. 'I'm sorry, Rachel,' Sam said, in my doorway. 'That's Chantelle in my car.' He paused and ran a hand through his hair. 'I'm so sorry about this...'

He stopped and bowed his head. 'We've been seeing each other.'

'Seeing each other?' I gasped. 'What do you mean?'

Looking back, I don't know why I asked that stupid question. Chantelle joined his sales firm last year. Looking back her arrival had coincided with the start of his extra late nights working at the office. Whenever I asked him why he needed to work so late he'd say Chantelle needed a lot of extra coaching. He'd clearly been giving her more than on-the-job coaching.

'We're going to spend Christmas with her parents,' he mumbled before I slammed the door in his face.

My Christmas at Aunty Karen's house was spent trying not to cry into my roast dinner and being told by my mother to look cheerful.

Olivia shook her head and scrolled through her phone apps. 'You haven't smiled properly in months. It's time to sort you out, Rachel.'

Connor nodded. 'Rachel, do what Olivia says. You can thank her at your future wedding.'

Kate went to sit on the rug. 'Come on, Olivia, we need details on Rachel's blind date.'

'He lives in Surrey so they might have to meet in London.'

'What's he called?' Connor asked, laying his cold flannel back over his face.

'Ben,' Olivia replied, opening WhatsApp. She paused before taking a breath and saying, 'You know my friend Sophie? Well he was her boyfriend.' We all went silent as she wiped her cheek. Olivia had mentioned Sophie a few times but had never gone into detail. The loss of her best friend to cancer six years ago was still a difficult subject for her.

Connor was the first to speak. He lifted his flannel and stared at Olivia. 'Is Ben in the right frame of mind for romance?'

Olivia nodded. 'Ben is in a good place now. He wants to find love again.'

Connor cast me a worried glance and when Olivia wasn't looking, I shook my head. This wasn't going to happen. The thought of dating her late best friend's boyfriend made me feel uncomfortable. 'Olivia, I'm not keen on this idea.'

'Do you have a photo of him?' Kate asked. Olivia ignored my objection. 'Ben's quite shy. He's one of those annoying people who lurk at the back when photos are being taken. I have a few, but they're not great and they're from years ago when he had long hair.'

'Is he good-looking?' Connor asked. 'Can we do a Facebook or Instagram stalk of this chap?'

I frowned at Connor who quickly placed his flannel back over his face. It didn't matter what Ben looked like because this crazy idea of Olivia's was not happening.

Olivia shook her head. 'Ben's not on there.'

Out of the corner of my eye, I could see Connor casting me an anxious look whilst lifting one of the corners of his flannel.

'Can we talk about something else?' I asked, feeling a little awkward.

Olivia was still tapping out a message to Ben. 'He's a bit

rough around the edges. Outdoorsy type of man. Brown hair, tall, with stubble although I think that's because he can't be bothered to shave.' She turned to me. 'How do you two want to contact each other to arrange the blind date?'

'Uh... I don't know,' I mumbled. 'Olivia, I don't want to go on this blind date.' This was going way too fast for my liking. I wasn't even sure I was into a man who was rough around the edges, either. Sam was the exact opposite. Everything about him was carefully curated – from his hair with the gelled quiff that took him an hour in the bathroom every morning, to his crisp-all-white trainers which he paired with a stylish black suit and a white T-shirt. 'Can I think about this?'

Olivia shook her head. 'I don't know why but I'm getting a weird sense of urgency with this.'

Connor lifted his flannel and winked at me. 'Olivia is going to write about you and Ben in her next romance book.' We all looked over at the pink vintage typewriter in the corner of the room. By day Olivia worked in advertising and by night she sat over by her typewriter and wrote spicy novels that she self-published on Amazon. She enjoyed using our respective dating experiences as fodder for her novels. When one of us was dumped or cheated on, Olivia added the love rat in question to one of her novels. Connor said he found it very therapeutic reading about his ex-boyfriend. Olivia turned him into a nasty villain and he died in a sword fight against the handsome, swashbuckling hero.

After Sam broke up with me, Olivia penned her first spicy thriller and a character called Sam had an unfortunate and troubling death.

Olivia nudged me. 'How can Ben contact you?'

'Ummm... I don't want to go on a blind date with him.'

Olivia grinned as she tapped out a message. 'He's going to

email you.' She pulled me into a hug. 'This is going to be great, and I want a mention at your wedding.'

Leaping up she went to the kitchen and brought back the bottle of fizzy cheap wine, cool from the fridge, and four plastic cups. The strong smell of her vanilla perfume filled the hot, stuffy flat air and gave our nostrils respite from our sweaty aromas. She'd obviously had a quick spray while getting the wine. 'Let's have a toast to the future Rachel and Ben.'

As she poured us all a glass, I decided that I wouldn't reply to his email. He'd get bored soon enough.

Connor sat up and dramatically threw away his flannel. 'Olivia, please have a brainwave about where I can take the hot waiter on a date?'

After a few glasses of wine and some suggestions on locations for Connor's first date, we forgot about the heat, my blind date and soon we were all dancing around the living room to Harry Styles' latest album. As Olivia and I collapsed in a sweaty heap on the sofa, she said, 'I can't wait to see you smiling again.'

'You don't need to fix me up with Ben to make me smile.'

She grinned. 'I like helping the people I love. Trust me on this.'

'I'm not doing it.'

She laughed. 'You said that after I'd told you about the charity bike ride.'

CHAPTER ONE

DECEMBER

'We're all worried about you,' revealed Maddie, my sister, handing me a generous slice of luxury chocolate Yule log. On her way to visit me, she'd stopped at Waitrose and bought us delicious festive goodies to eat. Maddie always came armed with cake and family gossip. Although, this wasn't what I wanted to hear.

'Maddie, I'm fine.'

'Drip, drip, drip.' She surveyed the three plastic buckets in front of us catching the drips from the leaks in the ceiling. The landlord had been promising to fix the ceiling for the past month, but his messy divorce had distracted him. Her gaze fell on the blankets over our laps, as it was colder inside than it was outside, and my greasy hair piled on top of my head in a messy bun. '*Fine* is not the word I'd use, Rachel.'

I said, 'I've even added tinsel to the buckets.'

Maddie gave me her concerned older sister stare. 'It's hard to see you living like this, Rachel. The last few months haven't been easy for you. I mean you've gone through something...'

I raised my hand to stop her. My face was heating up and a

wave of emotion was rising inside of me. 'Don't mention it or I will cry, and my tears will turn this delicious Yule log salty.'

She glanced over my shoulder at the selection of paintings against the wall. 'I see you're painting again.'

'It keeps me sane through all my job rejections.'

'You're not having much luck?'

I shook my head. 'Trying to get another job when Christmas is a few weeks away is not easy. I bet you wish you never came all this way to see me.'

Maddie rolled her eyes. 'Rachel, I would travel anywhere to see you. Oh and... Mum has started a secret family WhatsApp group chat titled *Rachel Needs Our Help*.'

A secret WhatsApp group chat is our family's way of dealing with problems. Before WhatsApp, we solved things by shouting at each other over plates of buffet food at a family social event, a wedding, a christening, an engagement party or at a funeral. We are a large family so there are a lot of these events.

If things were not resolved there would be a slew of lengthy phone calls, which would always result in someone either crying or hanging up in anger. We did try texts and emails, but WhatsApp was the game changer for the Reid family. It gave everyone, regardless of where they lived, a chance to have their say on a troubling matter in real time. And they could convey strong feelings via emojis. Although everyone wished Uncle Robert had not discovered the laughing face emoji as that had become his stock response to everything.

Everyone turns to WhatsApp when a family member becomes 'problematic'. That's how our mother has explained it to Maddie and me. She lives in Tenerife with our stepdad, Gary, and as unofficial head of the family, she likes to keep tabs on us all dotted around the UK and Australia. She creates a secret WhatsApp message chat which excludes the problem family member and everyone else is encouraged to give their views and advice on the situation.

Over the last few years, the family had solved various problems via family WhatsApp group chats. We navigated Uncle Robert's midlife crisis – which consisted of him publicly confessing his love for Aunty Karen's hairdresser.

Then we helped Aunty Flo deal with her rebellious teenage daughter Nadine. Through daily messaging on a secret chat, which excluded Nadine, the family were able to calm Aunty Flo down when Nadine ran away with her boyfriend, who had a penchant for stealing cars, to live with him in a tiny caravan. The family assured Aunty Flo that Nadine liked her home comforts too much and would return once life in the caravan got tough. Three days later Aunty Flo cheerfully informed the family that Nadine had come back hungry, tear-stained, clutching a load of dirty washing, and saying she never wanted to see another caravan or the boyfriend again for as long as she lived.

Recently the family WhatsApp chats had been about Aunty Bev. Mum had four sisters and Bev was the one who they all believed was the most 'problematic'. Every week Mum would set up a new thread titled, *Bev's Out of Control... AGAIN!*

The whole family, excluding Aunty Bev, would pile in with comments and suggestions on how to stop fifty-five-year-old Aunty Bev from going on crazy nights out, having an eye-watering number of male lovers, being tagged into saucy hot tub parties on Facebook and wasting a lot of money on expensive hair extensions. Even distant cousins in Australia voiced their opinions on how to control Aunty Bev, which I had always found extraordinary.

'Wow,' I said. 'I feel honoured to have made it into the Secret Family WhatsApp Hall of Fame. What's everyone said about me?'

Maddie took out her phone from the Mulberry handbag beside her and opened WhatsApp. 'Aunty Flo thinks grief can be cured by taking one of her fish oil supplements. Uncle Kevin doesn't believe you're grieving. He thinks you're really on drugs. Apparently, there was an article in the *Daily Mail* about increased drug use amongst people in their thirties. Aunty Polly has suggested you take up belly dancing. She says her neighbour was suffering from a low mood and they took up belly dancing. That neighbour now has a permanent smile on their face. Fay thinks you eat too much sugar. And Aunty Karen is worried you will turn into Aunty Bev.'

'How does Fay know I eat too much sugar when she lives on the other side of the world?'

Fay, our older cousin, is Aunty Polly's daughter. We were not close as kids. She emigrated to Australia after getting a nursing job. She's a regular on the family WhatsApp and always has a lot to say about everyone's lives. The time difference isn't a problem as Fay works nights and judging by how long she spends analysing family issues, she doesn't have a lot of nursing to do. When Fay is not on WhatsApp, she stalks everyone's Facebook and Instagram posts.

My sister grinned. 'Oh, and Uncle Robert thinks you might be pregnant. He also added a laughing face emoji.'

I rolled my eyes at Uncle Robert's input. 'Have you ever had a secret family WhatsApp group chat created about you?'

Maddie shook her head. 'No, although sometimes I wonder if I have missed out by not being the topic of a secret WhatsApp chat.'

'You could have had one about you last year,' I said, with a wink.

She smiled, reached out and covered my hand with hers. 'Still eternally grateful for what you did.'

'I'd do anything for you, Maddie, you know that.' I squeezed her hand.

We nibbled at our Yule log slices. 'Got any plans for Christmas?' Maddie asked.

Christmas Day for me would be spent rotating and emptying my plastic buckets, microwaving myself a supermarket Christmas dinner, and probably crying a lot about the empty space next to me on the sofa and the lonely pink typewriter over in the corner of the room.

'To get through it,' I said, blinking away stinging tears.

CHAPTER TWO

'Do you remember those amazing Christmases we had with Grandpa Eric and Nana Edith when we were kids?' Maddie had sensed it was time to change the subject.

A weak smile forced its way onto my face as I remembered spending Christmas with Nana and Grandpa. Mum used to be an air hostess. She got the job after Dad walked out and left us for a woman in Glasgow. Maddie and I would be left with our grandparents for several weeks at a time whilst she jetted off to the other side of the world. As Dad's parents had passed away a few years before, all childcare was down to Grandpa Eric and Nana Edith.

Mum dealt with her marital breakdown by flying to far-flung lands with her job and partying with her much younger cabin crew, as opposed to looking after us, her children. For seven consecutive years, Maddie and I spent a lot of time with Grandpa Eric and Nana Edith. No matter where Mum was in the world or how long she had been away, our grandparents would always made sure Christmas was a special time.

'Rushing downstairs on Christmas morning to find Grandpa dressed up as Santa Clause,' I reminisced. 'Complete with a gigantic stick-on white beard, a red jacket, huge black boots and a sack of presents slung over his shoulder. He'd always pretend we'd caught him in the act of delivering gifts. I loved how he always claimed his sleigh was on the roof and if we listened quietly, we could hear Rudolph making reindeer sounds. I never heard him.'

Maddie nodded. 'Nor me. Remember Nana's legendary roast beef and her Yorkshire puddings which would be so big they'd take up the entire plate?'

My mouth began to water at that delicious memory. 'Her roast beef dinners were unforgettable. What about her home-made mince pies and her Christmas chocolate stash in the pantry?'

'We'd eat so much chocolate before breakfast on Christmas morning.'

I chuckled. 'Dancing to Christmas songs with Grandpa by the tree, opening our presents but being more interested in Nana's fancy wrapping paper and going out at night to wish the stars a happy Christmas.'

Maddie beamed. 'Playing boardgames and cards with them both in the afternoon and Grandpa would win at everything.'

I laughed. 'He'd happily beat us at cards, bankrupt us at Monopoly and wish us a merry Christmas.'

Maddie twirled one of her blonde curls around her finger. 'Our cousins missed out. I can't remember any of them ever getting the chance to spend Christmas with Nana and Grandpa.'

'Grandpa once told me, you and I were their favourite grandchildren.'

Maddie began to giggle. 'Really?'

I nodded. 'He told me once Fay was "hard work", but I was a kid, so I didn't know what he meant.'

We both began to laugh, and Maddie picked up her phone.

'I found this old photo the other day of you and Grandpa.' She showed me the screen. I looked at Grandpa's sweet face, his twinkly blue eyes and his short dark hair that had started to turn silvery. A seven-year-old version of me was sat on his lap. We were both sticking out our tongues at the camera whilst wearing wonky Christmas paper hats. The photo flooded my body with some much-needed warmth.

'Aunty Karen says she must see Grandpa every day now.'

I stared at Maddie in shock. 'The last time I saw Grandpa he was fine. He was his usual cheery self, and he didn't act like he needed looking after. He burst out of his shed with such energy and pulled me into one of his huge hugs. I made him some food and we chatted before sneaking to the pub together.'

'Did Aunty Karen know you had taken him to the pub?'

'Aunty Karen was too busy getting a cut and colour at her local hair salon.'

Maddie shrugged. 'That was in the summer, Rachel. Maybe he's declined since then. Remember he's eighty now. People at that age go downhill rapidly. He's probably missing Nana Edith.' She placed her phone in her lap.

Our beloved nana died ten years ago leaving Grandpa to fend for himself. The death of Nana Edith had left a crater in all our hearts, especially Grandpa's.

'Well, Grandpa and I email each other every couple of weeks, and he still seems himself,' I say, recalling his latest email – he spent much of it moaning about Aunty Karen and Uncle Robert.

My eyes flicked to Maddie's phone. The photo of Grandpa and me was no longer on the screen. It had been replaced by a photo from years ago that featured a young man smiling at the camera. The face looked familiar, and it wasn't her husband Frank. It was Josh, her ex-boyfriend whom she dated when she was at uni. When they split up, she always used to say he was the nice one who had got away. She noticed me staring at her phone and fumbled with it.

'Why have you got a photo of Josh on your phone?'

Two rosy, pink circles bloomed over her cheeks. 'I was down memory lane and it popped up.' She turned to me and dropped her phone into her handbag. 'Look, I have a favour to ask.'

'Oh... a favour – interesting,' I said.

She reached out and rubbed my arm. 'I think it might help you and get you smiling again.'

My sister's words reminded me of Olivia. That was the phrase she liked to use after Sam dumped me. My breathing quickened, tears rushed to my eyes and my brain kindly played a showreel of everything that had gone wrong since he'd confessed to cheating on me with Chantelle.

'Hey, come on,' soothed Maddie, giving my arm a rub. 'I didn't want to make you upset.'

A loud sob escaped from my lips, and Maddie's face went blurry. 'My life took a downward turn after Sam. Flossy the Cat was put down, I was made redundant and Oli...' I tried to say her name, but I dissolved into tears. Maddie threw her arms around me. By the time I'd finished weeping into her shoulder, there was a huge damp mark on her cashmere cardigan, along with an intricate pattern of cake crumbs.

She handed me my box of tissues. 'Dry your eyes.'

I dabbed at my eyes. 'Sorry, one minute I'm okay and the next I am weeping.'

Maddie nodded. 'You need to listen to what I have to say. How do you fancy going on an all-expenses three-week holiday over Christmas?'

I cast her a puzzled look. 'Abroad?'

She shook her head of blonde curls which were so perfect and bouncy they gave the impression she'd stepped out of a hair salon. 'No. It will be a UK trip.'

'Where?'

Taking a bunch of her golden curls she secured them behind her ear. 'Frank is taking me to Malibu for Christmas and New Year.'

A year ago, Maddie had married Frank, a retired film actor and now a wealthy businessman, after a whirlwind romance. The way Maddie met Frank was like something out of a romance novel. She flew to New York and interviewed him – the CEO of this new promising media company – for the finance magazine she used to work for. After the interview, he asked her out for dinner. The next day he cleared his schedule and spent the day showing her around Manhattan. They started dating a week later as he flew her back to New York for dinner. Their wedding, which followed a few months of dating, was spectacular. It had taken the Reid family a while to recover from the lavish event and the free bar. Mum had claimed her hangover had lasted a week.

Following their wedding Frank took Maddie back to the States to live in California with him, but she had become unhappy after a few months. So he agreed to return with her to the UK. He bought a large country house in a little Surrey village called Harp Brook and filled it with beautiful and expensive things.

'Wow – you're going to Malibu for three weeks?'

Maddie nodded. 'Yes. I need someone to look after Humphrey over Christmas. As you know, my darling little dog still hasn't recovered from when Aunty Flo cared for him. Will you come, and dog sit for us? I don't want strangers looking after Humphrey. He can be a handful at times.'

I thought about Humphrey, my sister's beloved chocolate-coloured spaniel. The word 'handful' didn't accurately describe Humphrey. He had an endless amount of energy and should have been called *Houdini* given the number of times he escaped and ran away. When Maddie left to go live in America, Aunty Flo adopted Humphrey. She claimed the dog nearly drove her into an early grave as he went missing so many times during the few months Maddie was in America. She still joked that at one point she kept reusing the same *Missing Dog* poster.

'I don't think he's forgiven me for making him live with Aunty Flo.' Maddie ate a piece of Yule log and I thought about her offer. 'What is the likelihood of Humphrey escaping whilst you are away?'

'It won't happen. Frank has had the best high fencing erected around the back of the house.'

She flicked her eyes to the coffee table before I could arch my brows at her. 'What about the front of the house?'

Maddie let out a nervous laugh. 'Rachel, we're not going to turn the house in Fort Knox because of my dog. He'll be fine. I think now he's turned four he's calming down.'

'Calming down?' I stared at her in bewilderment. She flicked her blonde curls and inspected her pink nails.

We both knew Humphrey would do a disappearing act on me over Christmas.

CHAPTER THREE

'You're asking me to stay in your big house with Humphrey over Christmas?'

Maddie nodded. 'Just you and Humphrey. Oh, Frank and I fly next weekend.'

'Me – stay in your big new country house over Christmas? The same house that you and Frank don't fully live in because you don't want to spoil it.'

Their new manor house was split into two – the east wing and the west wing, as my sister referred to it. She and Frank lived in the east wing. They never entered the west wing because, strangely, Maddie claimed it was too beautiful to live in.

'How's married life?'

Something flashed across my sister's face. 'He wants us to...' She stopped.

'To what?'

She cast me a weak smile. 'To have a baby.'

'Oh... I see. How do you feel about that?'

Maddie let out a nervous laugh. 'I'll be fine. All relationships are a trade-off – aren't they?'

'Having kids is a big decision, Maddie. I wouldn't call it a trade-off.'

She sat up straighter and smiled. 'Ignore me. It's not going to be much of a holiday for Frank. He's trying to buy out that TV and film production company. Remember the one I told you about?'

'Yes, the American one which makes tearjerker movies? I tried to sit through that film you suggested I watch. After both the husband and the family dog died in the house fire and the much-loved grandmother got told she had some awful disease, I was a mess, so I stopped watching it.'

'You didn't get far with it then?'

I shook my head. 'Eight minutes.'

'This film company will add to Frank's growing media company empire.'

'When Frank takes over this film production company – will he get them to move away from making heart-warming tearjerkers?'

Maddie smiled at my description. 'Frank calls them wholesome and uplifting family films but you're right they're heart-warming tearjerkers. Anyway, this deal is consuming him right now and it's all he talks about. He barely sleeps as he's up in the night talking to his legal team back in the States.'

I thought about her offer. It would be a break from the constant dripping sounds, and if I was going to be sad and miserable over Christmas, I might as well do it in luxury surroundings. 'I suppose staying at yours will be better than staying here.'

'Exactly,' beamed Maddie. 'Humphrey will be over the moon. Oh, and don't worry about food. We will make sure the fridge and wine rack are fully stocked. Frank has also splashed out on a tree and decorations.' She squeezed my hand. 'You need a break. Oh, and Mum's not coming home for Christmas.

Gary wants them both to stay in Tenerife. He's invited his friends out there. She was nervous about telling you, so she put it on WhatsApp. Both Aunty Flo and Aunty Karen suggested I break the news to you.'

'I wouldn't have got upset if Mum had told me she wasn't coming home.'

'The family disagreed.'

'I'm thirty-two years of age. I am not going to dissolve if Mum decides to stay in Tenerife over Christmas.'

Maddie rubbed my arm. 'I told them you'd be fine. Mum thinks you need some family love.'

'What's she up to?' I arched my eyebrows at Maddie. If you knew our mother, you'd know how she would only start talking about "love" when she wanted something.

Maddie giggled. 'Stop it – Mum could be entering her caring era.'

'Worrying,' I said, nibbling a piece of chocolate log.

'There will be rules of course. The west wing will be out of bounds as we have a lot of expensive stuff in there. So, can I pencil you in for an all-expenses paid dog-sitting festive holiday? You'll need to be at ours for next weekend.'

'Yes, you can. Tell Humphrey there will be trouble if he's naughty.'

'No telling Humphrey off, Rachel,' Maddie said, picking her phone back up. 'He doesn't like being told what to do.'

As she began tapping something into her phone, I silently vowed to give Humphrey a masterclass in good dog behaviour.

'Will you be all right travelling down on Saturday?' Maddie asked as she rose from the sofa. 'We will cover your petrol costs.' She smiled and ran her hands over her fitted designer blue jeans. 'You remember how to get to the house?'

I nodded. 'It's on the outskirts of Harp Brook village. Down a little lane after the pub and after a half mile I come to a little row of cottages. The iron gates which lead to your house are a few yards after them.'

'Wow, you have a great memory and you've only been there a few times,' beamed Maddie.

'Have you made friends with the locals yet?' I asked, getting up from the sofa to check the water level in one of the buckets. It wasn't too bad.

'Frank hates them,' said Maddie. 'They don't like him either. When we first moved in, he did everything he could to make friends. Now we mostly stay in the house.'

'I'm sure the people of Harp Brook would love you both once they got to know you.' I went to sit back on the sofa.

Maddie leaned against the window frame. 'Frank has decided we need our privacy. We rarely leave the house.'

I glanced at my sister who was staring out of my flat window, and I got that familiar knot of worry in my tummy. Frank was the dream wealthy husband who showered her with designer clothes, sun-drenched holidays in Malibu, new cars, and luxury homes. Maddie lived a fairy-tale life. But for a while I'd sensed something in the paradise life they'd created wasn't quite right.

The Maddie stood by my window and the Maddie two years ago before Frank came along were two different people.

Before she met Frank, Maddie was lively and sociable. She was the centre of her little community in Northwest London and would always be at someone's house party, summer barbeque, having an impromptu coffee morning or raising money for her community. Her social media would be ablaze with photos of her mingling at a barbeque, or a birthday party or grinning with a small army of charity gardening volunteers. I couldn't recall the last time Maddie had told me she'd been out with her old friends. All she did now was stay inside her luxury home and she never used her social media anymore.

I could never tell Mum I was worried about Maddie's marriage as she would first scream down the phone at me, call for Gary to make her a new cocktail to calm her nerves and then lecture me on what a bloody good catch Frank was and how my sister would never have to struggle financially, like she did when Dad left us.

'Maddie, don't you miss strolling into town, going for a coffee or a pub lunch, bumping into some friends and having a nose in some local shops?'

Maddie shrugged, wandered around my living room and came to a stop at my makeshift Olivia shrine. I'd covered a little table with photos and personal things which reminded me of Olivia and made me feel she was still with me in some way. Maddie lifted one of the photo frames and smiled. It was the photo of Olivia and me at a line dancing event. Olivia had seen the event advertised and had one of her lightbulb moments – we both needed to experience line dancing. The next night we both dressed up as cowgirls and pulled two handsome cowboys – well... two lads from Brighton with rubbish American accents.

Two years ago, Olivia applied to be my flatmate. I didn't know her before that. We hit it off the second we met. Her flat-share interview started in the kitchen over a coffee and ended many hours later in a cocktail bar after a lot of dancing, squealing, and chatting. We had the same sense of humour, the same taste in men and I loved how she wrote novels in her spare time. I'd also never met someone who enjoyed talking as much as I did. In a matter of weeks, we went from strangers to flatmates to – as she put it – 'soul sisters'.

Maddie peered underneath the table at Olivia's pink vintage typewriter, along with a pile of her self-published novels. 'My favourite is the regency romance where the duke falls from his horse into an icy river and is saved by a beautiful maiden who nurses him back to health in her little cottage in the woods. Oh, my goodness, I was an emotional mess by the end when he goes back to find her.'

Pulling my knees into my chest, I wished Olivia could hear Maddie's unofficial book review.

My mind brought back that awful day at the end of September when two police officers came to my flat to inform me Olivia had been in a road accident. She'd been cycling to work and she collided with a car. Paramedics tried to save her at the side of the road, but nothing could be done. It was one of the worst days of my life.

Maddie touched Olivia's pink coffee travel mug, which I had kept. 'Whenever I came to visit, Olivia would always appear carrying this. Sometimes I wondered whether it was surgically attached to her hand.'

I smiled and blinked away tears. Maddie came to perch on the sofa arm. 'It must be hard living in this flat with all your memories of her and your dripping ceiling. Have you thought of finding somewhere new to live?'

'If I moved away, I wouldn't feel close to her.'

I felt my sister's warm hand on my shoulder.

'If I am honest, Maddie, the shrine for her over there is not working. I don't feel close to Olivia here, but I'm giving it time.'

'Rachel, I know you don't want to, and I get that it still hurts like hell, and you want to stay close to her, but you do have to move on with your life.'

'I'll think about it in the new year.'

Maddie continued. 'You're not tied to a job right now so you could go anywhere.'

'Yes, good point,' I mumbled.

'Why don't you leave project management and go back into catering?'

Years ago, after leaving college with an array of catering and cooking qualifications. I started a small mobile catering company. I turned an old blue camper van into a mini kitchen, and I made and sold food at festivals and weddings. I gave it up as it didn't make much money and Mum kept nagging me to get a proper job.

The idea did awaken something inside of me. Maybe I could go back to what I once loved. My mind reminded me of Mum's five-year job change nagging campaign. 'That would result in Mum setting up another WhatsApp chat about me and I would never hear the end of it.'

She nodded. 'How are things... romantically?'

'Non-existent. I blame Sam for cheating on me last Christmas.'

Maddie checked the time on her phone. 'I better be getting back. Remember to be at ours on Saturday morning. We leave at noon. Frank will give you a lecture on the house rules.'

I patted her on the arm. 'He doesn't need to do that. I know the rules. You're right about me needing a break.'

'Oh, and we now have a cleaner who will be coming in every few days. Frank also has a builder working on the new kitchen. The builder will be there. I'm sorry.'

'Will I be able to cook food?'

Maddie laughed. 'The new kitchen is being built on the end of the old one. Frank has kept the old kitchen, but he has said eventually it will become a playroom.'

My sister fiddled with her gigantic engagement rock and her wedding band. 'I'll get pregnant. We'll go back to live in the States so I can have the baby over there. Frank thinks the healthcare is better.'

'Living over there made you sad.' I reached out and touched my sister's arm. Her blue eyes were watery.

'It will be all right. He says I can split my time between here and the States.'

That familiar knot in my stomach returned.

'Thanks, Rachel, for the dog sitting. You can chill out and relax. Humphrey loves you so he will be thrilled. I told Frank you'd be the perfect dog sitter. Good as gold and no trouble.'

CHAPTER FOUR

'It's great you're going away for Christmas,' Kate said, as we sat in her car, and waited for Connor. We'd told him to be ready for ten in the morning. It was half past ten. Connor was always late. Olivia used to say Connor lived in a different time zone which was always half an hour behind everyone else. If Connor had been early, Kate and I would have worried about him.

Kate and I were rubbing our gloved hands to warm them up. My face was numb with cold, and I'd lost all feeling in my nose. Kate's car heater was struggling against the plummeting temperature. Overnight the Met Office had issued a slew of weather warnings about the arctic conditions causing havoc in the UK.

'It is, but I'm worried about Maddie.' I'd not slept properly since my sister had left a few days ago. That last conversation we'd had where she spoke about Frank wanting them to have a baby and them having to go back to living in America was on replay in my head. The way she'd looked at me had left me feeling uncomfortable.

Maddie had always been the golden child; excelling at school from a young age, gaining an array of impressive GCSEs and A-levels, going to a top university, securing an enviable job writing for a top finance magazine and marrying someone as high profile and wealthy as Frank. I loved her dearly and I'd learned from a young age that there was no point in being jealous of Maddie's achievements. She outshone everyone. This was a good thing. For many years Maddie took away my mother's focus on me which was a blessing. I got to do all the things as a teenager that Maddie was never allowed to do; go to parties with boys, drink cider, smoke cigarettes out of my bedroom window, go to music festivals, leave school with a collection of dismal GCSES, go to a local college and then leave to set up a mini catering business in a camper van.

However, through all this, Maddie and I were still close. She would always want to know everything about the parties I'd been to, the festivals I'd danced the night away at and the handsome young men I'd served hot dogs to.

'Have you spoken to her since she visited?' Kate asked. I'd updated her and Connor about Maddie's visit once she'd gone back to Harp Brook.

'I've messaged her a lot, but she tells me she's busy and promises we will talk before she goes on holiday.'

Kate blew into her gloved hands. 'Maybe she's worried about having kids. It's a big thing.'

I nodded. 'Maybe. I just know there's something she's not telling me. Anyway, I will be dog sitting Humphrey for three weeks over Christmas in Harp Brook and he will keep me busy,' I said, through chattering teeth. 'Frank and Maddie are off to Malibu so he can do some mega business deal with a film company.'

Kate smiled. 'Please tell me she has trained her naughty dog?'

I shook my head. 'Don't be silly. The day my sister disciplines that lunatic of a dog, pigs will be seen flying across the sky. Maddie said Frank will give me a lecture on their house rules when I arrive.'

Kate checked her pink face in the driver's mirror. Her gigantic purple bobble hat made me smile. A year ago, she'd taken up knitting during the lunch breaks of her stressful advertising job. At first, knitting was a way to reduce her soaring anxiety levels. She was mainly anxious due to a toxic boss and a ridiculous workload.

But the knitting soon became the catalyst for change. While she knitted hats, scarves and cardigans, Kate began to think about her life and how unhealthy it felt. After two bobble hats, four scarves and a cardigan, Kate handed in her notice at work. Three months later Kate was the new manager of a craft shop in town, selling wool, embroidery kits, ribbon, knitting patterns and an array of fabrics and materials.

Underneath her purple hat, her long blonde hair had been put into two schoolgirl plaits, each tied with sparkly purple ribbon from her shop. 'I wonder if Frank has hidden cameras set up,' she said, casting me an inquisitive look.

'Knowing Frank, he probably has. I'll ask Maddie.'

Kate threw a mischievous grin at me. 'Send me pics of the west wing.'

'I'm going to be a good house and dog sitter,' I explained. 'Something is going on with Maddie and I don't want to cause her any bother. She has told me everything in their country house is hideously expensive and you know how clumsy I can be. If they want me to live in the east wing all by myself then so be it. I'm going to chill and relax.'

'Don't you think keeping to the east wing is a bit boring?' Kate asked. 'I mean you're doing them a favour by dog sitting and they'll be hundreds of miles away. If he doesn't have hidden cameras, I think you should go wherever you fancy.'

'I don't want to get Maddie in trouble with Frank.'

Kate shrugged. 'The important thing is that you will be getting a break, Rachel.' She stared at her frosted windscreen. 'If Connor doesn't hurry up, all my hard work earlier to clear the windscreen of ice will be wasted.'

It was the day we had all been dreading – Olivia's birthday. She would have been thirty-three. This was the first birthday without her. Both Kate and Connor had booked the day off work so we could celebrate her birthday.

Connor yanked open the back door and climbed in. 'Morning both. Bloody freezing, isn't it?'

'Why did it take you so long?' Kate asked, grinning at him via the rear-view mirror.

'I was doing my hair and trying to find one of Olivia's romance books,' explained Connor.

'Why?' Kate and I both said in unison.

He brought one out of his pocket. 'I thought it would be nice to read from it.'

Kate and I spun around in our car seats to stare at him. 'Olivia hated anyone reading out her writing when she was alive,' I said, recalling Olivia running out of the room and hiding every time someone threatened to read an extract from one of her books.

Connor shrugged and hugged Olivia's romance book to his chest. 'I don't care what you both think. If she's looking down at us from heaven, she will love hearing me bringing her tale to life. You all know I had acting lessons as a child and took to the stage in my youth. Trust me, my reading will be epic.'

'Which book are you reading from?' Kate asked.

A huge grin spread across Connor's face. 'It's my personal favourite. *One Night with The Viking King.*'

'You can't read that out loud in a graveyard,' I screeched. 'Even Olivia said she had gone way too far with the spicy scenes in that book.'

Connor let out a heavy sigh. 'I was planning to read pages one to three. Calm down, Rachel. The saucy Viking King doesn't arrive until Chapter Two.'

'Right, let's stop arguing. What's the plan, Rachel?' Kate asked.

I pointed down the street. 'Olivia loved the coffee from Happy Beans Café, so I want to go and buy her a token birthday coffee.'

'Are we still placing it on her stone?' Connor asked.

'Yes, we are. We all assume the coffee in the afterlife is heavenly, but can you imagine Olivia's horror if it's not nice? She will appreciate our coffee gift.'

Kate started the engine. 'Olivia was our coffee queen and what better way to celebrate her birthday.'

'A vanilla latte and a special reading from one of your novels,' sighed Connor from the back of the car. 'I do hope you're grateful, Olivia. Oh, and if you could ask God to get a top talent scout to pop into your graveyard while I am reading and hear my voice, that would be great. Thanks, babe.'

Once Kate had parked outside Happy Beans Café, I ran inside with both Connor's and Kate's orders. There was a small queue and only one sweaty and flustered barista, so I took out my phone. A text message from Mum had arrived and it read:

Call Me ASAP.

As the barista had not made any progress in reducing the queue I called Mum.

'Thank goodness you've called,' my mother cried upon answering. 'We have a problem. Hang on a sec.' It sounded like she was clicking her fingers. 'Gary, bring me my iced coffee and my ciggies.' Mum cleared her throat. 'Karen doesn't want to care for Grandpa Eric over Christmas as she needs a break.'

'Hello, Mum, how are you?' I asked, which I knew would give her mild irritation. My mother lives life at a hundred miles per hour.

'Rachel, I haven't got time for greetings,' she snapped. 'Grandpa Eric needs to be included in the family's Christmas plans. We're not giving him to Bev as he will end up in a hot tub with a load of unsavoury people, so we have a problem. Has Maddie told you – I am staying in Tenerife this year.'

'Yes, she has. I'm off to Harp Brook to dog sit for her and Frank, so I can't be with Grandpa. Why don't you pay for him to fly over and spend Christmas with you.'

My mother let out a wail of frustration down the phone. 'He's not coming to Tenerife. Good grief, I need to relax. My father drives me insane at the best of times.'

'Well, ask Maddie if she and Frank will take him with them to Malibu.'

I heard a lighter and the noise of Mum sucking on her ciggie. 'Don't be ridiculous, Rachel.'

'I hear Aunty Karen is now caring for Grandpa Eric. When I visited him in the summer, he was amazing. Is he all right?'

Mum sighed. 'He's getting old, Rachel. Karen pops in every day. She says Grandpa is now hard work. I hate to say this, but she's told me some of the stuff he's coming out with, and I think he's losing his marbles.'

'Really? We talk on email a lot. He never sounds like he's confused.'

'Rachel, Grandpa needs to have someone to care for him over Christmas. The family on WhatsApp suggested that *you* look after him. It was your cousin Fay's marvellous idea. She said taking him to Harp Brook would give you some much needed company.' Mum took a glug of her iced coffee.

I recalled Maddie telling me that Fay thought I was consuming too much sugar. Irritation began to nibble away at me. My cousin Fay should stick to coming up with suggestions about her own life in Australia. My heart began to thump. 'Me? Look after Grandpa *and* Maddie's dog over Christmas in Harp Brook?'

'Yes, Rachel.'

The plan to chill out and relax over Christmas was crumbling. Why couldn't Mum come back from Tenerife and look after her father?

'Mum, I am going to Harp Brook for three weeks,' I cried, making the barista turn to see if I was okay. 'That's a long time for me to look after Grandpa and my sister's lunatic dog.'

Mum laughed. 'Rachel, you've got no commitments.' She coughed down the phone. 'You'll have time on your hands. It's also Christmas, an important time for family to be together. You're going through a hard time, and you need your family around you. That's another great thing Fay said on WhatsApp.'

It was then I erupted down the phone at my mother. 'My cousin Fay needs to mind her own business.'

'We're not discussing this,' snapped my mother. 'Robert and Karen have already bought Grandpa a train ticket. They will drop him at the station tomorrow. He'll be arriving at yours at lunchtime. We've booked him a taxi from the station to your flat.'

I recalled getting suspicious of Mum when Maddie told me she thought Mum was going through her caring era. I was right to get suspicious. She'd been planning this. '*Mum!*' I shouted, 'this is not fair. Grandpa can't stay in my flat. I have a leaky ceiling. It's a health hazard.'

'Life isn't fair, Rachel,' hissed my mother, before taking another swig of her iced coffee and a drag on her freshly lit cigarette. 'Do you think I enjoy being away from my wonderful and precious family at Christmas? I will be miles away in Tenerife having to entertain Gary's friends who are coming out here for the festive season. It will be exhausting for me.'

'But you like socialising in Tenerife! That's the main reason you went to live out there. Hang on, other cousins could look after Grandpa Eric.'

She exhaled loudly. 'Fay lives in Australia and we're not sending Grandpa out there. Her sister is about to give birth to twins after Christmas so she can't have Grandpa Eric either.' She took another drag of her cigarette. 'One of your other cousins is backpacking around South America and my sister hasn't heard from him for two weeks. Your eldest cousin has started shoplifting scented candles again and her sister has gone back to Ibiza to live with that divorced DJ – the one who has four children. Your youngest cousin lives in a squalid flat with three other male students and his sister is now a snake breeder. Rachel, do you see why Fay's suggestion of you caring for Grandpa works?'

There wasn't anyone else who could look after Grandpa. 'I suppose you have a point.'

'Grandpa won't mind a few leaks in the ceiling for a night. You can put him in your spare room overnight. Cheaper than a hotel.' In the background, she said to Gary, 'Is it too early for a cocktail? No? Can make you me one? Thanks, it's always a stressful call with Rachel.'

'Mum, I heard that,' I snapped. 'Can we not put Grandpa in a hotel overnight? The spare room is Olivia's bedroom.' My voice crackled. 'I haven't been in there since she...'

'Rachel, your grandfather cannot afford a hotel. He's a pensioner and not made of money,' snapped Mum. 'Why don't you sleep on the sofa?'

The barista had finished my order and was waiting for payment.

'I have to go, Mum.'

'Karen has created a WhatsApp chat for you titled, *Looking after Grandpa Eric*. She's invited you to join it,' Mum explained as my phone vibrated. 'The family will want daily updates on Grandpa so make sure you stay in contact. Oh, and don't lose your sister's dog either. It will break her heart and we don't want that. I've got to go. Gary wants me to join him in the pool. You wouldn't believe how warm it is out here.'

I carried the coffee order back to Kate's car, cursing my cousin Fay, my mother and the person who invented WhatsApp.

CHAPTER FIVE

'Happy birthday, Olivia,' Kate, Connor, and I all chorused, raising aloft our coffee cups. The vanilla latte I'd bought Olivia from Happy Beans Café sat on the top of her gravestone in its cute pink travel mug. On either side of her gravestone were bunches of pink flowers and two heart balloons with – *Happy Birthday* on them. The biggest arrangement was from Sonia, Olivia's mum. 'When did Sonia come up?' Kate asked, kneeling to inspect the flowers.

'She texted me earlier to say she was up here at eight in the morning,' I explained. 'The family are all coming back later this afternoon.'

We stood before Olivia's gravestone. Rummaging in my coat pocket I searched for tissues as tears spilled down my cheeks. Connor pulled me against him and stroked my hair. He began his speech. 'Olivia, happy birthday. I am missing your winged eyeliner, your ability to walk into any charity shop and find an amazing piece of clothing, your love of liquorice sweets and how, even though you were a dreadful cook, you never gave up cooking us all meals that gave the impression you'd been torturing a vegetable and a stringy piece of meat for hours.' He grinned at the stone. 'I hope you get to dance the night away in heaven tonight.'

With a nod and a little sob, I started my speech. 'Happy birthday, my soul sister. I am missing seeing you go wild on a dance floor and drinking dodgy green liquid shots. I miss sitting on the sofa in identical pink onesies, scoffing steak and onion sandwiches and talking about our future fitness goals. I am missing hearing you shout at imaginary people whilst you type out your romance books. I hope there are some fit angels up there for you to dance with as you celebrate your heavenly birthday.'

Kate rose to her feet and nodded. 'I still can't believe you're gone, Olivia. It's like you've gone travelling or are on an extra-long holiday. I keep expecting to see a photo dump on Instagram, filled with photos of you dancing on tables and lying on a towel looking pale and hungover. I am missing your laughter, your craziness, friendship and love.'

I rubbed Kate's arm. 'Me too.'

After placing his coffee cup next to Olivia's, Connor took out her romance book. Kate and I both nervously glanced around the graveyard for anyone who might not want to hear an extract from, *One Night with The Viking King*. He started to read, and I closed my eyes.

I remembered the day Olivia had come hurtling out of her bedroom with a huge smile on her face. 'I've finished it,' she announced. 'I can't believe I have written a medieval romance.' She giggled. 'My GCSE history teacher is going to be impressed with my historical knowledge when she reads it.'

'Do you think she will read *One Night with The Viking King*?'

She nodded. 'She's read all my other books on Amazon and always leaves me a thought-provoking three-star review. When she reads this one, she's going to feel guilty for predicting me a

C at GCSE history. She might go for a four-star.' We laughed before grabbing our coats and going out for a celebratory drink.

I wiped my tears away as Connor closed the book. He grabbed his coffee and smiled at the gravestone. 'Olivia, that was amazing. I felt like I was in medieval times waiting for my handsome Viking King to row across the sea. I did wonder whether a Viking king would row his long boat by himself. Surely, he would have had people rowing it for him.'

I placed a hand on his arm. 'Olivia doesn't need to hear your editorial criticism on her birthday.'

Connor nodded. 'As a reader, I did get a good idea of the Viking King's impressive physique with all those powerful rowing descriptions.'

Kate and I leaned against Connor, and we all gazed at Olivia's stone.

'I hope you enjoy the coffee, Olivia,' Connor said. 'Rachel put two sugars in it as she doesn't think heaven will have bad stuff like sugar.'

Kate smiled at me. 'We should have brought Olivia some vodka.'

I nodded. 'That will be next year's birthday.'

After Connor told Olivia's gravestone all about his latest online dating match, Kate talked about how she'd adopted a fourth cat called Bob. Then I began to tell Olivia's stone about Christmas. 'My family have conspired against me once again on WhatsApp, and I am now spending Christmas, looking after Humphrey, the dog, and Grandpa in Harp Brook.'

'Olivia, please make the wind blow the trees if you want Rachel to disobey her sister's rich husband and venture into the west wing,' Connor announced.

We all gasped and then laughed when the trees hemming the graveyard began to sway as the chilly wind raced around them.

'It's a sign,' said Connor. 'You must be naughty in Harp Brook.'

'Unlikely when I will be mostly tending to Grandpa and Humphrey.'

With tears in our eyes, we told Olivia how much we missed her. Connor poured her coffee around her stone as we didn't want to look as though we'd left a coffee cup on someone's gravestone. We linked arms and trooped back to the car.

'Do you remember that blind date she organised for you?' Kate asked, unlocking her car. 'Did you ever email that guy back?'

I shook my head and took out my phone. His email had arrived a few days after Olivia had messaged him. Even though I never replied to him I had kept it. I opened it:

Hi Rachel, I am assuming Olivia has told you about me and her idea of a blind date. If she hasn't then this is very embarrassing, and you must think I am her weird stalker friend. If this has happened, I will have words the next time I see her.

As you may or not know, I am Ben and Olivia has agreed to be my dating consultant. We've been friends since university, and I know the following about her:

1. She can't hold her drink.

2. She thinks she's the next Barbara Cartland.

3. She has a heart of gold.

4. She claims her odd-shaped nose was because she once banged it on a cupboard

40

but if you meet her mum, you will know the cupboard story is not true.

5. She loves Harry Styles and her own made-up dance sequences to his songs were questionable.

Hopefully, this will show you that I know Olivia very well and I am not a weird dude. If you want to go on a blind date, please get in touch. I know a great place for brunch and their coffee is out of this world.

Ben.

'Rachel?' Kate was nudging me. 'Are you looking at his email? Why have you kept it?'

I shrugged. 'I never replied to him. It didn't feel right. I did think about emailing him when she died but that felt awkward too. It wouldn't have worked.'

'Why not?' Connor asked.

Sam's face appeared in my head. 'My heart was still broken after what Sam did to me. It has taken me ages to get over him. Every time I open my flat door, I relive seeing Sam standing there about to break my heart.'

'Sometimes I wonder whether your flat is doing you any good?' Kate perused. 'So many memories for you to deal with every day.'

Connor tapped me on the shoulder. 'Where are you now on the romance front?'

'I would like to find someone,' I said, 'but my self-confidence isn't great, and I do spend a lot of my time getting upset about Olivia.'

'Have you got those leaks sorted?' Kate asked. 'All that water and dampness cannot be good for you.'

I shook my head. 'My landlord is ghosting me.'

'Where will your grandfather sleep tomorrow night?' Connor asked.

'My bedroom. I'm going to have to sleep on the sofa?'

Kate gasped. 'Rachel, you can't sleep in a room where half the ceiling is leaking.'

'She's right,' agreed Connor. 'The dripping will keep you awake and it's not healthy.'

There was only one other place. The thought of sleeping in Olivia's room made every muscle in my body clench. 'I can't sleep in Olivia's room. I haven't been in that room since her mum came over to take away her things.'

Kate reached over and laid her gloved hand over mine. 'You need a fresh start, Rachel. You're living in a flat which should have a public health warning stamped all over it and constantly reminds you of the past.'

'I disagree,' I mumbled. 'Being in my flat means I am close to Olivia.'

CHAPTER SIX

'Hello, Grandpa.'

He held out his arms. 'Hello, Rachel. I am sorry about this. The last thing you need over Christmas is a silly old bloke like me with you.' His twinkly blue eyes sparkled, his short fluffy white hair was neat on one side and unruly on the other, and his big smile stretched from ear to ear. I stepped into his hug, inhaling the comforting smell of his Old Spice aftershave, and resting my head on his old woollen winter coat, which he had always worn when Maddie and I were kids. His arms wrapped themselves around me.

Closing my eyes for a few seconds I savoured Grandpa's embrace. It felt like the sun had come out on my darkened little life. It was short-lived as I immediately became consumed by guilt for being frustrated at Mum the day before. How could I have been annoyed at spending quality time over Christmas with Grandpa Eric?

'You're not a silly old bloke. Come in,' I said after he'd released me. The taxi driver was busy hauling Grandpa's case to the door. After thanking the driver, I grabbed the suitcase and led the way. 'Excuse the buckets when you come into my flat.

The landlord assures me the leaks will be fixed by the time I return. I complained to him this morning.'

Grandpa came inside and closed the door. 'I offered to pay for a hotel for tonight, but your mother told me you wanted me to stay in your flat.'

I rolled my eyes. 'Don't listen to my mother, Grandpa. She knows about the ceiling.'

He shook his head. 'I'm sorry, Rachel. Why don't we book me into a hotel and save you the trouble of putting me up.'

'Grandpa – it's okay, you can have my bed tonight.'

We climbed the stairs to my flat. I deposited his suitcase in the living room as he stared in horror at the multitude of drips and buckets.

'Tea or coffee, Grandpa,' I said, to distract him. 'Are you hungry because I have made those afternoon tea sandwiches again. Do you remember the ones we had in the summer in your back garden?'

His eyes twinkled. 'I haven't stopped dreaming about those delicious sandwiches you made us that day.'

'Really?'

'You make food come alive, Rachel. A nice cup of tea too, please. The tea on the train was diabolical.'

He turned to my paintings set against the wall. 'These are beautiful.'

When Olivia died, I turned to my painting. Cooking and painting have always been a form of escapism for me. My love of painting started when I was little. Maddie and I used to sit at the top of the stairs, hugging our knees and listening to Mum and Dad argue about not having any money. After listening to their argument Maddie would lose herself in books and I would take out my paints. My canvases all show the world outside my flat window, tall dark office buildings which look like they are getting closer and are hemming me in. Their only redeeming feature is that at night the windows make them look like they are covered in pretty, orange squares. In the city it is hard to see the sky, what with the buildings and pollution. I normally improvise and create indigo skies with twinkling stars.

He turned to me. 'Can I have one for my bungalow?'

'Really?'

'I am proud of you, Rachel. You're very talented.'

His kind words made me go gooey inside. After gesturing for him to take a seat on my sofa I scooted into my kitchen to make a cuppa and grab my famous afternoon tea finger sandwiches that I'd prepared earlier, cured ham and mustard, cucumber with mint cream cheese and egg salad with cress. Each one carefully crafted, cut into a perfect finger shape, and arranged on a large platter dish.

Sandwiches are one of my favourite things to make. Making a well-crafted and delicious sandwich is an art form. Sandwiches are a way of showing someone you love them. The lengths someone goes to make sure the bread is fluffy; the crusts have been carefully removed and the filling ingredients provide a taste sensation is a sign of true love. The sandwiches that I make Grandpa always take me ages to put together but seeing him eat them gives me so much happiness.

I carried the platter of sandwiches into the living room and placed Grandpa's cup near him. Then I went back to fetch two plates. 'How was the train journey?'

He smiled. 'Robert drove like a madman to the station. I didn't think my pacemaker would survive. Anyone would think Robert was trying to get rid of me. Karen was going to have her hair cut. Lord knows why she keeps going back to that same woman after Robert admitted he was in love with her.'

'Mum says Aunty Karen loves the way that woman cuts her hair and she's spent years searching for the right hairdresser. Nothing is going to get in the way of a good haircut.'

45

Grandpa rubbed his face. 'I don't understand Karen's fascination with this hairdresser as she has always had short hair. It always looks the same to me.' He yawned. 'The train was bearable although I did sit next to a woman who told me that we're going to have a white Christmas. She reckons the snow could be bad in some places.'

I gasped. 'Snow?' This was the last thing I needed.

Grandpa nodded. 'It is going to be worse in the south. Isn't that where we are going?'

With a groan, I picked up my cup and took a sip. 'I hope Maddie has wellies as I have a feeling I'll be spending Christmas searching for her dog in the snow.'

Grandpa frowned. 'Rachel, we are Maddie's Christmas dog sitters. We'll both be looking for Humphrey in the snow if the little rascal runs away.'

I recalled the list of rules Aunty Karen had put on the WhatsApp chat about caring for Grandpa. One of which was that he couldn't go outside for long in cold weather. 'Aunty Karen has given me strict orders on keeping you indoors, Grandpa.'

The smile on my grandfather's face began to evaporate. 'Rachel, I might be eighty years old, but I am not a delicate antique.'

'I must look after you, Grandpa.'

He took another sip from his tea. 'What else have the family said?'

'They're worried about you. Don't worry, I am going to make sure you have a relaxing Christmas. You can put your feet up and eat the meals Aunty Karen has suggested I cook for you. And you can watch your programmes and sleep whenever you want, while I go off searching for Humphrey.'

'I don't want to have a relaxing time,' he barked, his voice tinged with what sounded like annoyance. 'I don't want you to be my Christmas carer, Rachel. I love my daughters, but they are wrapping me in cotton wool.'

'Sorry, Grandpa.'

He smiled. 'I'm eighty years old. I still live by myself. I cook my meals – albeit by shoving them in the microwave. I creak a lot going up and down the stairs and sometimes I need Karen to run me up to the supermarket. Occasionally in the summer, Robert and I will go to the cricket. I'm doing okay, I think.'

'Oh... Mum said Aunty Karen cares for you every day.'

Grandpa erupted into a proper belly laugh. 'She calls in a few times a week but that's it. I think she's telling porkies to your mother who lives in Tenerife and has no way of knowing what's really going on.'

We both tucked into our finger sandwiches. He held one aloft and studied it. 'I remember years ago when you and Maddie were little. Your mum would give your nan and me a list of what to feed you whilst she went on holiday.'

I grinned. 'We had to eat crusts, brown bread, and vegetables.'

He chuckled. 'The second your mother's car left the drive I told your nan to rip up the list.'

'Maddie and I loved coming to stay as we would eat biscuits, lollipops, jellied sweets, chips, and white bread sandwiches with no crusts.'

'How are you, Rachel?' he asked. 'I have been worried about you after what happened to your lovely friend, Olivia. Every day I think about how you're doing. No one should have to lose a friend like that at your age.'

Biting the inside of my mouth to stop myself from crying I nodded.

'The family are also worried about you,' he explained. 'I don't use that thing they call... ummm... Whatsit... Whats...'

'WhatsApp, Grandpa.'

He clicked his fingers. 'That's the one. Anyway, they all talk about you a lot on there. Bev told me.'

I laughed. 'Aunty Bev told you?'

'She's glad they never talk about her on there,' he quipped.

A giggle escaped from my lips as he winked at me.

'Aunty Bev and her wild party days are always being discussed on there.'

We both laughed and carried on eating, talking, and reminiscing. An hour later I noticed he was yawning a lot, so I suggested he go into my bedroom for a nap. Once the sounds of Grandpa's snores drifted into my flat I forced myself to enter Olivia's bedroom.

Kate and Connor were right yesterday. I couldn't sleep on the sofa with a leaking ceiling and the dripping sound. With Grandpa in my room, I would have to sleep in Olivia's room.

The last time I'd opened it was when Olivia's mum, Sonia, came over to collect a lot of her daughter's belongings. She took most of the stuff but let me keep a few things. After taking a deep breath I turned the handle and went into her room.

My eyes darted to the dressing table where I expected to see her, wearing her pink fluffy dressing gown, and curling the life out of her long black hair. She'd grin at me through the dressing table mirror and ask me what time we were going out to our favourite cocktail bar. There was just an empty stool.

The wardrobe next to her dressing table was empty with one door hanging open. If she had still been alive, it would have been overflowing with clothes, jumpers, belts, and bags. Olivia always said that her clothes rushed out to greet her when she went to her wardrobe.

Her double bed had been stripped bare. There were a few books in the little bookcase by the window. On one shelf was a basket full of old phone chargers and a collection of takeaway menus.

This room used to smell of Olivia's perfume. The second you entered your nostrils would be hit with its vanilla and earthy notes. It had been replaced by a faint musty smell. Sometimes I feel like going to buy some of her favourite perfume just so that I can feel like she's near me again.

I felt dizzy and sat on the bed until her room stopped swaying. Once the dizziness abated, I got up and went to collect fresh sheets and bedding. To fit the mattress cover I had to lift the mattress. Underneath the bed frame was a pink notebook. Bending down, I picked it up and a photo slipped out from it. The photo was of a young Olivia and a blonde woman I didn't recognise. They were dancing and laughing at the camera.

Flipping over the first page I gasped at Oliva's swirly handwriting. It read: *How I Got Over Losing a Wonderful Friend, by Olivia Lunn.* With a trembling hand, I turned the page.

This is a personal account of how I survived losing my wonderful friend, Sophie. One day I hope to publish this as I hope it will help others going through the same thing.

It must have been about her friend, Sophie, who dated Ben, the guy Olivia had been trying to set me up with. I closed it quickly as a wave of emotion was rising inside me. Reading this would turn me into an emotional mess. Grandpa needed me and tomorrow I would be driving us to Surrey. Maybe when I returned from Harp Brook, I could have a closer look at the notebook, or even pass it to Sonia.

I placed it on the dressing table, made the bed and left the room, shutting the door firmly behind me. Wiping a solitary tear, I went into the living room and checked on my buckets.

CHAPTER SEVEN

'You look tired, Rachel.' Grandpa took a sip from his morning tea. 'Are you sure you're well enough to drive to Surrey?'

'I'm fine,' I lied, avoiding his stare, and inspecting my piece of brioche bun. It had been difficult to sleep in Olivia's room. I'd spent the night scrolling through my phone in the dark and looking at pics of Olivia on my Instagram.

Shortly before she died, she'd started dating a new guy who worked in a pizza restaurant, and I don't think I'd seen her happier. One night after she'd returned from his flat, she'd summoned me into her room and asked me to be bridesmaid at her future wedding. We'd then cracked open a bottle of cheap wine from the fridge and spent hours sitting on her bed scrolling through bridal and bridesmaid dresses.

My last Instagram post of her was of us on this bed, with a giant bag of crisps between us, holding up mugs of wine and pulling funny deep-in-thought expressions. I'd added the caption – *Engaged in a lengthy debate about whether I would look better in sage green or purple orchid as a bridesmaid at a future wedding.*

Olivia spent the following day at work adding comments to

my post on how tired she was, how her post-wine headache wasn't going away and how the woman at who sat opposite her thought I would look great in a dreadful light peach colour.

I fell asleep against a damp pillow, clutching my phone.

Grandpa was an early riser, and he liked his breakfast cooked for him too. This meant my alarm had to be set for six thirty to make us both one of the breakfasts he enjoyed: a brioche bun filled with eggs and salmon. I also wanted to ensure we got to Harp Brook on time so that Maddie and Frank could head off to the airport.

After only three hours of sleep my eyes were puffy and sore.

'You know, Rachel,' said Grandpa, 'you have always been bad at lying. I don't know who taught you to lie because they did a terrible job.'

I laughed and he smiled. 'You and Maddie would squabble and fight like sisters do. Maddie would come rushing into the kitchen in tears saying that you'd stolen her little box of Smarties and eaten them behind the sofa. I would summon you into the kitchen. You'd stand in front of us, with Smarties juice around your mouth, and I would ask you whether it was true what Maddie had told us about you stealing and eating her box of Smarties. You'd avoid all eye contact with us and then you'd say in a squeaky voice, "I didn't eat her Smarties." Your nan used to whisper in my ear, "She's a terrible liar – isn't she?"'

With a sigh, I sank back into my chair. 'Am I that easy to read?'

Grandpa nodded. 'Like a book, Rachel. The trick to good lying is to maintain eye contact and not let your voice get high pitched.' He winked at me. 'Also, check that your box of Smarties is not still sticking out of your back pocket, and check it doesn't rattle as you walk away.'

We both began to giggle at my childhood Smartie theft

crimes. 'You're right, I'm tired, Grandpa. I'm a rubbish liar. Sleeping in Olivia's bedroom wasn't a great idea.'

'Do you need forty winks?' Grandpa smiled. 'A forty-wink nap always makes me feel better.'

'I'll be okay, Grandpa.'

After clearing away the plates, washing up and dragging our cases and bags downstairs into the hallway, I went for one final look around my flat to see whether I'd forgotten to pack vital things like a phone charger, my toothbrush, my favourite eyebrow pencil, or my paints, brushes, and spare canvases. Grandpa made his way down to wait by the cases.

I don't know what made me enter Olivia's bedroom, but I found myself in there. Wandering over to the dressing table I stared at the pink notebook. In the night I had thought about reading it, but I'd resisted. Now, it stared back at me. In a flash, I grabbed it and shoved it inside my handbag before racing out of my flat and closing the door behind me.

Dragging the cases and my bags to my car was like my own form of cardio workout. My paintbrushes had a mind of their own and flew out of the plastic bag, scattering all over the floor. By the time I had picked them up and heaved both cases into the boot, Grandpa was in the passenger side with his seat belt on. I got in beside him bathed in a light sweat.

He pointed out of the windscreen. 'First snowflakes.'

'Oh no.' I stared at the fluttery flakes landing on the glass and groaned. 'Let's hope it doesn't start laying.'

Grandpa chuckled.

Taking a deep breath, I started the car. 'Harp Brook here we come, Grandpa,' I said, as we pulled away from my flat. Reaching for the radio I went to turn it on. It was time to listen to some Christmas tunes, ignore the weather and enjoy a peaceful car journey. Grandpa cleared his throat as my hand travelled towards the radio button. 'I've never liked Frank, Rachel.'

I gasped, taking back my hand. 'What? Really?'

He nodded. 'I told Karen about how I feel, and she thought I was going senile. Our family has become blinded by Frank's money. Maddie should never have married him.'

After blowing the air out of my cheeks I stole a glance at Grandpa. He was trembling and chewing on his thumb. 'She's not our Maddie anymore.' His voice was crackly and tinged with sadness. Instinctively, I reached across and squeezed his hand. The knot in my tummy returned.

'She used to be bubbly and full of laughter,' he croaked. 'Always talking about her friends and her busy life. Maddie was the life and soul of the party. When I talk to her now on the phone, I hear her subdued voice and I listen to how they both sit in that gigantic house as the dust gathers on Frank's art collection. It breaks my old heart.'

The shock of hearing Grandpa confirm what I'd been thinking about Maddie made beads of sweat gather on my forehead. I wasn't the only one who was concerned for Maddie.

'Sorry, Grandpa,' I said, fighting the urge to pull the car over and hug him.

'Money isn't everything, Rachel. Though your mother and your aunty Karen would disagree.'

'I've also been worried about Maddie. When she came over to my flat the other day to ask me to dog sit. I saw something in her eyes. A sadness. I have this awful feeling something's going on with her.'

Grandpa patted his knee. 'I knew I wasn't the only one. The rest of them have lost all their common sense but you and I have kept ours, Rachel.'

He was quiet for a while. I drove and he gazed out of the window. At the motorway services, I stopped so Grandpa could go to the toilet, and I could buy myself a coffee. Once back in the car Grandpa smiled at me. 'We're similar souls, you and me, Rachel.'

'Really, Grandpa?'

He nodded. 'When your aunty Karen explained that the family wanted me to go spend Christmas with you, I was excited.'

Guilt wrapped itself around me as I drove out of the service station. Excitement had not been my first reaction. I had been more concerned about not being able to have a proper rest.

'We're the Christmas Dog Sitters and we are going to have a Christmas adventure,' he beamed, raising his fist in celebration. 'It's going to be great. As Nadine says, "Let's go large."'

He was worrying me with all this talk of an adventure and references to 'going large'. I needed to bring him down to Earth. This was supposed to be a relaxing break. 'Grandpa, I promised the family I would look after you in Harp Brook so we can't do too much adventuring.'

'This could be my last Christmas, Rachel.'

I turned to him. 'Don't say that, Grandpa.'

He shrugged. 'I am in my eighties now. I'm no spring chicken. We need to make the most of the time I have left. Please can we have a Christmas adventure?'

I was curious as to what his definition of a *Christmas adventure* included. For all I knew he could be referring to nipping down the local pub for a shandy, the odd game of darts which I knew he loved, watching the endless rotation of Christmas films on TV and stuffing his face with a Christmas dinner and all the trimmings. 'Okay, what would your ideal Christmas adventure include, Grandpa?'

'I would like to save someone's life, go on a dangerous expedition, dance with a beautiful lady under the stars, and do something amazing.'

I don't think I have ever gripped the steering wheel so tightly and struggled to remain calm on a motorway before. Aunty Karen's list of dos and don'ts when caring for Grandpa flashed across my mind. 'Make sure he has a blanket over his legs, has regular cups of tea brought to him, is fed three good meals and make sure all excitement is kept to a minimum.'

She wanted me to wrap him up in cotton wool and stick him in a chair next to a Christmas tree for three weeks.

He, on the other hand, wanted to spend Christmas living like an action hero from the films Frank used to star in.

A nervous laugh escaped from my lips. 'Oh, Grandpa, I don't think Harp Brook is going to be that exciting.'

'Rachel, I didn't want to tell you but...' He paused and I gulped.

'Tell me what, Grandpa?' My heart pounded against my ribcage.

'I'm lonely, Rachel, and it's making me very sad.'

His words hung in the air between us for a few seconds. 'Lonely?' I repeated and glanced at him.

'Your nan has been dead for ten years. I miss her every day but she's not coming back. I spend my days alone in my shed, listening to the radio and wishing I had someone to talk to, someone to laugh with and hold my hand. When I look out of the window in my living room, I see couples walking by chatting and laughing. Some days I even open the window just so that I can hear people again. The world is going on without me. It makes me very sad.'

The gloom in his voice brought tears to my eyes. I had to blink them away and stay focused on the stretch of the motorway. 'Why don't you go to the community centre? They have lots of events for seniors.'

He shook his head. 'Not that kind of lonely, Rachel. I would like to fall in love again.'

I gasped and imagined Mum's face hearing that her father wanted to have some romance over Christmas. That was *not* on Aunty Karen's list. 'Really?'

He let out a heavy sigh. 'I want to experience life again. Live dangerously for a few weeks and make Harp Brook a Christmas to remember.'

His words made every part of me clench. With the back of my hand, I wiped my forehead. It was glazed with sweat. All this car drama had sent my bladder into a tailspin. I was desperate for the loo, and I sensed Christmas at Harp Brook was not going to give me the relaxing break I needed.

CHAPTER EIGHT

Frank and Maddie's country home was set amid the rolling Surrey Hills and tucked neatly behind the picturesque village of Harp Brook. As we drove through, we admired the quaint red-brick cottages, the two snug country pubs, old church and the handful of shops on the high street.

Frank and Maddie lived in the biggest property in Harp Brook; a Grade II listed, red-brick, eight-bedroom manor house with a vast garden, a quadruple garage, stables, a gravel driveway, and iron gates.

Once Grandpa and I had passed through the gates, the beautiful old manor house came into view. Set against a backdrop of swirling snowflakes it was like an illustration from one of the winter fairy-tale picture books we had as kids. It made me gasp in awe. Grandpa muttered under his breath about Frank having far too much money.

Maddie was in the doorway waving at us and holding an excited Humphrey. As my car got nearer the spaniel escaped from Maddie's arms and raced towards my tyres, barking his head off. Slamming on the brakes to avoid running over Humphrey, I let out a yelp of frustration.

'That dog is out of control,' moaned Grandpa, as Humphrey jumped up at his car window. Humphrey's ears were way too big for his head and his pink tongue hung to one side as he cast us his best deranged dog look.

'Maddie told me he was calming down,' I groaned, turning off the engine.

Grandpa chuckled. 'She can't say no to that silly dog.'

Maddie squealed at Grandpa before throwing her arms around his neck. 'Grandpa – it's so lovely to see you.'

'Hello, Maddie,' he cried, giving her a kiss. 'Your Christmas dog sitters have arrived.' Humphrey barked and started to run in circles around them.

'How's married life?' Grandpa asked.

'Busy,' she said, planting a kiss on his cheek. 'Come inside, as it's cold out here and the snow is coming down.'

'Is Frank about?' Grandpa asked.

She pointed back towards their huge wooden front door, which was encased within an impressive stone arch. 'He's talking to the cleaner.'

Opening the boot of my car I was about to haul out our suitcases when Maddie raised her hand. 'Frank's driver will bring those in, Rachel. Leave them in your car for now.'

Normally I would have brought the cases myself, but Grandpa and I had both packed far too much and they needed a stronger pair of arms.

Maddie led the way through the front door and into the reception hall. Humphrey followed in a mad pursuit and nearly tripped up Grandpa.

As the reception hall opened, we were greeted with a vast curved staircase, made from solid oak, leading the way upstairs. To our right on the ground floor was the east wing, and three closed doors. One led to the large sitting room, which I recalled, from previous visits, was the room with the giant open fireplace, the high ceiling, teak flooring, and French doors opening out onto a sun terrace. One door was for the cloakroom and the other led to the annex.

To our left was a set of closed doors which led to the west wing. Maddie pointed to them. 'These will remain locked, and I have asked the cleaner to keep hold of the keys. Promise me you won't go in there.'

Both Grandpa and I nodded obediently.

We headed to the rear of the house and the large old kitchen. My bladder was about to burst, but loud voices drifting along the wood-panelled corridor as we approached distracted me.

'Please don't let me go, Mr Baxter,' begged a young female voice. 'I'm sorry that it happened again but I have nowhere else to put him.'

'Layla, I'm sorry, I have told you several times and it keeps happening. This is not acceptable,' Frank barked in his New York boardroom voice. His tone made me flinch and even Grandpa cast me an alarmed look. Maddie rushed ahead and clapped her hands. 'Frank, my grandfather and sister are here.'

As Grandpa and I entered the kitchen, Frank grunted in our direction. He was not one for warm welcomes.

Maddie and Frank were an interesting couple to look at. She was blonde, youthful, and ethereal looking with an enviable slim figure and porcelain white skin. Frank was twelve years older with grey hair, fashionable boxy black square glasses, a broad frame and tanned, leathery skin – a result of spending too much time in the sun on film sets during his acting career.

Frank's colourful past as an actor was not something our family ever mentioned. Well, they probably did in secret without Mum knowing. When Maddie first told me about Frank, I googled him and gasped at the old press stories of his wild lifestyle on and off the film set. Olivia and I spent many an evening going down Frank Baxter rabbit holes on Reddit and reading about Frank Baxter, the handsome young actor with a penchant for Hollywood poolside parties, drugs, affairs, and an array of scantily clad women. Maddie made it clear Frank was a changed man. He was now a successful CEO of a flourishing media empire and didn't want his chequered past to interfere with his business vision.

'Can you keep me on until after Christmas?' A young woman was stood in front of Frank, her hands clasped. 'Please don't get rid of me this close to Christmas.' They were both stood at the back of the kitchen, by the construction sheet covering the work site of the new extension.

I had always thought their old kitchen was impressive. Multiple Velux ceiling windows flooded the space with light, handmade cream wooden cupboards lined the walls, and a large kitchen island with two sinks and a marble worktop presided in the middle. In the corner were two cream Aga ovens. Frank liked everything to be new and perfect.

The sound of a young child grizzling filled the air and Humphrey began to bark. Everyone switched their attention across the kitchen to the curly-haired toddler who was chewing on his fingers and standing up inside in a travel cot.

'I have made it clear,' snapped Frank, 'that child is not to be brought along while you are cleaning this house. The quality of your cleaning is also questionable and at times I wonder what I am paying you to do.'

The young woman hung her head.

'I could find someone far cheaper and better at cleaning than you, Layla.' His voice had a hard edge to it.

Irritation bubbled inside of me. There was no need to talk to her in that way and certainly not in front of us all. Grandpa glanced at me, and I could tell he felt the same way.

Maddie went to Frank and whispered something in his ear.

Whatever she said pacified him as he let out a sigh. 'Layla, you can clean until the first of January. I will make sure my wife's family inform me if they catch you cleaning my house and looking after your child at the same time.'

An awkward silence descended upon the kitchen. Maddie smiled brightly at her husband. 'Frank, come and say hello to Rachel and Grandpa.'

He nodded at us. 'Hello, Rachel and Eric. Sorry, I need to go sort out the builder. He's meeting me out the front. I'll be back shortly.'

Frank strode away leaving Maddie, Layla, Grandpa, and me in the kitchen.

Layla spoke to Maddie. 'Thank you for letting me stay on as your cleaner, I appreciate it.'

Maddie smiled. 'Don't worry, I'll talk to him on holiday. You do a great job, Layla, I don't want you to go.'

'It's a temporary blip with Zac,' said Layla, pointing to her son in his travel cot. 'I promise. It's not been easy for us lately.'

My bladder was going crazy. I desperately needed the loo. 'Maddie, can I use your toilet?'

She nodded. 'Use the cloakroom off the hallway.'

Humphrey raced after me as I sprinted down the corridor. After closing the toilet door on Humphrey I locked it and had one of the most satisfying wees of my life.

As I sat on the loo, Frank was shouting again. 'Your other clients might accept your shoddy work, but I won't. You need to think about who you're working for and how damaging a complaint from me will be. I will think twice about using your firm again.'

A male voice replied, 'I'm sorry you feel that way. The plasterer I hired hasn't done the best job, so I am going to sort that. I'll do my best to rectify the situation next week.'

'Make sure it's finished for when I return,' Frank snapped.

His footsteps drifted away. An uncomfortable feeling passed over me as I washed my hands.

On the previous occasions Frank and I had met he had either been engrossed on his laptop or talking on his phone. At their wedding, he barely spoke to me, but I'd assumed that was because it was his big day and the wedding planners had not followed his strict instructions.

After drying my hands, I groaned at my dishevelled reflection in the mirror. My long brown hair was greasy and lifeless. It had been tied in a messy bun at the top of my head earlier this morning but during the journey it had escaped and now hung over my shoulders. My skin was paler than ever and the old navy-blue sweatshirt I wore had a few stains. Why had I arrived at Maddie's posh house in such a state? This was the sort of place you dressed up before visiting.

Frank's voice drifted under the door. He'd returned and it sounded like he was talking to someone on a phone. 'You're my lawyer. Deal with it.'

I was not warming to my new brother-in-law. The sooner he left for his holiday, the better. As I came out of the cloakroom, I felt that same knotted feeling in my tummy and a little inner voice whispered, *Who has Maddie married?*

CHAPTER NINE

'You're to stick to the east wing,' explained Frank, gesturing for me to follow him into the living room. He was wearing a fitted white shirt with jewelled cufflinks and smart black jeans.

In the short time I'd known Frank, I've never seen him looking rough or dishevelled. 'The west wing is out of bounds.'

I didn't answer him as I was too busy gawping at the gigantic Christmas tree in the corner of the room. The tops of the branches brushed against the high ceiling. Silver glass baubles and crystal ornaments hung from every branch. They did not like the cheap decorations I'd bought from the supermarket. The tree gave the impression it had been custom designed for one of those glossy country life magazines Maddie used to have on her coffee table before she met Frank.

It was a beautiful living room with an open fireplace at the far end, tall French windows, cream drape curtains, plush brown leather sofas, and several oil paintings on the walls. I couldn't see Maddie's influence in the décor. It was all Frank. Even the paintings on the walls were of historic battles. I'd never known my sister to be interested in military artwork.

'I don't want any of the locals setting foot inside the house or in the grounds,' Frank explained. 'Only you and Eric are to stay at the house. There's everything you could want here, and no need to go into Harp Brook village.'

'Sorry,' I said, thinking I'd misheard him. 'What did you say?'

Frank cast me a fake smile. 'You and Eric are to stay here in the house.'

'Why?'

He took a step back and stared at me. Running a hand through his grey hair he began to walk towards the open fireplace. 'I don't see why you would need to go into the village. There's enough food and wine in this house to feed you and Eric for three months, let alone three weeks. The garden and grounds are big enough for daily walks and if you prefer to exercise inside you have full use of our gym. I have every TV channel, every streaming channel, every subscription, and the best wifi.'

'For three weeks, you want us to stay here and not venture out?'

Frank nodded. 'I don't see a problem with that.'

'But what about walking Humphrey?'

He shrugged. 'The grounds and garden are big enough for Humphrey. Maddie walks him out there every day.'

'Well, that sounds great, but Grandpa and I *will* be venturing into the village,' I said, defiantly.

Frank gazed out of the French window. I followed his gaze. Huge snowflakes were descending from the sky. If the snow carried on it would be unsafe for Grandpa to walk into Harp Brook, but I did have the car.

'I will leave that decision with you, Rachel,' he said, quietly. 'However, my wife assured me you would abide by our rules and keep your elderly grandfather safe.'

An uncomfortable silence fell upon us, and he turned away to stare up at a painting above the open fireplace. He spoke first, maintaining his gaze on the artwork. 'The builder will be here Monday to Friday. The cleaner every three days.'

Maddie showed Grandpa and me where we would be sleeping. The ground floor annexe with its rose-coloured bedroom, an en-suite toilet and a shower room would be where Grandpa would be sleeping. 'I am going to sit here and take in the beautiful snowy view,' said Grandpa, pointing to a gorgeous royal blue chair by his bed, overlooking the garden. 'You girls go on ahead.'

Maddie took me upstairs. She was wearing a crimson dress which was gathered at her slim waist and grazed her brown leather ankle boots. 'Sorry about Frank earlier,' she whispered as we crept along the east wing's landing. 'He gets power crazy sometimes.'

'Is that what you call it?' I cast her a worried glance.

She pushed open the door to my bedroom and I gasped. It was a spacious room with abundant natural light due to the tall windows, a fireplace, an en-suite and a giant wardrobe. The windows commanded a spectacular view over the east side of the garden and grounds.

'Apologies, I haven't spoken to you much since my visit last weekend,' she explained. 'We've had Frank's company social media team here and they've been filming us in the house.'

'Oh,' I said, running my hand over the beautiful sage green bedding which was adorned with embroidered silk woven peacocks walking through an array of ferns and green shrubs. It was magnificent and so soft to touch. Maddie sat on the edge of my bed and stared at the beautiful, embroidered birds. 'I gave you the peacock bedding.' She smiled. 'Did you know the peacock is a symbol of rebirth?'

'Maddie, I don't need a rebirth, I just need a rest.' I took her hand. 'Do you know that I've been worried about you?'

She smiled. 'Me? Don't be worried, I'm okay.'

I recalled Kate asking about cameras. 'Does Frank have security cameras?'

'Yes, but that is a touchy subject,' explained Maddie. 'He's having the old ones replaced when we get back from our holiday. There are cameras outside, but they are not up to his high standards. Frank has great plans for his security system. He wants an American firm to come over and install cameras in every room.'

'Even in the west wing? The part of the house you and he don't use?'

Maddie rolled her eyes. 'Everywhere.'

'He's told me that Grandpa and I are to stay here for three weeks and preferably not go into Harp Brook.'

'Given the snow, I think that's sensible, Rachel. There's a snowstorm forecast for Christmas Eve according to Frank.'

I glanced at my sister. She was squeezing her hands together so hard her fingers were almost white. 'Are you okay?' I asked.

She nodded and let out a nervous laugh. 'Pre-holiday nerves. Ignore me.'

'What is going on with you and Frank?'

'Nothing, we're fine.'

I studied her face. 'You can tell me, Maddie.'

She held my gaze. 'I'm overthinking everything. A lot is going on. Listen, did I tell you that Olivia was the reason why Frank and I chose to live in Harp Brook?'

'Olivia?'

Maddie nodded. 'Remember Frank and I came back from the States after... everything over there had got to me.' She took a breath. I sensed the memory of her being so unhappy out in

California last year was still painful. 'About that, Rachel, I wanted to say thanks for keeping what I was going through out there to yourself and not telling the family.'

'You don't have to keep thanking me, Maddie,' I said, 'I'm just glad Frank listened to you and was decent enough to set up home over here.'

'Anyway, Frank and I were looking for houses over here to buy. He'd seen this house and was organising for us to have a viewing. You and Olivia had come to London to meet me for brunch. Remember?'

'Yes, I do.' A memory came rushing back to me. The previous day had been particularly tough as my cat, Flossy, had been put down after suffering a stroke. I'd woken up to find her unable to get out of her basket. My vet managed to see her at nine in the morning. It was severe and the best thing was to have her put to sleep. In the afternoon I'd been told my job was at risk due to a cost-cutting restructure and in the evening Connor and Kate messaged me to ask whether I knew that Sam had proposed to Chantelle live on Instagram with Rupert holding up the ring box. I mainly spent that brunch crying in the loos of the café.

'Well, you were in the ladies, and I happened to mention we'd found a house in a place called Harp Brook. Olivia said she'd rented a house there once and it was beautiful.'

'Oh, wow,' I said, trying to think whether Olivia ever told me she knew Harp Brook. 'She never mentioned anything to me.'

Maddie smiled. 'You were going through a hard time back then.'

I nodded and she came over to pull me into a hug. 'I hope you get a chance to have a break, Rachel. You need a rest.'

The urge to tell her about Grandpa wanting to live

dangerously and have a Christmas adventure was strong, but it would worry her on holiday. I remained silent.

We walked towards the bedroom door. 'I've always been jealous of you, Rachel.'

I laughed. 'Maddie, how can you be jealous of me when you live in these surroundings and your husband is... Frank Baxter.'

She held my gaze. 'You've always been free to do the things you wanted to do.'

Reaching out I touched her shoulder. She nibbled on her thumb nail. Her glassy blue eyes were trying to tell me something. I opened my mouth, and she swiftly left the bedroom. 'The driver will be here any minute. Have fun, Rachel.'

Frank and Maddie's sleek white chauffeur-driven Mercedes headed down the drive and away from the manor house. After Maddie had cried buckets over leaving Humphrey and Frank's chauffeur had nearly put his back out while lifting out my suitcase, they'd finally left for the airport.

Grandpa was talking to Layla and keeping Humphrey distracted with a ball in the kitchen. I was standing by the front door. The Mercedes was getting smaller and smaller as it travelled down the driveway. The talk with Maddie in my bedroom upstairs had not put my mind at rest. It had left me with a thudding heart. The snowfall had eased and there was only a thin covering on the ground which was one good thing.

My phone began to vibrate. Taking it out of my pocket, I saw that it was Mum. She was facetiming me. I pressed the accept button and she appeared from her sun lounger looking bronzed in a bright pink bikini. 'Have Maddie and Frank left yet?' she asked, before sipping on a colourful cocktail.

I nodded and flashed the phone camera towards the driveway. 'Just left.'

'Oh, it has been snowing then,' Mum said, peering closer at her phone screen.

'Yes, but it has stopped now.'

'Isn't their manor house beautiful?' cooed Mum. 'I am so proud of Maddie living like royalty and now going off to Malibu. Some days I must pinch myself. She's living a perfect life: she's married Frank Baxter and she's surrounded by luxury. She will never endure what I went through with your father.' She took a mouthful of a cocktail, placed it on the table and took up her lit cigarette. She took a drag. 'Guess what?' she said, before coughing and erupting into a cackle of laughter.

'What?'

She laughed and pointed her phone at the sunbed next to her. 'Guess who has come out and joined us in Tenerife?'

I stared in horror as Aunty Karen and Uncle Robert grinned and waved back at me. They were both in swimsuits with a drink in one hand and a ciggie in the other. Aunty Karen was in a bold tangerine one-piece suit with frilly edges which didn't match her orange hair and Uncle Robert was in navy shorts. His dark hairy chest resembled a sample from my local carpet shop.

'What are they doing with you?'

Mum laughed. 'They needed a break from looking after your grandfather. It was your cousin Fay who suggested Karen and Robert fly out for Christmas.'

Aunty Karen held aloft her cocktail. 'Cheers, Rachel, and Merry Christmas.'

Uncle Robert chuckled as he held his drink up. 'Be a good girl, Rachel.'

Irritation at my family made me prickle. I was here in Harp Brook with Grandpa, confined to the Manor House with a mad dog and a head full of worries about my sister, and they were all partying in Tenerife. I opened my mouth to start shouting about my cousin Fay when Grandpa yelled something from the kitchen. 'Got to go, Mum. Bye.'

After ending the call, I went to shut the front door. It was an old, cumbersome door and tough to close. As I battled with the door something shot past my legs in a flash of chocolate brown. 'Humphrey!' I yelled, but it was too late. Maddie's dog raced away up the driveway.

CHAPTER TEN

I chased Humphrey but gave up after he disappeared into a flurry of snowflakes. 'Grandpa, Humphrey has escaped,' I groaned, walking into the kitchen.

'Sorry, Rachel,' Grandpa said, 'Humphrey stopped playing ball with me and his ears went up like two satellite receivers.' Grandpa held up his two index fingers and wiggled them about. 'That dog scooted out of the kitchen, and I knew he was about to run away.'

Layla giggled at Grandpa's description. Resting my elbows on the marble work surface I placed my face into my hands. 'They've been gone six minutes, and Maddie's dog has run off.'

'Ah, well,' chuckled Grandpa, 'leave him. He'll come back when he's hungry.'

'He's a dog, Grandpa, not a cat,' I said, blowing the air out of my cheeks. 'You can't let dogs wander about anymore. I am blaming my mother, Fay, and that stupid door for this.'

'What have your mother and Fay got to do with the dog?' Grandpa asked, rising from a chair he'd been sitting on.

'Mum rang me whilst I was watching Maddie and Frank leave. You'll never guess what's happened?'

Grandpa stared at me.

'Aunty Karen and Uncle Robert have gone to Tenerife to spend Christmas with Mum and Gary. Fay suggested the idea. She's so annoying. Why can't she mind her own business in Australia?'

Grandpa walked over to the work surface where the kettle was. 'You know where I would rather be?' He turned and smiled. 'Having tea with you two. Let's have a cuppa and if the dog's not back, the search party can begin. Layla – do you want a cup of tea?'

Her smile began to disappear. 'I should be cleaning. Mr Baxter said...'

Grandpa waved his hand at her. 'Mr Baxter has gone on holiday for three weeks. Rachel and I are in charge now. You look like you need a cuppa.'

I cast Grandpa a worried look. 'Do you think we should be going after Humphrey?'

Grandpa was taking out three cups. 'He might have nipped to the loo outside.'

The image of Humphrey bolting down the gravel drive, his large ears rotating as he ran, giving him more speed, appeared in my mind. 'Humphrey was not going to the toilet.'

Grandpa gestured for me to take a seat. 'Calm down, Rachel. Let's have a cuppa.'

After taking a few sips of Grandpa's tea my hunched shoulders sunk. 'You have always made good tea.'

Layla took a sip and gave Grandpa the thumbs up. He nodded before taking a mouthful. 'Tea making is one of my many talents. Being a Christmas dog sitter is going to be tough, so I'll make sure we all have plenty of tea inside us.'

'Tough?' I exclaimed. 'Grandpa, Humphrey has already bolted, and this is day one.'

Layla smiled and fiddled with the gold chain around her neck. I noticed a tiny L hanging from it. She had striking dark eyes that reminded me of black coffee. Her nails were long and a bold pink colour. On top of her head her black hair was coiled into a tight bun. The sides were perfect and smooth with not a strand out of place. She was wearing a pink sweatshirt, blue jeans, and white trainers.

'Do you live locally, Layla?' I asked, keen to know more about her.

She shook her head. Her young face had become creased and shadowy. 'If you'd asked me a month ago, I would have said yes and that I live with my boyfriend, Ryan, in the flat above the Harp Brook Inn.' Pausing, her fingers returned to playing with her chain. I sensed she was nervous. 'We've split up and...' She took a breath. 'He threw me and my baby son out two weeks ago.' After wiping her sweaty forehead, she took a mouthful of tea. 'Zac's biological dad never wanted to be involved so it's always been just Zac and me.'

'What?' I gasped, glancing at Layla and her baby son in his travel cot. 'Your boyfriend did that to you right before Christmas?'

'That's terrible,' said Grandpa. 'I'm so sorry, Layla.'

She stared down into her cup of tea. 'Ryan kicked us out because I found texts from other women on his phone. They were sending him photos of themselves.'

'Did you confront him about the texts?'

'Yes, and he got angry.' A solitary tear trickled down her face. She wiped it with the back of her hand. 'He said Zac and I are annoying, and we were getting in the way of him enjoying himself.'

'Where have you been living,' I asked, glancing at Zac playing in his travel cot.

She let out a heavy sigh. 'Zac and I have been sofa surfing.

Well, he's all right as he's in his travel cot, but I have been living on the sofas of friends.'

I instantly thought of Maddie. She'd be horrified if she knew. 'Have you told my sister about this?'

Layla shook her head. 'Mr Baxter knows but I don't think he's told her. He told me it wasn't his problem. This is why I have had Zac with me on cleaning jobs. Ryan would normally look after him, but he doesn't want anything more to do with us. Christmas is coming and my baby and I are going to be homeless. Plus, there is a lot of snow coming and do you know what the icing on my "crap life cake" is? I don't even...' She let out a large sob. 'I don't have a sodding hood on my coat.' She dissolved into tears.

Instinctively I jumped out of my seat and put my arm over her shoulder. 'Hey, Layla, don't cry. Come on, dry your eyes.'

Grandpa and I exchanged worried glances. 'Do you not have any family you can stay with?' I asked.

'I don't have any family,' Layla said. 'My mother stopped speaking to me when I was seventeen because she listened to my stepfather. He hated me.' Layla flashed us both a brave smile and wiped her face. 'I've only just started speaking to my biological dad, but I have never met him. I can't really turn up on his doorstep.' She sniffed. 'I'll be okay.'

'How old are you, Layla?' I asked.

'Twenty-one. It's going to be okay. Sometimes baby Zac looks at me when we're crashing on a friend's sofa, and I wonder what he's thinking. I tell him, "Don't worry, Mummy is going to sort this mess out."' More tears streamed down her face.

I studied her and thought about all the things I'd moaned about lately; having to look after my grandpa over Christmas, the state of my hair, being forced to stay in a luxurious manor house for three weeks and seeing my family on WhatsApp enjoying themselves in Tenerife. I wasn't homeless and I had somewhere to sleep tonight. Layla's issues put things into sharp perspective. Without hesitation and any thought about what my brother-in-law might think or say, I placed my hand over Layla's. 'Stay here, Layla, until you find somewhere permanent or until my sister and her husband return after Christmas.'

She wiped her damp cheeks and glanced at both of us. 'What? Really?'

Grandpa nodded. 'Rachel's right. How can we live in this huge manor house with the empty rooms and enough food to last for weeks knowing you and your baby son are homeless over Christmas.'

'You can have the room Maddie was going to put me in,' I explained. 'It's the bedroom with the peacock bedding. I will find another room.'

'Are you sure?' Layla gasped. 'You don't know how much this means to me.'

I smiled at her. 'Don't worry. There's room for all of us.' She stood up and gave both Grandpa and me a hug. 'You've made my year, both of you.'

Warm tingles shot up my spine at seeing Layla's happy smile.

Grandpa went over to say hello to her baby son who was playing with a soft toy.

'How old is he, Layla?'

She smiled. 'Nine months.'

'Ah. Nice to meet you, young man. You're staying here for the next few weeks, and I have my eye on you so no trouble.'

Layla chuckled as Zac handed Grandpa his toy and babbled something in baby language. A worry about Frank finding out flared up inside my mind but I suppressed it. I couldn't let Layla spend Christmas homeless or sleeping on sofas.

CHAPTER ELEVEN

A thought hit me – I remembered Humphrey was still missing. With a heavy sigh, I grabbed my coat, a dog lead and car keys. 'I'll be back. I'm going to find Humphrey.'

Grandpa leaned over and picked up his coat. 'Let's go.'

'We don't both need to go. Stay here, put your feet up and relax.'

Grandpa shook his head and cast me a mischievous grin. 'I do enough of that at home. As I said before, I am ready for an adventure.'

Layla took our cups to the sink. 'I'm going to finish the cleaning and see if the person who I am currently sofa surfing with can drop my stuff over. Good luck finding Humphrey. He burrows under a hole in the fence at the bottom near the gates. I've told Mr Baxter that he should get the fence fixed as it leads onto the road, but he doesn't listen.'

Silently cursing Frank, I made my way to the front door. Grandpa stepped outside, after me. 'This door is so hard to close,' I yelled, trying to pull it shut. Somehow, I managed to give the old door a huge yank that secured it.

Grandpa took his flat cap out of his pocket and put it on.

'That crafty dog will have worked out our weakness – shutting that door. This doesn't bode well.'

'Great,' I sighed, giving the old door a huge yank.

The snow had stopped falling which was a relief. There was only a thin coating on the ground. Once in my car, we crawled down the gravel drive at a snail's pace, looking across the grounds for Humphrey. Maybe he hadn't chosen to leave the driveway. I was certain the white snow would make it easier to spot a brown spaniel. 'I can't believe we have lost Humphrey and I've invited their cleaner to stay for Christmas,' I said, feeling anxious. 'Two of Maddie and Frank's rules broken already. If Frank is going to watch us on his security cameras he is in for a shock. Maybe I should message Maddie and tell her?'

Grandpa shook his head. 'Let them enjoy their holiday. They don't need to know.' He gave me a mischievous wink.

'Maddie said Frank has security cameras.'

Grandpa let out a sigh. 'Frank has other things on his mind like that business deal he's trying to win. He'll be too wrapped up in that. Rachel, he was too busy to even talk to us earlier. Trust me on this.'

We headed out of the gates and turned into the lane to go into Harp Brook village.

'Where would a dog like Humphrey run away to, Grandpa?'

With a chuckle, Grandpa shrugged. 'Maybe he's got a lady dog friend?'

I drove slowly past the row of three little cottages with their snow-capped roofs, which were directly after the gates to the Manor House. Grandpa and I both scanned the front gardens for a sighting of Humphrey. Once past the cottages, I headed into Harp Brook.

'Do you think he ran to the village?'

'Park up,' ordered Grandpa. 'It will give us a chance to have a look around the village. Might even pop in for a pint.' He grinned and gestured towards one of the pubs, The Nag's Head.

'We need to find Humphrey first, Grandpa. Aunty Karen gave me strict orders to restrict you to half a shandy on Christmas Day.'

'Rachel, it's Christmas. A time to enjoy ourselves.'

'Oh, yeah,' I mumbled, scanning the road and houses for Humphrey. 'I keep forgetting.'

After parking near the church, we both got out. Grandpa went to look at the Church noticeboard. I walked up and down the high street, shouting, 'Humphrey!' and scanning the road. There was no sign of the little spaniel.

Grandpa came to meet me. 'There's a Senior Christmas Tea Dance on Monday afternoon in the church hall,' he announced cheerfully.

I rolled my eyes. 'Now is not the time for checking out social events, Grandpa. Where is Humphrey? I don't think he would have come this far.'

Grandpa shrugged. 'When Flo had him, he was found five miles away one time. He'd been missing for eight hours mind. That dog will travel.'

'Five miles away?' I gasped.

There were a few little shops behind us. I went into the first one, a cute gift shop selling cards, pieces of beautiful pottery, scented candles, stationery, and jewellery. The doorbell jingled as I entered it. A woman behind the counter with bushy brown hair and a cheery smile beamed at me. 'Hello, can I help you?'

'We've lost our dog,' I said. 'We don't think he's come this far but can I leave my mobile number in case anyone finds him?'

The woman chuckled. 'My dog is always crawling under our fence and running away. I feel your pain.' She grabbed a piece of paper and a pen.

'He's called Humphrey and he's my sister's dog. I'm not from Harp Brook.'

She beamed at me. 'I thought I didn't recognise you,' the woman replied. 'Who is your sister?'

'Maddie Baxter.'

The woman's cheery disposition evaporated before my eyes. 'Oh, I see,' she said. The tone in her voice had changed. It was no longer bright and welcoming. 'It's the Baxter's dog.' Her dark eyes narrowed. 'You are her sister?'

I nodded. 'I'm Rachel. My sister and her husband have gone away for Christmas. My grandpa and I are dog sitting. Do you want my mobile number?'

She scribbled it down and circled the surname Baxter several times. 'I'll keep an eye out,' she mumbled and hurried into the back of her shop.

As I left her shop, I wondered why everything had changed when I told her I was Maddie's sister. I recalled Maddie telling me that Frank disliked the people of Harp Brook. Knowing Frank, he'd probably shouted at one of them.

Despondent, I went into the next shop. It was a pharmacy and given the number of people waiting for their prescriptions, I decided to go find Grandpa instead. He was back looking at the church noticeboard and not searching for Humphrey.

We decided to drive back towards the Manor House. I was feeling anxious. Where was Maddie's dog? We were past the first cottage when Grandpa suddenly shouted, 'HUMPHREY,' and pointed into the garden of the second cottage, before the gates to the Manor House. I pulled over, turned off the engine and bolted from the car. Humphrey was standing in the garden by a little girl. She had blonde plaits which were sticking out of a red bobble hat, and they reminded me of Kate. Humphrey was wagging his tail and gazing up at her with his large brown eyes.

'Humphrey, come here,' I said, entering the garden with my hand outstretched.

The little girl grinned at me. 'He is my friend.'

'He's a naughty dog,' I said, getting closer to Humphrey and praying he didn't decide to make another break for freedom.

'I was sad,' the little girl announced. 'He made me laugh.' Her eyes were like large blue buttons, and she had a sweet, heart-shaped face.

'Why were you sad?' I asked, noticing Humphrey was transfixed by her. The little girl nudged a stone with her red welly boot. I didn't like to press her, so I changed tactic. 'This dog is called Humphrey.'

She smiled. 'Humph-wee.' The way she pronounced it made me laugh.

'Excuse me, who are you?' A male voice called out, making me jump. A man was striding towards me. 'Is this your dog?'

I nodded. 'Sorry, he escaped, and I have been—'

He was tall and wore a grey woollen hat. At the edges, I could see wisps of brown hair sticking out. His chin was coated in stubble and as he got closer, I was taken aback by his captivating green eyes. The man didn't let me finish. 'Can you keep your dog under control? I don't like finding my daughter, Rosie, with a strange dog.'

'I'm sorry,' I said, grabbing Humphrey's red collar.

'Daddy, don't shout at the lady,' his little girl said, tapping him on the leg. 'I like this doggy. Can we keep him?'

'No, Rosie, we can't keep him.' The man took a closer look at Humphrey and glanced at me. 'This dog looks familiar.'

'He's my sister's dog,' I said, guiding Humphrey back towards the car and wishing I'd grabbed his lead from the back seat.

'You could try putting a lead on him,' the man called out in a patronising voice. 'That would be a start in controlling him.'

Turning my head back I glared at him. 'Thanks for the advice.'

Humphrey climbed into the back seat of my car and sat wagging his tail and panting.

'He's had fun,' exclaimed Grandpa, turning around in his seat. 'Look at him, he's a happy chap after his adventure.'

I climbed in the front, yanked my door shut and refused to look at Humphrey. He'd caused me enough stress for one day.

CHAPTER TWELVE

In the afternoon I made us all a slow-cooked casserole with beef, vegetables, and my handmade horseradish dumplings. Maddie was right when she told me the house was fully stocked with food. In the utility area, behind a door in the kitchen, was a row of giant American fridge-freezers, stocked with every food imaginable. There were also cupboards filled with tins, soups, pasta, rice and an array of flavourings, spices and herbs.

Later Grandpa and Layla laid the wooden table in the corner and kept praising me for the delicious smell coming from the casserole. Earlier I'd asked Layla what she'd been eating, and she said that she often went hungry as buying Zac baby food and nappies was her priority. She felt bad about asking the people who let her sleep on their sofa for food.

After I'd served us all a bowl of casserole and offered everyone a piece of crusty bread, we all dived in. To see Layla wolfing down my casserole brought tears of happiness to my eyes. Blinking them away I glanced at Baby Zac playing in his travel cot and Humphrey asleep in his basket by the kitchen island. That was not where his dog basket normally lived but given what had happened earlier, I'd decided to not let him out of my sight. The house felt peaceful and calm.

'So, Layla, have you always been a cleaner?' I asked, feeling the warmth from the casserole engulf my body.

She shook her head. 'I started out doing a hairdressing apprenticeship.'

Grandpa mopped up some casserole sauce with a piece of bread. 'Why did you stop?'

She smiled and pointed at Zac. 'I needed a job which fitted around him. Cleaning houses in the mornings worked in the early days when he was tiny as he would sleep a lot. Ryan didn't have to do much when he looked after him for me.' She took out something from her handbag which was slung over the back of the chair. 'I still carry around my hair dressing scissors and combs.'

'You should go back to it,' Grandpa suggested.

Layla sighed. 'Eric, I would love to go back to it. Whenever I stay on someone's sofa, I always offer them a quick trim. Some take me up on my offer.'

Grandpa ran his hand through his white tufty hair. 'What do you think, Layla? In your professional opinion – should I go shorter? A buzz-cut maybe?' His eyes twinkled with excitement.

Layla giggled and then studied Grandpa's hair. 'Eric, I think a little tidy up and maybe comb both sides as opposed to just one.'

She had a point. Grandpa's hair was neat on the right side and unruly on the left.

He smiled. 'Everyone at eighty should embrace their wild side.'

'Worrying,' I said, jokingly, as Layla got up and went to smooth down Grandpa's hair.

'How did you and Ryan meet?' I asked, putting my greasy hair up into a messy bun.

'I met him on a night out with my mates,' said Layla. 'It was my first night out after having Zac – he was three months old.'

'Do you think you and Ryan will have a reconciliation?' Grandpa asked.

Layla shook her head. 'He said some nasty things. Zac and I are not going back there.' She studied Grandpa's hair at the back of his head. 'Blimey, Eric, it's quite long. I could trim it so it's above your collar.'

'Deal,' said Grandpa, 'I want to look my best for the ladies of Harp Brook.'

Layla gasped at what Grandpa had said and I rolled my eyes.

After dinner, Layla put Zac down upstairs in her new bedroom. I raced upstairs and fetched my bag and suitcase from Layla's room and went to search for another room to sleep in. I stared at the doors leading to the west wing. What was behind those doors? I was intrigued and nosey at what sort of expensive furniture lay behind them. All the doors were locked, which was what Maddie had said. I tried to bend down and peer through the keyholes, but I couldn't see anything.

I decided that I didn't want to sleep in Maddie and Frank's master bedroom, so I walked along the hallway and found myself crossing over into the west wing of the house. The doors would probably be locked like the ones leading to the west wing downstairs, but I decided to find out. Feeling anxious and with a trembling hand I turned the handle on the first door I came to. It wasn't locked. I skipped a breath as I entered.

Flicking the light switch I gasped. My eyes were met with an explosion of colour. A spacious room stood before me with walls painted in a gorgeous royal blue colour and adorned with beautiful oil paintings of peacocks set in gold frames.

In the centre presided a king-sized bed with burnt orange silk bedding. A vast fitted wardrobe stretched the length of one wall, and a dressing table nestled against another wall. On each side of the tall window opposite the bed were two full length dusty-pink draped curtains.

Leaving my suitcase and handbag by the bed, I pulled them across and let my eyes roam. On the dressing table were Maddie's face creams and make-up bags. I assumed this was the room where she got dressed.

Sliding back the wardrobe doors, I saw that it was full of all her clothes. They were in strict colour order, which made me smile. Below the clothes were racks of shoes, all neatly stacked. Maddie had always loved an organised and tidy wardrobe. There were numerous full-length mirrors dotted about the room.

I spotted little constellations of photos. One was of us both on holiday in Greece three years ago. We'd run off to Greece for a week at the last minute, just the two of us. Frank wasn't on the scene, so it was just Maddie and me. That was the holiday we spent daydreaming about opening our beach café. I would do the cooking and she would cover the front of house. We spent hours at a little bar planning out our business idea on Maddie's phone and sipping cocktails. It stayed a daydream as life got in the way but thinking of that holiday gave me a warm fuzzy feeling. In most of the photos, we had a colourful cocktail in our hands, sunburnt noses, and goofy smiles.

There were several of us as little kids stood with Dad before he packed his things and left. He didn't stay with the tall woman from Glasgow. After a year he left her for his now second wife and has been happily married ever since. I wondered whether Mum knew Maddie had these photos up of Dad. Tiny knives of guilt pricked my heart as I stared at Dad's face, his messy brown hair and his friendly smile. We'd lost touch over the years, which nibbled away at the edge of my mind. But Mum had told us it would upset her if we contacted him.

On a mirror tucked away at the back of the room were three photos of teenage Maddie standing with Josh, the guy she'd dated while she was at university. He'd worked at the café on the campus. Mum disliked him from the moment she laid eyes on him. 'He's got nothing going for him,' I remembered her saying. 'Maddie, you have to aim high in relationships or you will end up with someone like your father.' I stared at the photos. Josh's long arms were wrapped around a grinning Maddie. He was tall with black curly hair and a boyish smile. Josh and Maddie were together for most of her years at uni. She said they knew each other inside out and he was the only guy to make her laugh so much her sides ached. I struggled to visualise Frank doing the same to Maddie. I wondered whether he was okay with her having photos of her ex-boyfriend on her mirror.

Surveying the room I sighed with contentment. It was nice to see Maddie had somewhere to be her colourful and vibrant self. A worry ballooned at the back of my mind. Was Frank as controlling as he was with everything else when it came to designing their house? Did Maddie not get a say in decoration? Had she agreed with Frank that she would have one room hidden away upstairs that would be styled and designed by her to make him happy? The thought left me feeling uncomfortable.

After catching sight of my reflection in one of the mirrors and groaning at my washed-out and grubby look, I collapsed on the bed. Lying down I was hit by a wave of exhaustion. It had been quite a day. The bedding was a myriad of embroidered lavender and blue flowers. It smelt of Maddie's expensive flowery perfume. I hoped she was okay on her flight wherever it was over the Atlantic.

Closing my eyes, I let my mind wander. It replayed what Maddie had said earlier about Olivia knowing Harp Brook. My chest ached for Olivia. I wished she was still alive. She could have come with me to Harp Brook. We would have had such a laugh, drinking Frank's expensive wines, eating our body weights in chocolate and dancing to Christmas songs around the manor house. Rubbing my chest, I sat up and pulled up my handbag by its straps. I took out Olivia's pink notebook. Maybe if I read some of her book it would feel like she was here with me.

I flicked over the first page and read what Olivia had written.

Step One. Change Me on the Outside.

When my wonderful friend died, I took drastic action and dyed my hair from brown to black and then cut it to above my shoulders. Side note: my hair touched my lower back before Sophie passed away. This was a drastic move.

Cutting and dyeing my hair wasn't something I did to help me grieve. I did it because I was angry and took out all my frustration on my hair.

After days of yelling up at the sky, sending God a lot of angry prayers and crying about how unfair life felt after watching my best mate die, I became a tornado and destroyed as many personal possessions as I could. This felt shockingly good. From smashing up photo frames, burning random things in the back garden to hacking my clothes to pieces, I was furious with life.

One day after collapsing into an emotional heap on my bedroom floor, surrounded by broken belongings, I decided to channel my fury in other ways. Seconds later I got the idea about my hair and went on the hunt for some kitchen scissors and hair dye.

This is not the approach I would advise. Kitchen scissors do not give you a stylish cut. Grief makes you do all sorts of strange things. Even though my hair looked terrible for days after and a hairdresser had to spend a good hour fixing the mess I'd made, the change in how I looked helped me.

When I stared at myself in the mirror, I was no longer the sad, grieving friend whose world had caved in around them. There was someone new staring back at me and I had a strange sense of detachment. My grief for Sophie didn't go away. It will live inside me for the rest of my life. But after my drastic haircut, I created a new version of Olivia. This helped me to move on with my life.

Changing myself on the outside was the catalyst for easing the pain inside of me.

Having nice hair was a big thing for Olivia. She spent a small fortune on washing, styling, and maintaining her black silky locks. She must have been hurting a lot when she cut her hair off. I read on as she joked about sitting in the chair at the salon post her kitchen scissor cut and her usual hairdresser nearly fainting at her jagged ends.

After coming to the end of the chapter I reminded myself of my reflection in one of the full-length mirrors. My hair was piled up on top of my head in a greasy knot. Since Olivia had died, my hair had become something I groaned at when I entered the bathroom back in my flat. I was always too exhausted to do anything with it so I simply wound it into what I felt was a bun shape and cursed it every time I went to the toilet. If Olivia was here, she would have something to say about it.

I was the sad, grieving friend staring at herself in the mirror. Looking away I caught sight of the pink notebook lying on the bed. I had spent too long staring at the person in the mirror. An idea sprang to mind.

Leaping off the bed I raced downstairs and went into the

kitchen to find Layla making everyone a cup of tea. 'Zac's out like a light,' she said, cheerfully. She pointed to the baby monitor. 'I always carry it with me now that we're little nomads.'

'Layla, how do you fancy giving me a haircut?'

She looked shocked. 'Really? Now?'

I nodded. 'What do you think?'

'What sort of haircut? Remember, I never finished my apprenticeship.'

Taking a deep breath, I let the words on the tip of my tongue tumble out. 'Chop it to my shoulders – yeah?' I'd always had hair which reached down to my lower back, so this was going to be quite a change.

Grandpa chuckled as he walked into the kitchen and caught sight of me sitting on a kitchen chair whilst Layla cut my hair. 'Short haircuts are great when embarking on an adventure,' he cried, lifting his hands in the air. 'Let's go large!'

Layla giggled. 'Eric, you sound like one of the teenagers from the pub.'

He punched the air. 'My granddaughter, Nadine, is always telling me to go large. I've no idea what she means but it feels good to say it.'

Later after I'd showered, washed, and blow-dried my newly cut hair, I looked at myself in one of the full-length mirrors and gasped. Layla had cut my hair to my shoulders. It now gave me an unexpected bolt of happiness.

The person staring back at me was different to the washed out one who looked in this mirror earlier.

I noted the way the ends of my hair flicked up in little curls on my shoulder and when I turned my head, my hair looked alive and glossy. As I left the room to go downstairs and model my new hairstyle now I'd washed it, I smelt a hint of vanilla. It made me stop, press my forehead against the wood and whisper, 'Hope you like it, Olivia.'

Both Layla and Grandpa clapped and cheered as I twirled about the kitchen showing off my new shorter cut. Even Humphrey barked at me, but I scowled at him as he was still in my bad books.

CHAPTER THIRTEEN

'Oh God, you've cut your hair off,' cried Mum, from her sunbed. She was wearing a bright red bikini, and her mahogany skin was darker than the day before. 'Karen put down that cocktail and come here quick,' Mum called out. 'Rachel's chopped off her beautiful long hair.'

'Mum, it was never beautiful,' I said, as Aunty Karen clip-clopped in heels towards Mum to peer down the phone screen at me.

'Oh, Janice, I like it,' cooed Aunty Karen, grinning at me and giving Mum a prod. 'It suits her.' Aunty Karen was wearing a pink frilly number which clashed with the angry red sunburn strap marks on her shoulders.

'I'll have to tell Fay,' Mum muttered, fumbling with her phone. 'Hang on a minute.'

I rolled my eyes with frustration as Mum tapped something out on WhatsApp. In the background, Aunty Karen was telling Uncle Robert to stop ogling the woman in the bikini from the villa next door to Mum's.

Mum screwed up her eyes and read what she'd typed. 'Two

days with Grandpa Eric and Rachel has cut all her hair off. He's hard work at eighty.'

She smiled sweetly at me. 'Where's Dad, Rachel?'

I fiddled with my phone and pointed it at a happy Grandpa, who was sitting with Humphrey on his lap, on the sofa in the east wing's living room.

'Get that dog off your sister's expensive sofa,' my mother screeched so loudly that she woke up Humphrey. 'For goodness' sake, Rachel, get that dirty dog off the sofa. It probably cost Frank thousands.'

I ignored her. 'Grandpa, do you want to say hello?'

He waved and gave Mum a thumbs up.

Mum peered at her phone screen. 'He looks pale. Are you feeding him properly?'

'Yes, he had a cooked breakfast this morning and last night he had a casserole.'

The sound of Zac grizzling as Layla brought him into the living room made Mum sit up on her sun lounger and cast me a puzzled look. 'Did I just hear a baby crying?'

'It's Layla's baby.'

Aunty Karen clip-clopped at speed back towards Mum. 'Is there something I should know, Janice? Why has Rachel got a crying baby?'

'Layla is Maddie and Frank's cleaner, Mum. She has a little boy called Zac.'

'Cleaner?' Mum gasped. 'Why is the cleaner there with her baby son? Have you opened a creche at your sister's palatial home?'

With a heavy sigh, I glared at my mother. 'It's fine, don't worry.'

'How did you sleep? Did you feel like royalty in Maddie's satin bedding?'

'It was very relaxing,' I said, although I left out the bit about

Zac crying for most of the night and keeping me awake. Even though he and Layla were in the east wing, I still heard him. Layla had apologised over breakfast saying that with the constant change in Zac's life he was out of his routine. I told her I'd not heard him.

Mum had got distracted and was clicking her fingers at Gary. 'I'll have another gin and tonic please. Make it large. I'm stressed, so bring me my ciggies as well. I tell you, parenting is hard work.'

'I have to go now.' I was getting irritated with my mother, so I told her I needed to walk Humphrey.

Mum nodded. 'Do not lose that dog, Rachel. Maddie doesn't want to come back from her gorgeous and relaxing holiday in Malibu to find her dog is missing.'

'Enjoy your Sunday, Mum.' I cast her a fake sugary smile.

In the background, Aunty Karen shouted, 'Tell Rachel to make sure Dad is near a toilet. His bowels play up a lot.'

I ended the call and looked at Grandpa. 'Aunty Karen says your bowels play up a lot.'

He chuckled. 'What does Karen know about my bowels? She pops her head around the front door and shouts, "Everything all right, Dad?" I shout "Yes"; she says, 'Great" and she gets back in her car and goes home.'

Rolling my eyes I walked to the door. 'Humphrey, walkies.'

After I returned from walking Humphrey, Grandpa suggested we all play cards. Layla and I joined him in the living room. Zac crawled about as Layla, and I tried our best to beat Grandpa at rummy.

He won every time.

It made me smile and remember those Christmases Maddie

and I spent with him and Nana. He would do the same then – beat us at every opportunity.

'I've missed playing cards,' said Layla. 'My nana used to play cards with me when I went to stay at her house.'

'Was she any good?' Grandpa asked before laying down a perfect hand of rummy and winning the round.

Layla grinned. 'She had little mirrors placed around the room so she could always see my cards.'

I gasped at Layla. 'Your nana cheated?'

Grandpa cast me a knowing smile and I found myself looking around for strategically placed mirrors. Had Grandpa used mirrors with us? To my horror I spotted one hidden behind Layla and one in the branches of the tree behind me. I reached for it, crying, 'Grandpa, you've been cheating all this time.'

He began to belly laugh. 'I have been fooling you for years. If I ever tell you where to sit before a game of cards, check for mirrors. Your nana Edith used to tell me off. "Eric," she'd say, "how can you trick those little girls?" and I would say, "With ease."'

I turned to Layla. 'Thanks for telling me about your nana and her little mirrors. I have seen my grandpa in a different light now.'

She broke into a fit of giggles. 'Sorry, Rachel, I can't believe you never worked out what Eric was doing when you were little.'

'Nor can I.'

Layla leaned back against the sofa. 'Living with my mum and stepfather was hard so it was nice to escape to Nana's house. I twigged early on what she was up to with the mirrors.'

'Maddie and Rachel didn't,' interjected Grandpa, making us all laugh.

It was nice seeing Layla smile and joke with Grandpa. I looked up at the gigantic Christmas tree and its twinkling lights and the pressure of the family, Aunty Karen's list of rules for looking after Grandpa and my worries about Maddie slipped away.

After cards we had some lunch and Zac went down for a nap. Then Grandpa beat us both convincingly at Scrabble.

'Thank you,' Layla said to us once the Scrabble board and tiles had been cleared away. 'Today, I've felt festive and happy.' She smiled. 'It's been tough for me these past few weeks. I never thought I'd be playing games in this beautiful house with two lovely people, eating delicious food and not worrying about where Zac and I are going to live.'

I gave her hand a squeeze. 'This is just the start of our Christmas together, Layla,' I beamed.

Grandpa nodded. 'Layla, I like you already and we're not going to stop smiling all Christmas.'

'Is that a promise, Eric?' Layla asked.

Grandpa grinned. 'Sure is. The Christmas Dog Sitters never break their promises.'

While Grandpa told Layla all about how he used to spend a lot of time setting up his mirrors, when Maddie and I were little, and how he'd call us into the room, wondering whether this would be the game that we realised what was going on, I found myself thinking about Maddie. Was she okay in America? Would she have a nice Christmas?

With a twang of sadness, I recalled Maddie phoning me from California in floods of tears and sobbing about how much she hated her new life. The memory left me uncomfortable, so I leapt to my feet and decided to bake a pie for tea. I was overthinking the Maddie and Frank situation again. She had said there was nothing to worry about. I was reading too much into that glassy-eyed look she'd given me before she left.

CHAPTER FOURTEEN

It was Monday early morning. Grandpa and I were in the kitchen having a cup of tea after devouring my sausage, cheese, and egg muffins.

He was dressed for the day, whereas I still had my Christmas pyjamas on – red ones adorned with brown reindeer. I'd seen them in the supermarket the day before Grandpa arrived.

Layla and Zac were still upstairs, and Humphrey was snoozing in his basket by my feet.

Before coming down for breakfast I'd read a second chapter of Olivia's pink notebook, titled: *Happy Pennies.*

She'd written down a huge list of what she called her *Happy Pennies.* It made me smile as it included things like ordering coffee from the sexy barista at the café – even though his coffee-making skills were questionable; buying herself flowers; going swimming to see the hot lifeguard wink at her from his chair; eating chips with curry sauce; dancing to Harry Styles in the kitchen; and going to her local writers group where she would have a giggle with the flirty thriller writer.

So many of Olivia's happy pennies featured lusting after

attractive men. Olivia claimed that she had made a determined effort to fill her day-to-day life with as many happy pennies as she could. This was what prompted me to go downstairs in my reindeer pyjamas. They made me feel happy.

There was a loud knock at the front door which made us both jump. 'Who the hell is that?' I gasped, checking the time on my phone. 'It's just started getting light outside.'

'The police?' Grandpa said, stroking his white stubble-clad chin. 'I would love to be interrogated; it's been a life dream of mine for years.'

I cast him a worried look and padded into the hall to begin the arduous process of opening the old front door. It was so heavy that I had to grab the handle and lean back.

After a lot of huffing and puffing, I got it open and stared at the person on the doorstep. It was little Rosie's dad. The patronising man from Saturday who had made a smart-ass comment about me using Humphrey's dog lead. He wasn't wearing a hat this time, and he had thick dark brown hair. His green eyes surveyed my tousled new shorter hair and my reindeer pyjamas.

I found myself distracted by his broad shoulders, his stubble and his large hands. My cheeks warmed. 'Can I help you?' I said in a sugary voice.

He opened his mouth and I yelped. Something furry darted through my legs and shot up the drive. 'Humphrey!' I shouted.

The man glanced behind him at Humphrey who was now a brown speck up the driveway and turned back to me. 'Still not got control of that dog, I see.' He arched an eyebrow.

I glared at him. 'Look what you made me do.'

He shifted his weight from one boot to another and cleared his throat. 'I'm the builder.'

'Builder?'

'Yes, I'm working on Mr Baxter's new kitchen. That's my

van over there.' He pointed to a blue van parked at the side of the house.

'Oh... right,' I mumbled. 'You're the builder.'

He nodded. 'I need the side gates opening so I can get around the back. Mr Baxter assured me there would be someone here.'

'Side gates? What do I need to do?'

'Open them... perhaps?'

My cheeks had become red hot. With a flick of my hair, I turned on my heel, grabbed my boots from inside the hall, shoved my feet into them, pulled on my coat and stormed past him.'

'What are you doing?' He asked.

'Opening the gates for you,' I snapped.

He arched his eyebrow a second time. 'They're electric. You press a button... inside the house.'

To my relief, Layla appeared in the doorway, with Zac on her hip. 'Rachel, I'll show you.'

Without looking at him I stormed back into the house and followed Layla. 'That man is so rude,' I snapped.

Layla turned to me and grinned. 'Your face is as red as your pyjamas. I can see he's pressed all your buttons.'

Once the gates had been opened, I stomped upstairs to get a shower, wash my hair, and put some clothes on so that I could go find Humphrey.

Grandpa joined me in the search for Humphrey. It felt like the film *Groundhog Day;* however this time the snow had melted away. 'I bet he's gone back to that builder's cottage,' I said as we crawled along the gravel drive.

We drove back and forth past the three little cottages peering out to see whether we could see Humphrey again but there was no sign. Once in the village, I parked up and we searched up and down the high street. There was no sign of him. The third shop was a bakery with a small café out the back. 'Do you fancy a cuppa, Grandpa?'

He nodded and we stepped inside. Grandpa went to sit down, and I approached the counter. The young man behind the counter grinned at me. 'Hello, what can I get you?'

'One tea and a flat white please.' I surveyed the rows of freshly baked loaves of bread and crusty rolls to the right of him. 'Your bread smells fantastic. Can I buy one of your sourdough loaves?'

He smiled. 'Thanks. I can't take credit for the bread as that's all my wife's handiwork. I'm the barista of this fine establishment. Are you visiting? I know most of the regulars, but I haven't seen you in here.'

'Grandpa and I are dog sitting over Christmas for my sister. Her dog escaped this morning and we're out looking for him.'

The man smiled and began making my coffee on the silver machine behind him. 'Leave me your dog's details and I will watch out for him.' He reached over and grabbed a brown paper bag and a pen. 'Write your name and a contact number plus a description of your sister's dog.'

I scribbled down my details and a description of Humphrey. 'Her dog has a reputation for escaping so this could be a regular occurrence.'

'Who is your sister?'

'Maddie Baxter.'

He cast me an odd look. 'You're Maddie Baxter's sister?'

'Yes, why?'

With a shrug, he went back to his coffee machine. Once he'd made my coffee, he took out a black circular tray and placed the loaf on it, along with Grandpa's teapot. 'You're new to Harp Brook?'

I nodded. 'Yes. Maddie and her husband have gone away for Christmas. This bakery café of yours is fabulous. I think

99

Grandpa and I will enjoy coming here. We're looking for things to do so if you have any ideas…'

The man presented me with the card machine. I tapped my card. 'Word of advice,' he said, 'stay away from the landlady in the pub down the hill. It's called *The Harp Brook Inn*, and she's called Vanessa.'

'Why?'

He shrugged. 'She's not a fan of your sister's husband and she's not one to hide her feelings.' Leaning against the counter he placed my coffee on the tray, plus a milk jug and an empty cup and saucer for Grandpa.

'Oh, I see.'

'You and your grandfather look like nice people. Vanessa is one to avoid.'

With a smile, I took hold of the tray. 'I'm Rachel by the way.'

He gave me a cheerful smile. 'Darren. Nice to meet you, Rachel. My wife, Abi, is out the back sorting out more bread.' A woman poked her head from around the loaves and waved. 'Hi, I'm Abi.'

Darren gestured towards his wife. 'What you can't see is that my beautiful wife is pregnant. Baby is due in January.'

'Congratulations,' I said. 'Is it your first?'

Abi laughed. 'I wish. It will be our third child.'

'The more the merrier,' joked Darren.

I smiled before taking the tray over to where Grandpa was sitting. After unloading the tray, I told Grandpa what the guy behind the counter had told me.

'Well, we'll have to go meet this Vanessa,' chuckled Grandpa. 'I came here for an adventure and a tussle with an angry landlady sounds like fun.'

'Grandpa, you're a bad influence.' I laughed. 'I wonder why she hates Frank?'

'He probably complained about her pub or the food she serves,' Grandpa said, pouring out his tea.

I nodded. 'You're probably right. So... what are we going to do about Humphrey?'

Grandpa shrugged. 'Don't worry about it. He'll turn up.'

'I can't just leave it. I think when I get back to the house, I will make some missing dog posters with my mobile number on them and pin them around the town.'

Darren came to our table carrying a mobile phone. 'Abi has had an idea about your runaway dog. Why don't we stick a photo of the dog and your contact details on Harp Brook's town Facebook page.'

'That would be great.' I took out my phone and scrolled through my photos. 'Ah, here's one of Humphrey. He's been microchipped so if he's handed to a vet, they will be able to see who he belongs to.'

I showed it to Darren, and he grinned at Humphrey looking angelic. After sending Darren the photo, my name, and my contact number he put a post on the town's Facebook site and sent me a link.

After our drinks, we thanked Darren and Abi and left the café. We did one more scan of the high street before getting back in my car.

'I used to love driving my car,' Grandpa said, as I turned into the Manor House drive entrance. 'Your mother made me sell it a few years ago as, according to her, I was too old to be driving.'

'Well, you're not missing much, Grandpa.'

There was no sign of Humphrey back at the house. Anxiety crawled over me. Even though I grumbled a lot about Humphrey I didn't want him to come to any harm. Maddie and the family would never forgive me if something happened to him.

The kitchen was filled with the sounds of drills, hammers,

wood being sawed and men laughing, all drifting out from behind the construction sheet. I needed something to do so I pressed my face near to the sheet. 'Does anyone want a tea or a coffee back there?'

In a few seconds, the sounds of heavy boots got closer to the sheet. It was flicked back, and a young guy with blond spikey hair grinned at me. 'We thought you'd never ask.' Behind him, I could see the new kitchen. It was a huge space with giant windows on either side. In the ceiling, there were a myriad of wooden rafters.

The smart-ass builder whom I spoke to earlier glanced at me and I scowled at him, 'Two mugs of tea please,' said the blond guy. 'My name's Tom and my boss who, I have been told you've already met, is Ben.'

'Hello, Tom and... Ben. I'm Rachel and I better get to work making your teas.'

After sorting out mugs of tea for the builders I created some 'Missing Dog' posters and printed them out in Frank's ground floor office. Layla was off to a cleaning job in town, and promised to pin them up.

As time passed there was still no sign of Humphrey. I left my phone out on the kitchen table and at one point tried to telepathically communicate with Humphrey. This didn't work. I decided to lose myself in making Grandpa and me my legendary steak and caramelised onion stacked sandwiches for lunch.

They were one of Olivia's favourite lunches and they were one of my happy pennies.

On weekends we'd still be on the sofa in our PJs at lunchtime. Our Saturday and Sunday mornings always went at a glacial pace. We used to watch something on Netflix, idly swiping through photos of men on her dating apps, social media stalking someone we both knew, brainstorming her next novel or making pointless online clothing purchases. I'd decide to make us some lunch and she'd persuade me to make steak and caramelised onion sandwiches.

Once, as we sat on the sofa savouring every bite, she said, 'Rachel, you are wasting your time with a career in project management and also the world is missing out on your wonderful cooking.'

'Being a project manager is a proper job,' I replied. 'Keeps my mother happy.'

Olivia shook her head. 'Do what makes *you* happy.'

'What? Making life better one sandwich at a time?' I said as a joke.

With a nod she said, 'Exactly that.'

Her words echoed in my head as I caramelised the onions and savoured the sizzling sound and the sweet aroma they put into the air. Closing my eyes for a few seconds I remembered how Olivia would stand by me while I was cooking the sandwiches. She'd laugh and admit to drooling. I would giggle as she grabbed a sheet of kitchen roll to catch her slobber.

Once they were cooked, I placed the sandwiches on plates and called Grandpa. As I took them over to the kitchen table, I was sure I could smell a hint of vanilla.

His eyes grew wide and a huge smile stretched from ear to ear. 'You're spoiling me, Rachel.'

'I've made sure the steak is at that melt-in-your mouth stage and I have cut it up small so don't worry about your dentures.'

Watching him devouring his sandwich filled me with happiness.

After, he seemed preoccupied and quiet. 'Are you okay, Grandpa?'

'The Senior Christmas Tea Dance is on this afternoon at the church hall. His face lit up. 'Dancing makes me happy. I haven't done it in years.'

I thought back to Olivia's notebook. If this was one of Grandpa's happy pennies, then I had to help him. A worrying thought bloomed at the front of my mind as I recalled Aunty Karen's list and how she said he wasn't to do anything strenuous. Grandpa was eighty years old and even though he claimed he could still walk fast; he was slow, plus his bones creaked a lot. The most he was going to do at the Senior Tea Dance was sit on the sidelines and watch the dancing couples. 'Let's do it.'

'I haven't brought my smart suit. Karen made me take it out of my bag as she said I wouldn't need anything like that. She didn't see me sneaking in my fancy shoes, though.'

Leaning back in my chair I studied Grandpa. He was the same height as Frank and roughly the same build. If my brother-in-law did not have security cameras in the master bedroom, this plan of mine might work. 'I have an idea. Come with me.'

CHAPTER FIFTEEN

Grandpa and I entered Frank and Maddie's master bedroom in the east wing. We were in search of Frank's wardrobe and, hopefully, a collection of suits.

The room, like every other in the manor house, was impressive. It was presided over by the biggest four-poster bed I had ever seen, made up with beautiful cream silk bedding. An elegant white sofa was positioned by a tall window, framed by two full-length linen curtains. On the back wall was an enormous dark wood wardrobe. There were a few arty photographs in elegant frames of Frank's mother, who lived back in California. In her youth she had been a professional ballet dancer, so all the photos were of her in *Swan Lake* or *The Nutcracker*.

There were no photos of anyone from our family which wasn't a surprise: none of us are professional ballet dancers.

My heart pounded against my ribcage. I was invading Maddie and Frank's privacy by being in their bedroom. I turned to look at Grandpa. He was my moral compass and would tell me if what I was planning was wrong. 'I thought we could borrow one of Frank's suits, but now we're in here I feel like it is a bad idea.'

Grandpa beamed at me, and his twinkly blue eyes shone. 'Rachel, you think too much. Frank won't miss a suit and it will only be for a few hours.'

We opened the wardrobe and gasped in wonder at the array of suits. There were jackets and trousers in every shade of grey and blue and a variety of fabric textures. 'Wow – Frank likes a suit,' I murmured.

Grandpa beamed at me. 'Those ladies at that Senior Tea Dance are in for a treat.'

I looked around the room. 'I can't see any cameras.'

Grandpa grinned. 'If there was a camera in here, I would do a little dance for Frank.'

I stared at him in shock. 'Is that your wild side at eighty coming out again?'

He chuckled. 'Definitely.'

That's when I wondered whether Grandpa was the right person to use as a moral compass.

With the help of several safety pins and one of Frank's belts, I managed to get Grandpa in a posh grey, double-breasted suit.

'Wow, you look good, Grandpa,' I gushed, as he gave me a twirl. He went up to the full-length mirror and stared at himself. 'It's a shame your nana is not here to see me in such finery. She loved a decent suit on me.'

'She would be very proud, Grandpa.' I placed my hand on his shoulder as he went a little blurry. Wiping away a stray tear, I croaked, 'She's probably looking down on us.'

Grandpa cast me an uncomfortable look and fiddled with the red bow-tie I'd found him. 'Let's hope she's not able to see me at the Senior Tea Dance.'

'What do you mean?'

He grinned and gave me a wink. 'I'm in the mood for a bit of romance.'

I let out a silent groan. Maybe I should have followed Aunty Karen's advice and kept excitement to a minimum. It was too late now. As we turned to leave the master bedroom, I took another look around the impressive room. Once again it felt very Frank-inspired. There were so many personal touches for him and his late mother. It was like Maddie had been forgotten.

'Are you coming?' Grandpa asked, gesturing towards the bedroom door.

I nodded and suppressed the familiar knot of unease.

We made our way downstairs. I helped him put on his smart black shoes. As I was tying the last shoelace my phone began to ring. I grabbed it and saw that it was an unknown number. Maybe Humphrey had been found?

A woman answered. 'Is that Rachel, the owner of the brown spaniel? One of our regulars saw a post on Facebook about your dog.'

'Yes, it is.'

'We have your dog. Come down to the Senior Tea Dance in the church hall. One of the ladies has him as he turned up at her house.'

'What?' I screeched. 'I am coming down now.'

'Grandpa, Humphrey is at the Tea Dance.'

Grandpa began to clap his hands. 'That dog knows how to enjoy himself.'

I needed to grab my car keys and they were in the kitchen. 'Let's go get my keys.' We made our way into the kitchen, and I looked up in shock as I saw Ben and Tom standing sipping cups of tea.

Tom's face lit up at Grandpa in a designer suit. 'Great suit.'

Loving the attention, Grandpa did a twirl and then a couple of model poses that made Tom and Ben laugh.

'I've borrowed it from Frank,' announced Grandpa. 'It was Rachel's idea. Don't tell him. I am off to the Senior Tea Dance to break a few hearts.'

As I snatched my keys from the island counter, I noticed Ben giving me a worried look. Inside I was a ball of nervous energy. Letting Grandpa borrow one of Frank's suits was a risk – but what I didn't need was a smart-ass builder looking at me like I was a naughty child. 'Mr Baxter loves his suits,' exclaimed Ben. 'Do you think that's wise – letting your grandfather borrow it?'

Irritation at Ben the builder prickled at my neck and cheeks. Who the hell did he think he was? Had I asked for his advice? I snapped, 'You stick to building the kitchen out there and I will sort out Grandpa.'

Tom turned away to chuckle and Ben stared at me.

As I drove us into Harp Brook, I couldn't shake an uncomfortable feeling I had about the Christmas Senior Tea Dance. Grandpa was sat in the passenger seat of my car, dressed in Frank's suit, and practising complicated arm gestures. His movements flooded me with worry: Grandpa was not going to sit on the sidelines.

We parked the car and Grandpa was like an excitable child in his eagerness to get inside. 'Come on, Rachel, let's go large at the Senior Tea Dance.'

In the little hall attached to the church, a six-piece band was setting up. Chairs and tables had been set out around the edges to make a dance floor. Under the twinkly lights, I could see a lot of senior partygoers in some fabulous and colourful outfits: lots of sequinned dresses, silver shoes, and multi-coloured bow ties.

I immediately felt underdressed in my jeans, an old blue shirt, boots, and coat.

Grandpa nudged me and pointed. There was Humphrey gazing up at an older lady in midnight blue, who was sitting on her own at a table. Grandpa and I made our way through a throng of tea-dance goers.

The band started to play, and the church hall came alive. A few couples left their chairs and walked onto the dance floor. I'd been a *Strictly Come Dancing* fan for years and I found my gaze drawn to the dancers.

Once the band finished their first song, I joined Grandpa who was standing by the older lady. Now I was closer, I could see that her midnight blue dress really was beautiful and she had grey curly hair which was pinned up at the back.

Grandpa outstretched his hand and introduced himself. 'I'm Eric.' He pointed at Humphrey. 'That's my granddaughter's dog and he's been missing all morning.'

The lady beamed at Humphrey. 'This dog is the reason I am here.'

Grandpa asked if we could sit at her table. She nodded and smiled at the prospect of our company. 'My name's Dorothy. My husband passed away ten years ago, and we both enjoyed ballroom dancing.' Dorothy gave Humphrey a pat. 'I've been feeling a bit lonely lately. My daughter saw this event advertised and she's been urging me to go.' Dorothy smiled at Grandpa. 'But it felt too overwhelming to come here so I'd decided to stay at home and carry on being lonely.'

Grandpa gave her a knowing nod. 'I've been doing the same.'

Dorothy turned to him. 'Really?'

'My wife passed away years ago and all I do is sit at my living room window and watch the world carry on without me.'

'Eric,' she gushed, her eyes dancing with excitement at him.

'That's exactly it – watching the world carry on without us.' She pointed to Humphrey. 'Well, I was having my morning cup of tea and this little chap turned up.' She stroked Humphrey under his chin which he clearly loved. 'I don't know how, but he managed to get upstairs, but he did! And you wouldn't believe this, but he came downstairs with one of my silver sandals in his mouth.'

Grandpa laughed and clapped.

Dorothy chuckled. 'It was a sign. My daughter thinks I am mad viewing things as signs. Seeing him gently place the shoe by my feet did something to me. I rose from my armchair and went to choose an outfit.'

The band started to play 'It's Beginning to Look a Lot Like Christmas' and Grandpa stood up. He offered his hand to Dorothy. 'Shall we?'

Her eyes widened. 'Are you sure, Eric?'

'Dorothy,' he said, in a suave voice, 'I've been known to cut a rug in my time. This song is perfect for a slow fox-trot.'

'Oh, Eric,' gushed Dorothy, as Grandpa led her by the hand onto the dance floor.

To my amazement, they both assumed their positions with their arms high, like they're told to do on *Strictly*. Grandpa started with his left foot forward, right foot forward and then they did a quick step to the left. They started slowly but soon they were gliding effortlessly around the floor. I leaned forward in my chair watching Grandpa dance like a pro. It was like seeing a different version of him. He and Dorothy were so good, other couples stopped to stare at them.

Grandpa and Dorothy never returned to the table until the final song had finished. They were the stars of the event, and everyone applauded them at the end. As they made their way back to the table, I sneakily put Humphrey on his lead and gave him a pat for doing something nice for Dorothy.

Grandpa and Dorothy began talking to each other as soon as they sat down. It was like they were long-lost friends.

Grandpa was clearly enjoying himself, so we stayed until the event organisers started asking us to leave. We walked Dorothy out and I noticed she had looped her hand through Grandpa's arm.

I placed Humphrey in the back of the car and waited for Grandpa to finish saying goodbye to Dorothy. Her daughter was picking her up, so I assumed he was being a gentleman and making sure she got a lift safely.

A car pulled up and I noticed it was the lady from the gift shop. She beamed at Dorothy and Grandpa before glancing at me. Her eyes widened and her mouth opened. 'It's you, you're–'

'Maddie Baxter's sister. We met in your gift shop. That's my grandpa.'

The woman frowned and quickly led Dorothy away from Grandpa. 'Come on, Mum. These are not the kind of people you should be fraternising with.'

Dorothy glanced back at Grandpa and cast him a sad look. Grandpa had hung his head. He was crestfallen.

'Grandpa, get in the car,' I ordered.

'Why did her daughter take her away like that? Dorothy and I have had a wonderful time.'

I started the engine and swung out of the car park. 'Not sure – but we will get to the bottom of it.'

CHAPTER SIXTEEN

Overnight the snow returned. We all awoke to a thick layer of snow outside and giant snowflakes pattering against the windows. My bed was warm and cosy, so I allowed myself to spend an extra twenty minutes in it.

Propping up my pillows behind me I took out my phone and saw that the Met Office had issued several weather warnings in the area. Waiting for me in my email inbox were a slew of job application rejections which made me groan. My redundancy money would soon come to an end, and I would be forced to use my savings if I didn't find work.

On the general family WhatsApp chat Maddie had shared several photos of the fabulous house Frank had hired out for their Christmas in Malibu. It commanded a view across the shimmering blue ocean and was hemmed in by palm trees.

In one Maddie was standing by the pool like a swimwear model with her enviable slim figure and her golden curly hair. My sister looked relaxed and happy. Her bikini was a gorgeous burnt orange colour and reminded me of the bedding I was laid on. Our cousin Fay had been busy reviewing the photos overnight and had posted:

Great pics, Maddie. I bet Rachel is jealous as hell seeing these whilst caring for Grandpa and your dog back in Harp Brook.

'Fay, mind your own business,' I murmured, stopping myself from replying to Fay's comment with something salty and inflammatory.

Distracting myself, I moved on to Facebook and saw that I'd been accepted by the admin to join the Harp Brook town group. Scrolling down I saw Darren's post about Humphrey from yesterday.

The face of Ben, the builder, appeared in my mind. I recalled the moment on the doorstep from the day before and the run-in we had in the kitchen about Grandpa borrowing Frank's suit. His green eyes, square jaw, his smile and his smart-ass comments made my heartbeat quicken. Before I had the chance to think about what I was doing I was searching for him on Facebook, I wanted to know more about him. He was bound to have a pretty wife or girlfriend.

The email from Olivia's friend appeared in my mind. He had been called Ben and he'd lived in Surrey. I dismissed the thought. Ben is a popular name and there must be loads of Bens in Surrey. What was I doing? I stopped myself and closed Facebook. Feeling embarrassed at myself I got up and went for a shower.

Grandpa and Layla were already downstairs when I entered the kitchen. Layla smiled and pointed to the construction sheet. 'The builders are here early. I opened the gates.' Sounds of the radio and Ben laughing with Tom drifted out.

Grandpa cast me a weak smile. Humphrey was pretending to be asleep in his basket by the table. He slyly opened one eye as I walked past.

'You okay, Grandpa?'

He rose from his chair. 'Take a seat and I'll put the kettle on.'

Layla waved at us both. 'I've got to go get Zac up as I am cleaning the pub. See you later.'

Once Grandpa had made a pot of tea and I'd made some homemade pancakes covered in fruit and maple syrup, we settled at the kitchen table. He let out a heavy sigh after eating a raspberry rolled in a piece of pancake. 'I didn't like the way Dorothy's daughter led her away so quickly.' He scratched his fluffy white hair. One side was in desperate need of a comb. 'Dorothy and I had a connection.'

'You both were fabulous dancers,' I said, remembering them looking like professional ballroom dancers. 'You had perfect posture and I think if you'd been on *Strictly,* you would have got nines and tens. When did you learn to dance like that?'

He leaned back in his chair. 'I used to go to dances regularly with your nana. She'd had ballroom dancing lessons as a girl, and she taught me everything. Back in the day we even won a few competitions.'

I remembered Nana teaching me to cook in her kitchen. She was a great teacher, but she didn't hold back with her feedback. There were a few times when she pointed out my baking skill weaknesses and I'd run off to have a little cry. 'I bet Nana was a tough teacher at dancing.'

Grandpa chuckled. 'I lived in fear of putting a foot wrong.'

We ate some more pancakes, and I thought about Nana and Grandpa being ballroom competition winners. Mum never told us much about Nana and Grandpa's lives before they had children. 'I wish I'd known Nana had been into ballroom dancing back when we were little.'

Grandpa nodded. 'At least you got a chance yesterday to see me in action. I need to tell you something?'

'Yes?'

'I think I'm in love with Dorothy.'

I stared at him. How could he go from reminiscing about Nana to revealing his love for Dorothy in the blink of an eye? He reminded me of my youngest cousin, Stanley, who was always telling Aunt Polly he loved a different girl at university each week. 'In love? Really? After one Christmas Tea Dance?'

He nodded. 'When you're my age, Rachel, you don't have time to mess about. I would like to see Dorothy again.'

I let out a silent groan. This was all I needed – a lovesick grandfather.

'She feels the same way.'

'Grandpa let's slow down,' I said, raising my hands. 'We don't know anything about Dorothy and–'

He interrupted me. 'I might not be here next Christmas, Rachel. None of us know how long we have left in God's waiting room. I might drop down dead tomorrow.'

'Grandpa, don't talk like that.'

'It's true. Rachel, I want you to organise a second date for me with Dorothy before Christmas. I am free the rest of this week and next week.'

I needed to distract him. 'We need to pop the suit back in Frank's wardrobe.'

'Oh, well... we might have a problem there.'

My heart began to pound. 'A problem with the suit?'

Grandpa nodded. 'I didn't say last night when you were helping me out of it but there's a tear in one of the trouser legs.'

My heart went berserk. He'd torn one of Frank's expensive suits. 'What? You've torn Frank's suit? Why didn't you say?'

He fidgeted in his seat. 'You looked tired, and we'd had enough emotion for one day. I felt it go as I twirled Dorothy around.'

In my head I could see Frank holding up his torn suit trouser leg and demanding I pay him thousands of pounds to repair it and asking why I had disobeyed him. My heart began to thud. What the hell was I going to do?

'There's also something else.'

I groaned. 'What?'

'I found something in the inside jacket pocket.'

'Like what?'

He got up from the table. 'I'll be back.'

Panic set in as I glanced at the snow falling on the Velux windows. With all the snow, how would I get Frank's trousers fixed?

With a flick the construction sheet opened, and Ben stepped into the kitchen. 'Any chance of a cuppa?'

The memory from yesterday where he'd made that silly comment about whether it was wise for me to let Grandpa borrow Frank's suit rushed back to me. For a few seconds I considered telling him to make the tea himself, but I decided to be the bigger person and rose from the table to switch on the kettle.

Ben pointed at Humphrey. 'You found him yesterday?'

'Yes, he took a lonely widow to the Senior Tea Dance.'

Ben looked a little surprised. 'Really?' He scratched his head. 'How did he do that?'

I explained about Dorothy and how Humphrey had brought down a silver shoe from her wardrobe.

'I heard your grandfather say he'd torn Mr Baxter's trousers.' He arched one of his eyebrows at me, which was infuriating.

'Why are you earwigging on my conversations?'

He shrugged. 'You both speak in loud voices so...'

'Haven't you got enough building work to be getting on with?' I interrupted him and raised my eyebrow at him.

'I bet you're worrying about getting that torn suit trouser mended?'

I wasn't going to give him the satisfaction of knowing the

torn trouser leg was on my mind. 'No, I'm not,' I lied. 'My brother-in-law will be cool with it.'

'Cool?' Ben questioned. 'He doesn't strike me as the kind of guy who would be cool with you and your grandfather vandalising his suit.'

A red filter slipped in front of my eyes. 'We were not vandalising his suit.'

Ben's eyes left my face and were focused on something behind me. Shock swept over his face. I felt a tap on the shoulder. I whirled around to see Grandpa holding up a pair of fluffy pink... handcuffs. 'I found these.'

'Oh God, Grandpa,' I gasped, snatching them from him. They were the last thing I expected Grandpa to find in Frank's pocket. 'Let's put these away.'

I turned to Ben who was looking awkward. 'Excuse me, whilst I deal with this.'

'I'll make my own cuppa then.'

'Come on, Grandpa, let's go sort this issue out,' I said, gesturing for us to leave the kitchen. My face felt red hot. Ben did not need to see a pair of fluffy pink handcuffs. What must he think of us?

'I had to show you them,' hissed Grandpa, as we entered the hallway.

'Grandpa, let's put them back,' I said, feeling uncomfortable. Guilt nibbled away at me. 'We should never have borrowed Frank's suit. Whatever Frank and my sister get up to in their spare time is none of our business.'

Once we had put the handcuffs back into the pocket of the suit and I'd sweated profusely at the noticeable tear in the trouser leg, Grandpa suggested we go play cards in the living room. He raised his hands. 'No cheating, I promise. You look like you need to calm down. My news about Dorothy must be shocking.'

I sent Grandpa a look of bewilderment. It wasn't his newfound love for Dorothy that had produced the damp patches under my arms – it was the damage to Frank's suit, which probably cost hundreds of pounds, even thousands; plus the memory of Grandpa holding up fluffy pink handcuffs in front of the builder.

We sat down and started to play. 'I will never forget your nana Edith, Rachel.'

'I know that, Grandpa,' I said, surveying the dire hand of cards he'd dealt me.

'We haven't been here in Harp Brook that long, but I already feel like a new man,' Grandpa said, studying his cards. 'I have my energy back and it's been fun to have a laugh and a giggle with you and Layla. Yesterday at the Tea Dance, I felt like a young man again.' He looked up from his cards. 'Rachel, I want to say thank you.'

'I haven't done anything.'

He shook his head. 'You've done more for me in a couple of days than your aunty Karen and uncle Rob have done for me in years. Back home, I feel ancient and alone. Here, I feel alive and ready for adventure. Dorothy and I have a future together.'

'Grandpa, I don't want you to rush into anything with Dorothy. Take it slowly. You've only known her for five minutes.' I was sounding more like a mother talking to her lovesick teenage son than a granddaughter to her grandpa.

CHAPTER SEVENTEEN

Connor and Kate were facetiming me from Happy Beans Café after work. 'How's everything going in Harp Brook?' Connor gushed in a mock-posh voice. 'Are you lady of the manor yet?'

I sat down on the edge of my bed. It was nice to see their grinning faces. Their timing was perfect. It was early evening and I'd come upstairs to have a little break from Grandpa.

'So,' said Kate, 'are you relaxed and chilled out? Hang on – have you cut your hair?'

Connor gasped. 'Wow – you look sassy and chic!'

I let out a nervous laugh. 'Thanks. I like it shorter.'

'Right, tell us about your break so far?' Kate asked.

'We've been here four days and I've broken almost every rule.'

They both laughed. 'When you're on holiday, rules must be broken,' cried Connor.

'This is not a holiday though,' I groaned and gave them a detailed account of the events so far.

Connor scratched his head. 'Crikey, Rachel, you and Grandpa Eric have been busy.'

Kate giggled. 'I would have paid good money to have been a

fly on the wall when you were chatting up the handsome but annoying builder with Eric behind you holding up a pair of fluffy pink handcuffs.'

I tried to lie. 'He's not handsome.'

They both burst out laughing.

'Nice try,' said Connor. 'We know you, Rachel. So, it's kinky times for the newlyweds.'

'I feel guilty for telling you about the handcuffs. That's Maddie and Frank's private business,' I explained. 'I am going to be in so much trouble when he finds out about the suit.'

'What are you going to do about Eric and Dorothy?' asked Kate. 'Harp Brook's answer to Romeo and Juliet.'

I shrugged. 'No idea. The snow has been a godsend as we can't go out anywhere, but Grandpa has spent the day telling me about his love for Dorothy.'

'Does your family know any of this?' Kate asked.

Connor nudged her. 'Rachel's not going to casually update the family WhatsApp with, "Having a great time, Grandpa is in love with a local woman called Dorothy. I've allowed the cleaner to move in. We've torn one of Frank's designer suits and Grandpa found a pair of Frank's pink handcuffs which he waved about in front of the builder. Merry Christmas, fam!"'

Kate chuckled and nodded. 'Yeah, you're right. Janice would go crazy on her sun lounger.'

'Grandpa claims he feels like a new man down here in Harp Brook.'

Connor chuckled. 'You need to watch Grandpa Eric.'

I nodded. 'It's like having a teenage son who is in love with his new girlfriend.'

They both laughed.

'I better go. Grandpa will want his tea.'

'Good luck.' Connor waved and Kate grinned.

❄

Once tea had been cleared away, Grandpa went to the living room to watch TV and I stayed at the table talking to Layla.

'How are you doing?' I asked, pouring us both a glass of wine. Since arriving at Harp Brook, I'd not touched a drop of wine. After the stress of the past few days, I was gasping for a glass.

Layla smiled. 'Much better, thanks. It's been a godsend staying here. You and Eric are so nice and he's hilarious. He's told me all about Dorothy.'

'I think Grandpa needs to slow down.' The wine, a delicious Sauvignon Blanc, slipped down my throat with ease. 'Do you know anyone who can repair suit trousers?'

Layla took out her phone. 'Let me think. Kay who runs the gift shop does a bit of repairing on the side.'

I groaned. 'She's not a fan of me or Grandpa. I will need to work on her.'

'Oh, before I forget, do you want me to leave the electric gates open tonight so tomorrow we don't have to get up early for the builders?' Layla asked. 'I fancy a lie-in.'

'Do you think that will be okay?'

She nodded. 'They can come and go as they please.' Her phone vibrated with a message. I prayed she was not back talking to Ryan.

'How are things with you, Layla?'

With a shrug she said, 'The usual. People are still letting me down. I must have been bad in a past life or something.'

As her phone bleeped a second time I asked, 'Are you seeing anyone?'

'After what Ryan did to me – no. Most fellas run a mile when they know I have a kid.'

I decided to change the subject. 'Okay, look I'm keen to get to know Harp Brook a bit better. Do you know many of the locals?'

Layla nodded and cast me an uncomfortable look. 'Not many like Mr Baxter.'

'I'm sensing that. Do you know why?'

She fidgeted in her chair and when she spoke, kept her focus on her wine glass. 'I think it's the way he comes across.'

I nodded. 'That sounds about right.'

She picked up her phone. 'I didn't know he used to be in films.'

'Yes, action films. A long time ago.'

Her nails tapped softly on the screen as she scrolled through a page on her phone. 'There's an article out today about him,' she explained. 'I often google him. He's being interviewed about his plans to buy out this film company and how he's worked hard to change his public image.'

She showed me her phone screen. There was a glamorous photo of Frank and Maddie standing together with the ocean behind them. 'He says he's looking forward to raising a family and living life by his strong values of transparency and kindness. And he says he's excited about making good, wholesome films.'

I wanted to know more about life inside this house. 'Do you clean both the east and west wings?'

Layla fiddled with the tiny L on her chain. 'Yes – why?'

'I just wondered. I've always been curious about the west wing.'

She shrugged. 'There's nothing special in the west wing. It's identical to the east wing, there's a living room, a cloakroom, and a study I think.'

'Oh, I see. I'm just being nosey.'

'I'm not allowed to show you,' Layla said. She touched her

necklace. 'Mr Baxter had it written into my contract and Mrs Baxter said I had to keep hold of the keys.'

'Written into your contract?'

She nodded. 'Mrs Baxter spends...' My phone began to vibrate and interrupted Layla. It was my mother. 'Excuse me, Layla, my mother is on the phone.'

As I stepped away to talk to Mum, my Maddie anxiety crackled inside of me. Why had Frank written it into Layla's contract that the west wing was not to be shown to anyone?

'Rachel, we are all worried about how you're coping in the snow,' explained Mum, coming through over WhatsApp video call, cocktail in hand. It was night over there and she was sitting outside with the pool lit up behind her. She was wearing a bright blue halter neck vest top which accentuated her dark tan, and her shoulder-length brown hair was full of curls. 'You're not keeping everyone updated on what's happening.'

'Mum, I've been busy, and I spoke to you at the weekend.'

I walked into the living room, as she would probably want to talk to Grandpa.

'Pass me to Dad, please,' Mum ordered.

'Grandpa,' I said, 'Mum wants to talk to you.' As I handed the phone to him, I arched my eyebrows and put my finger to my lips to remind him that there were things we'd agreed to keep quiet about. To my horror he stared gloomily down the camera at Mum.

'Dad,' Mum said, 'you look sad. What's going on?'

'Dorothy,' he said, making my entire body flinch.

'Who the hell is Dorothy?' Mum barked.

'A beautiful lady who I danced with yesterday. We had a wonderful time together and I think I am in love.'

'What the hell is going on?' Mum cried. Instinctively I grabbed the phone from Grandpa. I needed to do some urgent damage control. Mum was busy shouting for Aunty Karen. 'Karen, we have a problem. Come here quick.'

I smiled at Mum. 'Nothing to worry about. I took him to the Senior Tea Dance in the afternoon.'

Mum frowned. 'Aunty Karen specifically told you to keep excitement for Dad to a minimum.'

'He had one short dance and I helped him back to his seat.'

Aunty Karen's heels were clip-clopping towards the phone. 'What's up, Janice?'

'Rachel took Dad to a Tea Dance for the elderly.'

'Mmmm... Rachel's not read my rules on caring for him,' said Aunty Karen, bursting into view. Her cerise sun dress matched her angry pink sunburn. 'Carry on.'

'Dad told me he's in love with the old dear he danced with.'

'He's losing his marbles,' hissed Aunty Karen. 'Ignore him. He says all sorts to me.'

Mum turned back to the camera. 'Rachel, please review Aunty Karen's rules on caring for your grandfather.'

'I think we need regular updates,' hissed Aunty Karen.

Mum nodded. 'You got that, Rachel? Right, we better go off to that fish restaurant, Karen. Gary says it's the best on the island.'

Once the call had finished, I turned to Grandpa. 'We agreed to keep things quiet. I am now in trouble.'

'Ignore them, Rachel. I need to see Dorothy again.'

As I walked out of the living room, I thanked my lucky stars that Grandpa had not told Mum what he had found in Frank's suit pocket.

Layla had disappeared upstairs, which was a shame as I wanted to find out more about the secretive west wing. I made a mental note to speak to her again about it.

CHAPTER EIGHTEEN

Grandpa wasn't up when I came down for breakfast. There was no radio being played. Voices drifted out into the kitchen from behind the construction sheet. I heard Tom say, 'She's a bit feisty – isn't she?'

Ben replied, 'I think she's struggling. She clearly has no control over her grandfather or that naughty dog.'

I could feel my defences rising. How dare he say that I am 'struggling'? Some things hadn't gone to plan but I was in control.

Tom chuckled. 'I can't believe her grandpa was walking about with a pair of Baxter's fluffy pink handcuffs.'

'I might rename her Little Miss Chaos. I wonder what we'll witness today,' Ben said.

What the hell did he just call me? *Little Miss Chaos*? A red filter slipped in front of my eyes.

'I'm starving,' Tom moaned. 'I forgot my lunch today and I didn't have any breakfast.'

'Same here,' said Ben, before striding through the sheet and coming face to face with me. Shock swept across his face.

'Sorry,' I said, in a sugary sweet voice, 'you'll have to excuse me as I am struggling out here so I can't make you a cup of tea.'

He cleared his throat. 'I'm sorry you heard that.'

I scowled at him before marching out of the kitchen. Once I'd sat in the living room and tapped out a lengthy and angry message to Connor and Kate about 'know-it-all' builders, I calmed down.

Kate responded with several laughing face emojis, and Connor sent me a message which read:

You'll be kissing him soon.

After muttering things about Connor's humour, I ventured back into the kitchen. The radio was on behind the construction sheet and there was no sign of Ben.

I decided to seek my revenge on them both using food. If they were hungry then they could suffer with the delicious smell from the wonderful breakfast I was about to cook for Grandpa and me. With an evil smile I walked out to the fridges and selected ingredients for a full English fry-up.

Soon there was a delicious aroma wafting out from the kitchen and Grandpa appeared with a huge smile on his face. 'This is going to be the breakfast of dog sitting champions,' he cried, rubbing his hands together with glee as I checked on the sizzling sausages under the grill.

Seeing both Ben and Tom's hungry faces as they came into the kitchen to wash out their mugs gave me so much pleasure as I laid the table for breakfast.

Grabbing my plate piled high with sausages, bacon, eggs, tomato and hash browns, I grinned at Ben and Tom. 'Little Miss Chaos is hungry.'

As Grandpa tucked into his fry-up, he pointed to Ben and Tom hovering by the sheet. 'Why not give some to the fellas?'

I glanced over my shoulder and let out a silent chuckle. Turning back to Grandpa I said, 'I don't think there's enough, Grandpa.'

He glanced at the pile of spare food still on the grill and gave me an odd look. I ignored him.

When I sat down and started to tuck into my food, Grandpa nudged me. 'You really should offer the fellas some food.'

I shook my head. 'No, not after what I heard them saying about us this morning.'

Grandpa leaned closer. 'What did they say?'

'They said I was struggling to control you and Humphrey.'

Grandpa put down his knife and fork and scratched his white chin. 'I quite like that.'

I rolled my eyes.

He continued. 'I like how the fellas over there think I am difficult to control.'

'Grandpa, Ben called me *Little Miss Chaos*.'

To my horror Grandpa chuckled. 'That's funny.'

'You're supposed to be on my side.'

Grandpa touched my arm. 'It's Christmas, Rachel, and the fellas are hungry. Let's give them some of this delicious food.'

Ben and Tom's faces lit up when Grandpa announced they could help themselves to what was left.

Layla came into the kitchen with Zac on her hip. Her face looked creased and shadowy as she warmed his milk. 'Hurry up and heat, I don't have all day,' she muttered, clearly exasperated. Once he had his bottle she came over to the table.

'Are you okay?' I asked.

She checked her phone. 'I'm meeting someone later. Just a bit nervous.'

'Ryan?'

'God, no – I am not speaking to him.' She took out her

phone. 'I got to take Zac to my friend's house and then meet him...' She stopped and gave me an awkward look.

'You got a date?'

She shook her head. 'No.'

'There's loads of food left over from breakfast.'

She shrugged. 'I'm not hungry.'

There was something she wasn't telling me. Anxiety nibbled away at me. I hoped she wasn't in any kind of trouble. Even though I'd only known Layla for a few days, I liked her a lot and I would worry about this conversation for the rest of the day.

Once Zac had finished his bottle and been fed some yoghurt with chopped up banana, she took him away upstairs and they left soon after.

I cleared away breakfast and took Humphrey out in the snow in the grounds at the back of the manor house. As I trudged, I thought about Layla and how young she was to be living such a turbulent life. The urge to help her in some way when my sister returned was strong.

Humphrey and I were at the top end of the back garden. He was busy burrowing into a snow drift when his ears shot up like two antennae. I remembered Grandpa talking about his ears going up like two satellite receivers. He was going to run away. I tried to grab him, but he shot past me. 'HUMPHREY,' I roared and gave chase. He sped across the garden and raced across the driveway.

Running in snow is hard and it's even tougher when you notice a familiar tall builder staring at you from the side of the house.

I ignored him and carried on half running and half stumbling through the snow. I wanted to give up and let Humphrey go but Ben's gaze was on me. In my head, all I could hear were his words, 'She's struggling to control both an out-of-control relative and dog.' I was not going to give him the satisfaction of admitting I couldn't control Humphrey.

'Are you okay, Rachel?' Ben shouted as I raced past him with a heaving chest and a pink face. Humphrey was a brown speck in the distance, travelling at a high speed.

'I'm fine!' I shouted as Humphrey disappeared. I wished I'd not eaten a large breakfast to punish a certain builder. In my side a painful stitch made its presence known. Staggering down the driveway, I clasped my abdomen and gasped for air. Humphrey would get such a telling off when I got hold of him. All dog treats were going to be banned.

I was seconds away from giving up on chasing Humphrey when I heard shouts and barks coming from the road. Panic took hold of me. Oh God – had Humphrey been run over.

'Humphrey!' I screamed and picked up the pace. The gates were open. On the road outside was a car which had smashed into the tree on the opposite side.

Humphrey was barking and jumping up at the driver window. A terrifying thought flared across my mind. *Did Humphrey charge into the road and cause the car to swerve and crash?* Ignoring my stitch, I ran as fast as I could towards the car.

An older woman was stood on the verge holding on to a bored looking Labrador and staring in horror at the car. 'I don't have a phone,' she cried. 'We were passing when I saw the car across the road and heard that dog barking. Someone is trapped inside.'

I felt my back pocket. Damn! My phone was still in the living room. Running back to the house would take me ages. I could try the row of cottages up the road. Ben wouldn't be in – he was back at the manor house – but his neighbours might be.

As if by magic I turned around and there was Ben. Relief flooded through me and washed away my earlier irritation. He must have followed as I chased Humphrey. His phone was pressed to his ear. 'There's been a road accident.'

The driver was slumped over his steering wheel. I tried to open his car door, but couldn't. Hearing me tugging on the door made him lift his head and turn towards me. His ashen white face and trembling hands against the wheel made tears rush to my eyes. 'Help,' he mouthed.

Ben was still on the phone to the emergency services. He also tried to yank open the car door, but it wouldn't budge.

I pulled at the passenger side door. To my relief it opened, and I climbed inside.

The driver cast me a weak smile. His forehead had a nasty bloodied gash to it and a column of red was trickling down his face. 'I can't feel my leg,' he croaked.

We couldn't move him, so we had to make him as comfortable as possible where he was.

'It's okay,' I said. 'Help is on its way. Are you cold?'

His hands were shaking, and lips had a bluish tinge. He nodded. He had dark hair, flecked with grey, eyes like two cups of black coffee and grey bushy eyebrows.

I took off my coat and placed it over him. I looked inside his glove compartment and found a pack of tissues. Carefully I balled some up and placed it over his wound to stem the flow of blood.

'I lost control. One second, I was driving, and the next I hit a patch of ice, and the car was careering towards that tree.' He cast me a frightened look. 'I woke up and this country lane was silent. No cars or people about. I got scared. I thought I'd die here, alone and cold. Then that little brown dog turned up out of nowhere. He knew I was in trouble. As soon as he started barking you arrived.'

I smiled as Humphrey was barking outside the car. 'That's Humphrey.'

'He's a clever dog.'

I smiled. 'Naughty and clever.'

Ben opened the passenger door and stuck his head inside. 'Help is on its way.' He looked at me. I was shivering as it was icy cold, and my coat was keeping the man warm. Ben took off his coat and placed it around my shoulders.

'My name is Derek,' said the man, 'I was on my way to meet my daughter for the first time.'

'The first time?'

He nodded. 'I didn't realise I had a daughter until she tracked me down on Facebook a year ago. An old girlfriend of mine never told me she was pregnant with my child. She moved away and raised our daughter by herself for twenty-one years.'

'Oh wow – that's amazing you two have finally got in touch.'

He shook his head. 'I should be there now but look at me. She will be waiting and thinking I've let her down.' Resting his head against the wheel he let out a sob. 'I didn't want to let her down. I can't believe I've crashed the car and now I can't get to her.'

His emotion made my chest ache. I gave his arm a rub. 'Hey, come on.'

The wail of the fire brigade's siren could be heard in the distance.

'Derek, please don't get upset. We can fix this,' I said. 'Do you want me to get a message to her? I can go meet her for you.'

He looked at me. 'Would you do that?'

'What's her name and where are you supposed to be meeting her?'

Ben and I stood as the firefighters rescued Derek from his mangled car. An ambulance also arrived, and they took the Derek to hospital. He waved at me as he was stretchered into the ambulance. Once they had driven off, I turned to Ben. 'Will you take Humphrey back for me?'

'You okay?' He looked concerned.

I nodded. 'There's something I need to do for Derek.'

'I'm sorry about calling you Little Miss Chaos. You were great back there. The way you spoke to that guy when he was trapped and frightened...'

'You were not so bad yourself,' I said, remembering his heroic arrival.

He took the dog lead and nodded as I hurried off towards the high street.

Outside the bakery café was a familiar figure in a bright pink puffa coat, jeans and trainers. It had started to snow. I sensed she was wishing she had a hood on her coat as she pulled up her collar. When I got closer, I could see she was dabbing at her eyes.

'Layla,' I called out, 'I need to talk to you.'

Layla shook her head and began walking off in the opposite direction. 'Not now, Rachel, I am a bit upset.'

I chased after her and grabbed her by the elbow. When she turned around, I could see she had been crying. Her dark eyes were swollen and pink. 'People always let me down,' she sobbed. 'The guy who I was going to meet. He didn't show up. Like the rest of them...'

Placing my hands on her shoulders I shook my head. 'Derek was in an accident. He's okay. They've taken him to hospital.'

She stared at me. 'Derek... you know about...'

I nodded. 'He was on his way to meet you. His car skidded on some ice outside the gates. Humphrey was the one who alerted me. I sat with Derek until the ambulance arrived. Look, Derek wanted you to know he didn't let you down.'

Layla burst into tears, and I pulled her into a hug. 'Oh, Layla, don't cry, it's going to be okay.'

'Everyone lets me down at some point,' she sobbed. 'It's a shock to hear that Derek actually cares.'

'Derek cares, so do I. Come on and dry your eyes. You are freezing cold.'

Together we walked back to her friend's house to collect Zac and then back to the manor house.

Once inside the house, Layla and Zac went upstairs and I made everyone a hot tea. After I made a huge fuss of Humphrey and told Tom, Ben and Grandpa about what had happened with Layla and Derek. They listened intently. When I told them about how I'd gone to find Layla to give her Derek's message, Grandpa reached out and squeezed my hand.

Later as Tom and Ben were making their way back through the construction sheet, I caught Ben's eye. With a cheeky grin I said, 'You see – it's not all chaos here.'

CHAPTER NINETEEN

Later in the afternoon I updated the family on WhatsApp about the morning's events.

I got a mixed response. A few of the cousins congratulated me on helping Derek in his hour of need and getting a message to Layla.

Aunty Flo claimed Humphrey never did anything heroic when she was looking after him. Although, as Mum pointed out, she had no idea what Humphrey had got up to when he stayed with her.

Uncle Robert sent a laughing face emoji.

Mum reminded me that losing Humphrey would break Maddie's heart.

Fay was more concerned about her unplanned weight gain, despite dieting, this side of Christmas.

And Aunty Karen reminded me in capital letters that Grandpa should not be left on his own.

After cooking tea and clearing away, I went to sit on the sofa in the living room with Grandpa. We sat together and Humphrey curled up at our feet.

'Maybe we've got Humphrey all wrong?' Grandpa said,

before leaning over to give him a scratch behind the ears.

I shook my head. 'It was a coincidence. I think Humphrey was planning to run away and I think the car accident distracted him.'

I showed Grandpa what the family had said on WhatsApp about the drama from this morning. He shook his head at the responses from my mother and Aunty Karen. 'Some days I struggle to understand the actions of my own daughters. I don't know why those two can't say something nice to you for once. It wouldn't hurt them to say, "well done, Rachel."'

I tried to change the subject. 'Let's not talk about Mum and Aunty Karen. What do you fancy for dinner tomorrow night?'

But Grandpa wanted to talk about Mum. 'Your mother has been angry at your father for too many years. This is why she's so bitter the whole time.'

'I'd say power crazy and bitter.' I thought about the way Mum controlled everyone on WhatsApp.

Grandpa shook his head. 'She's still cross at your father. I think his betrayal has made her poisonous. What your father did was wrong, and he hurt your mother a lot, but she can't carry on being bossy and nasty to everyone.'

'Don't worry, we all ignore her,' I said, with a nervous laugh.

'You don't ignore her though – do you?' He stared at me. 'You and Maddie have spent years trying to please her.' He lifted his hands to gesture to the house. 'This situation Maddie has got herself into is your mother's doing.'

'Really?'

He nodded. 'Your mother has spent years making Maddie marry someone with money and I think it's made Maddie depressed.'

'We don't know what's going on with Maddie.'

Grandpa shook his head. 'I know something is going on with Maddie. Frank worries me.'

Grandpa was getting upset so I gave his hand a rub. 'We're going to have a nice Christmas, Grandpa. I know the last few days have been a bit chaotic, but I am hoping things will settle down and we can relax.'

He grinned. 'Relaxing is for wimps, Rachel.'

I let out an inner groan at the mischievous glint in his twinkly eyes.

'I wanted to come visit you when your lovely friend passed away.' He held my gaze. 'You needed your grandpa, and I had my suitcase packed. Karen refused to get me a ticket as she claimed you were not in fit state to care for me. That was nonsense.'

I smiled and fought back tears as his kind face went blurry. 'That's nice to know, Grandpa.' I let him put his arm around me and I snuggled up to him.

'Are you okay, Rachel?'

I wiped a tear which was making its way down my cheek. 'I'm a little better down here. Focusing on Layla has helped.'

'Well, that's good to hear.' He smiled. 'I'll always be here for you and Maddie. All those years your mum worked away and left you with your nana and me made us all close. There were times when your nana and I discussed letting you move in permanently with us. We thought you could go to the local school and see your mum when she was home. She left you both for such long periods and we didn't like ferrying you back and forth.'

'I bet Mum was against us moving in with you.'

He nodded. 'She wouldn't have had control. Now, I want you to promise me something.'

'What's that, Grandpa?'

'Stop letting your mother control you.'

I sat up and stared at him. 'I'm not doing that.'

He looked at me with watery blue eyes and stroked my face.

'You are, my girl, and it makes me sad. That life you lead in London is not you, Rachel. You are unbelievably talented, and it breaks my heart to see you trying to please your mother. The world is waiting for you, Rachel.'

Layla entered the living room holding her phone. 'They've operated on Derek's leg. He should be fine.'

I stood up and gave her a hug. 'I'm pleased he's going to be okay. How are you feeling?'

She smiled. 'I'm better than I was this morning. Thank you for coming to find me.'

'I didn't know it was you until he told me. Although, looking at you know I can see you both have the same dark eyes. He said you contacted him last year. What made you find him?'

She fiddled with the L-charm on her necklace. 'I was lonely. Everyone had either deserted me or was being horrid to me. I'd always wondered about my biological father. I thought – life can't get any worse so what have I got to lose? I remembered some stuff Mum had told me over the years. So, I tracked down Derek.'

I put my arm around her little shoulders as she talked. 'We started messaging each other. A few weeks ago, after Ryan had kicked Zac and me out, I decided to arrange a meeting with Derek.' She lowered her head. 'Yesterday, I honestly thought he was like all the rest.'

'I don't think he is, Layla. He was emotional in the car.'

'Well, hopefully we can meet again soon.'

'Are you going to visit him in hospital?'

She shrugged. 'He wants me to. They say he will be there for a few days, but I don't want to take Zac. The hospital he's in is a long way away.'

'Layla, I will help you.'

Her face lit up. 'Really?'

'We will get you to visit Derek.'

CHAPTER TWENTY

It was light outside. I'd slept late which was unusual for me.

Before going to sleep I'd taken out Olivia's pink notebook and read one of her chapters. It started:

Grow your outer world

Do new things, meet new people, and do things to help others. My outer world shrunk after I'd lost Sophie. I locked myself away, stopped seeing friends, going out and doing new things. I think this happens because your mind can only cope with so much when you're grieving. Losing a good friend is catastrophic. To process and make sense of what's happened you hide away from the world. As a result, your outer world shrinks.

It made me think about my life after Olivia had died and before I had come to Harp Brook. My outer world had shrunk. I stopped doing the things I loved and chose to sit in my flat and watch the drips from the ceiling.

Olivia had written out a lengthy list of all the things she'd done to grow her outer world. She'd attended a new writer's group, raised money for Cancer Research and forced herself to join a gym. That made me smile as she'd written at the side:

You don't have to exercise at the gym. I preferred to wear fancy gym clothes, walk about with a towel to give the impression I was on a warm down, and talk to handsome men lifting weights.

Closing her notebook, I lay back in bed and thought about what I could do back home to grow my world. The thought of returning to my flat, the leaky ceiling, my lazy landlord and city life was no longer appealing. It wasn't long before I fell asleep.

Next morning, as I got out of bed, I decided that somehow today I would get Layla to the hospital.

'Morning, Rachel,' Ben said, as I walked into the kitchen. The kitchen was empty apart from us. He was pouring hot water into two mugs with tea bags inside.

I didn't see Grandpa. 'Is my grandfather not up?'

Ben gestured towards the hole in the wall. 'He's back there. Tom's showing him the new layout for the kitchen. Don't worry, I made sure he put on a coat as even though we have heaters it's still a bit chilly. Can I make you a cuppa?'

With a sigh of relief, I smiled. 'That would be nice.'

'Look,' Ben said, 'we haven't got off to the best start. Shall we start again?'

'That would be good.' I leaned against the island as he reached for another mug. 'Is your daughter enjoying the snow?'

He turned around and smiled, which set off a fluttery sensation inside my chest. It was quite a smile, full of fun and a hint of mischief. 'Rosie is loving the snow. Although the sledge I made us goes far too fast.'

'That sounds cool. A handmade sledge. Doesn't she like going fast?'

He laughed. 'That's the worry – she wants it to go faster. Do you like sledging?'

'Love it,' I gushed. 'Rosie sounds like me when I was little. I was a speed demon from a young age. I reckon I have still got it when it comes to sledging speed.'

Ben grinned. 'Fighting talk. Be careful or you might find yourself up against a sledge pro like me.'

He poured milk into the cups and I imagined the thrill of having a sledging race against him. My heartbeat quickened at the thought... until my mind reminded me that he probably had a beautiful wife who would not be impressed at our sledge race.

He stirred both mugs. 'Rosie's school is shut again and that's causing me childcare issues.'

'Must be tricky.' I pictured Ben with a pretty wife and Rosie all larking about in the snow. 'Does your other half work full time as well?'

He brought over my mug of tea, and I noticed how he kept his eyes fixed on the floor. 'It's just me and Rosie. My mum is helping me out again but I'm not sure whether she can do it tomorrow.'

'Oh, I see,' I said, sliding onto one of the chairs at the kitchen table and hiding my excitement at hearing him say he was a single father.

'Do you have kids, a partner?'

I shook my head. 'No, just me.'

He took a sip of his tea and grinned at Grandpa and Tom's laughter from behind the construction sheet. 'Sounds like they're having fun.'

'It's nice to hear him enjoying himself.'

Ben looked at me. 'I can tell you're close to your grandpa.'

'Grandpa and my sister, Maddie, are my family favourites.' Humphrey leapt up from his basket and started barking at me. 'Calm down, Humphrey,' I exclaimed, 'you are so bossy. Let me finish my tea.'

The dog took one look at me and hurried out of the kitchen.

A mobile phone began to ring, and I knew it wasn't mine by the ringtone. Ben put down his tea and checked his pockets. 'Ah, where is it?' He stuck his head through the sheet. 'Tom, is my phone in there?'

Heavy boots come closer and then Ben answered the call. 'Hello, Mum, everything okay?'

He gasped. 'What? You can't find her? She must be in the house... She was there when I left earlier.'

'What? Her wellies have gone, and the back door is open. I'm coming back.' He let out a heavy sigh and walked back into the kitchen. 'Mum can't find Rosie. I need to go home.' He ran his hand through his wavy brown hair. 'Sorry, I'll be back. Rosie is nearly seven and thinks she's an adult.'

'Oh, no, do you want me to come with you?' The words tumbled out of my mouth to my surprise.

'Really?' He seemed taken aback.

I grabbed my coat and sunk my feet into a pair of wellies that I'd been using. 'I used to go on adventures by myself a lot when I was little. Is your van around the back or out the front?'

'Bizarrely I left it out the front when we arrived.'

Without a thought about Humphrey, Ben helped me open the front door and as I tried to close it, Humphrey shot out. Before I could shout and scream with frustration, he darted down the snow-covered driveway.

I trudged to Ben's blue van. 'Leave him. He'll be fine.'

Ben's van did a better job of driving down the snowy driveway than my car would have done. An older woman was waiting outside Ben's cottage as we pulled up. Ben clambered out and I followed. 'You found her?'

The woman shook her head. She was tall like Ben, with brown curly hair. 'Her coat and wellies are missing. She left me a hand-drawn picture of her in the snow.'

'Is the sledge still there?'

His mum nodded. 'I left her alone for two minutes. I thought she was in the back room with her dollies.'

Ben strode away and headed into the back garden shouting, 'Rosie!'

Ben's mum ran her hands through her hair. 'I'm so worried. You hear these stories of children being taken. I hope she's okay.'

Reaching out I placed my hand on her arm. 'We'll find her. She can't have gone far.'

'I was doing some housework and I thought it had gone quiet in the lounge. Rosie has this independent streak in her. She'd been talking about going on an adventure when I arrived to look after her. I thought she was referring to something in one of her books.'

'She sounds like me when I was her age.'

Ben came back. His face was taut with worry. 'Rosie!' he bellowed across the snow.

'We should call the police. Oh, Ben, I am so sorry, I feel terrible. If anything has happened to our beautiful little girl, I will never forgive...'

Ben wrapped his strong arms around his mum and pulled her close. 'Hey, come on. We will find her.'

I surveyed the lane and remembered Derek's car from the day before. The tree he'd gone into was nursing a huge dent. Opposite Ben's cottage and across the road was woodland. 'Would Rosie have crossed the road and gone into the woods?'

Ben shook his head. 'No, she would never cross this road by herself. Maybe she's headed into town. I'll go ask the neighbours.'

My heart was pounding in my chest. If I was Rosie and I was desperate to go on an adventure – where would I go?

Whenever Maddie and I went to stay with Nana and Grandpa in the summer holidays I was always the one who wanted to go off on an adventure. Maddie never wanted to cause Nana and Grandpa any worry so she would always say no when I begged her. After Maddie had said no, I would sneak out of the house to go on an adventure by myself. My adventures always ended up in the large forest at the end of Grandpa and Nana's garden. I used to love the smell of the trees, their branches which always formed a protective canopy above me, and the crackling of twigs under foot.

It was then I heard a dog barking in the woodland opposite. That dog bark sounded familiar. 'Humphrey?' I recalled how Humphrey had stopped Rosie feeling sad the other day. Was Humphrey with Rosie now? It was a long shot. I ran across the snowy road and entered the woodland. 'Humphrey, come here.' He was still barking.

In a flash Ben was behind me. His loud footsteps thundered behind me. I followed the barking and pushed my way through the snowy bushes until I came to a clearing. There sat on a log was Rosie with her red bobble hat on, her red coat and matching wellies. Beside her was Humphrey, wagging his tail and gazing up her.

Relief flooded through me. 'Ben, she's here,' I cried, as he appeared from the bushes.

'Rosie,' he gasped and ran to her. 'What are doing out here in the cold and on your own?'

She smiled. 'I went on an adventure and Humph-Wee came to find me.'

'Rosie,' Ben said, sitting down beside her on the log. 'You can't go on adventures by yourself. You mustn't cross that road by yourself.'

'I like going on adventures with Humph-Wee,' she said, stroking Humphrey.

'Let's get you home with Nana,' ordered Ben.

Humphrey refused to walk with me or let me grab his collar.

He only had eyes for Rosie, which made her giggle. 'Humph-Wee is naughty.'

Once we got across the road, Ben's mother rushed to greet Rosie and scooped her into her arms. 'I've been so worried, Rosie.'

'Sorry, Nana, I went on an adventure with Humph-Wee.'

Ben's mum looked down at Humphrey. 'Oh, he's adorable.'

'Looks can be deceiving,' I said, which made Ben chuckle. 'He's the naughtiest dog ever.'

Ben turned to me. 'He's a hero now in my eyes. I feel bad for calling him a naughty dog.'

I waited for Ben in his van with Humphrey on my lap. Ben was having a stern word with Rosie inside.

He came out grinning and climbed in beside me. 'Well, that was fun.' He reached over and stroked Humphrey. 'Thanks, little fella.' As he pulled his hand back, he held my gaze and a fluttery sensation engulfed my chest.

CHAPTER TWENTY-ONE

When we got back to the manor house I checked the visiting times at the hospital. Layla was in the living room playing with Zac. 'Layla, do you have a car seat for Zac?'

She nodded. 'Yes, I do.'

'Let's go visit Derek. I will stay in the car and look after Zac for you.'

'Oh, Rachel, you don't have to do this.'

'Layla, I want to help you. Get your things and whatever Zac needs. Grandpa can stay here with Humphrey and guard the house.'

The main roads were clear so getting to the hospital wasn't too bad. Zac babbled away in the back for the first twenty minutes but soon he fell asleep. Layla fidgeted a lot in the passenger seat. She kept wringing her hands and squeezing them until they turned white. 'Are you nervous?' I asked.

She nodded. 'Yes. I don't know what to say to him?'

'You'll find the words. You message each a lot – don't you?'

Her fingers touched her tight hair bun. 'It's different when you're face to face though. 'Are your mum and dad still together?'

I explained about how Dad left us when Maddie and I were young and how we now had the odd birthday and Christmas card from him.

'Do you ever feel like contacting him?' Layla asked.

'Mum has always told us not to...' I stopped and remembered something Grandpa had said. I'd not contacted Dad because of Mum and how she always told us speaking to him would be like a form of betrayal to her. A lot of the time it was easier to go along with what Mum wanted. I turned into the hospital car park and realised Grandpa was right. I had been letting Mum control me. 'I'd like to contact him.'

I explained about what happened with Dad.

Layla studied my face. 'Their marriage problems were their business. Not yours and your sister's.'

She was right. 'Layla, for a twenty-one year old, you're wise.'

Layla looked up at the hospital building. She placed her hand on her chest. 'My heart is going berserk.'

'You can do this.'

'I know I can.'

'You and Derek have a lot to catch up on.'

She nodded and glanced at a sleeping Zac in the back. 'Be good for Rachel,' she whispered. Before opening the door, she leaned over and planted a kiss on my cheek. 'Thank you for being here for me, Rachel.'

'Always, and I mean that, Layla.'

A different Layla returned an hour later. She had a huge smile across her face and her dark eyes were shining.

'Well, how did it go?'

She looked at me and her huge grin lit me up inside. 'Derek and I talked non-stop. Even the nurse commented on how we both liked to chat. We discussed a lot of things and he's keen to meet Zac.'

'That's amazing.'

'My life doesn't feel as dark now. I mean, it's far from perfect... I don't have a permanent place to live, I have a young baby and I'm struggling to find cleaning work, but I have Derek now.'

I reached over and pulled her into a hug. 'This is the start of your new life, Layla.'

'He thinks he will be out just before Christmas. His leg is badly broken, and he might have to undergo other ops, but the doctors are positive he might be okay.'

'Does Derek have a family?'

She shook her head. 'This is the bizarre thing. He's gone through some dark times too and he said finding me again has brought some sunshine into his life.'

Our journey back home was an emotional but happy one. Layla talked about all the things she wanted to do with Derek in the future. It made me tearful. She sounded happy and her face was no longer creased and shadowy. Her dreams also made me think about Dad. A little part of me wanted to write to him. I wasn't sure what I would write but I was sure it would come to me. When we got back Grandpa and Humphrey were pleased to see us. I cooked us all a chicken casserole and over dinner Layla told Grandpa all about her visit to Derek.

'I'm so pleased for you, Layla,' gushed Grandpa, taking her hand in his. 'You'll have to invite Derek over on Christmas Day.'

Layla glanced at Grandpa and back at me. 'Really?'

I nodded. 'I don't see why not. I mean we have far too much food for just us three and there is room for him to stay over.'

Layla got up and came to hug me. 'I am so glad you came to stay, Rachel.'

I rubbed her hand. 'So am I, Layla.'

❄

'Rosie and I were wondering whether you'd come sledging with us on Saturday,' Ben asked the following morning, as I made him and Tom a cup of tea.

A huge grin took over my face. 'Me? Sledging?'

'The other day you claimed you have still got it when it comes to sledging so here's your opportunity to show us.' He arched his eyebrows suggestively.

'I don't have a sledge.'

Ben smiled. 'There's an old plastic one in my garage. You can use that. Well – what do you say? Rosie and I thought it would be a nice way to say thank you for helping us when Rosie went on her little adventure.'

'I would love to. Thanks.'

Ben pointed to Humphrey. 'Oh, and "Humph-Wee" must come with us. Rosie's order.'

'He would be honoured to join us,' I said. 'Do you know any good hills for sledging?'

'I know the best hills,' chuckled Ben with a wink. 'We'll pick you both up at ten?'

Grandpa entered the kitchen. As much as I wanted to, I couldn't take Grandpa sledging. The snow was deep, and it was very cold outside. 'Grandpa, Ben and his daughter have asked me to go sledging tomorrow morning. Are you all right to stay here?'

I waited for his protest but to my surprise, it didn't come. 'Go for it,' said Grandpa, raising his fist. 'Go large!'

Ben laughed. 'I love that, Eric.' He turned to me. 'I better go get on with the job. See you tomorrow, speed demon.'

Grandpa and I sat at the kitchen table together. I made him pancakes and a pot of tea. As he spread jam on his pancake, he hummed away to himself. This made me suspicious. 'Why are you so happy?'

He looked up. 'It's Christmas, Rachel. Just feeling festive.'

'Have you been thinking about Dorothy?'

His twinkly blue eyes brightened at the mention of her name. 'I will see Dorothy again soon.' He leaned in and whispered, 'I saw you talking to Ben.'

'Yes,' I whispered back.

Grandpa gave me an exaggerated wink. 'I think he likes you.'

'He's just being friendly.' Inside, my chest felt like it had been taken over by butterflies.

Grandpa gave me the thumbs up before saying, 'I like him, and it would be useful to have a builder in the family as Robert is useless. All the shelves he put up in my living room are wonky.'

Layla walked into the kitchen carrying Zac on her hip. 'Morning,' she said in a happy sing-song voice. 'How are we all?' Her black hair was no longer coiled up in a tight bun. It was loose and full of soft waves. She looked fabulous.

'Wonderful,' announced Grandpa. 'How are you? I like the hair. It suits you like that.'

'Aww thanks, Eric,' she gushed. 'Derek is doing well, and he's texted me this morning. I still can't believe what we did yesterday, Rachel.'

'We're a team. What are your plans today, Layla?' I asked, before nibbling on a pancake.

'I'm cleaning up at the pub as they had a private party last night.' Layla went over to a cupboard to take out Zac's feeding cup. 'My friend Trish has said she'll look after Zac for me.'

'Is that the Harp Brook Inn?'

'No,' said Layla. 'The Nag's Head. I used to clean at the

Harp Brook Inn but Vanessa... said she didn't need me anymore.'

I remembered Darren from the café warning me about Vanessa. 'What's she like – Vanessa, the landlady?'

Layla stayed with her back to us. 'A lot of the village listens to her. She... umm... dislikes your brother-in-law.'

'I had heard that.'

It was the way Layla glanced at me which caught my attention. Her phone in her back pocket began to vibrate which was frustrating. I sensed Layla knew more. The moment was gone as she answered her phone, gave Zac his drink and left the kitchen. I didn't see her again as Humphrey needed his morning walk.

When I returned, I decided it was time Grandpa and I ventured back into Harp Brook. 'Do you fancy a drive into town, Grandpa?'

He rose from his chair with a smile on his face. 'I thought you'd never ask.'

'I know we have stayed in for a few days. Driving in snow is not one of my strengths and I didn't want to put us in any danger.'

Humphrey began wagging his tail and looking hopeful at me. 'I walked you half an hour ago. Be good here and guard the house.'

We managed to drive down the driveway and get into the village. I also managed to park outside the bakery with the café. 'Wait till I come around to help you out, Grandpa,' I ordered before getting out of the car. The pavement, despite being gritted, was still a bit tricky and I didn't want Grandpa to fall.

Once inside the café, I asked Grandpa to go sit down while I got the drinks.

Darren smiled as I approached the counter. 'Back again?'

'Pot of tea for two and I think we'll try two of your toasted tea cakes, please.'

'Coming right up.' He turned and began filling up a red teapot with hot water. 'Not many people are venturing out so it's nice to see you and your grandfather.'

'How's life in Harp Brook?'

He shrugged. 'The primary school reopened today which was a blessing for Abi and me. The twins might love snow days but it's tricky when you're trying to run a business.'

'When do they break up for Christmas?'

He loaded up our tray. 'Next Tuesday. The nativity play is on Monday and we're praying the snow doesn't shut the school again as our two little ones will be mortified.'

'Aww, do they have parts?'

He nodded. 'Shepherd number 3 and Sheep number 2.'

'Amazing, I hope they have a great time.' I tapped my card against the card machine.

'There is another issue with the nativity play,' he explained, sorting out our teacakes.

I was about to carry the tea over to Grandpa but stopped to listen.

'They had a lady who was going to paint the background scenery – the night sky and the stable – but she's been taken to hospital, so they've asked the PTA to help.' He pointed towards the back of the shop. 'Abi is on the PTA and her painting skills are not great.'

A voice from the back shouted, 'I heard that.'

We all laughed. Darren carried on. 'She's struggling to find someone to paint...'

As he talked, I recalled Olivia's words, *Grow your outer world.* I could paint something for the school. It would get me out of the house, and I might meet a few new people in Harp

Brook. Before he'd finished the words flew out of my mouth. 'I paint and I would love to help the nativity play.'

'Abi!' shouted Darren. 'I think we've saved the nativity play.'

A head poked out from behind a tray of freshly baked loaves. Abi grinned. 'This sounds exciting.'

I took out my phone and brought up some photos of my paintings. Abi squealed when she saw them. 'Rachel, are you free tonight, by any chance?'

CHAPTER TWENTY-TWO

Grandpa insisted that I take him along to meet Abi and a few other members of the PTA in the school hall. 'You will need someone to pass you a paintbrush or two,' he explained.

'It might be boring to listen to Abi and me talk about painted scenery; and then I will have to apply a base layer of paint.'

Grandpa shook his head. 'Robert painted my living room last summer. Now, that was boring.' I smiled as he put on his coat. 'Gave a whole new meaning to watching paint dry. Your aunty Karen thought it would be nice for me to sit there as Robert painted my walls magnolia. I might be in my eighties, but I can still entertain myself. Please let me come so I can watch this artwork of yours take shape.'

Harp Brook Church Primary School was on the outskirts of the village. It was easy to find, and the school car park had been cleared of snow. Abi had told me to meet her in the school hall at 6pm, so Grandpa and I made our way there. The walls were covered with children's festive artwork, Christmas decorations, achievement certificates and photos.

In one corner was a pile of PE mats which reminded me of

my school days when my friends and I would do cartwheels instead of practising boring forward rolls as the teacher had asked.

A small group of parents turned around and stared at us. Two of them began whispering to each other and glancing at us. They didn't come across as friendly as they carried on relaying secret messages to each other. I was sure one of them mentioned 'Frank Baxter', which made me silently groan.

Abi appeared and cast us both a huge smile. Her red hair was pulled up into a ponytail and she was wearing black maternity dungarees which struggled to cover her enormous baby bump. 'Hello, both, come and join me up here.' She leapt up the three steps which led onto the stage and waved us up.

Grandpa took the steps up to the stage before me and I was about to follow him when I heard someone say in a loud voice, 'Abi, isn't there anyone else who can paint the scenery?'

I spun around to see a tall woman with long brown hair standing behind me with her arms folded across her chest. Her face was emotionless and cold.

Abi came to the edge of the stage. 'Denise, Rachel here is an amazing painter and she's offered to do it for free.'

'You know how people feel about *her* family,' the woman said, glaring at me.

What the hell did she mean? 'Excuse me,' I said, as my face began to heat up.

The woman spoke directly to Abi. 'I don't want anyone related to the Baxters painting the set for the play.'

Abi groaned. 'Denise, we have no one else and the nativity is on Monday.'

I glanced at Grandpa on stage. He was glaring at the woman. An awkward silence descended upon the school hall. Denise rolled her eyes before storming out of the school hall, followed by the group of whispering parents. My plans to grow my outer world were crumbling all thanks to my power-hungry brother-in-law.

'Rachel, I'm sorry,' said Abi, gesturing for me to come onto the stage. 'Denise is the sister of a lady called Vanessa.'

'Ah, Vanessa, who runs the pub. She's not a fan of my brother-in-law – right?'

Abi nodded. 'I try to stay out of town drama.' She led me over to where the backdrop to the play would need to be.

'Town drama? Do you know what happened between Vanessa and my brother-in-law?'

Abi wiped her sweaty forehead with a tissue and cast me an awkward look. 'I just want to make sure the children get to have a nativity play on Monday. My twins are in reception, and this is a big deal for them. As I said earlier, I try my best to avoid town gossip.' She smiled and rubbed her bump. 'Once the nativity is out of the way I can concentrate on Christmas and then the arrival of this little one.'

Abi seemed a nice person and this wasn't the time or place to find out why Frank had squabbled with Vanessa. If I was a betting person, he had probably been rude to her, and she'd taken it badly. I smiled. 'Let's get this nativity play sorted.'

The scenery would need to be painted on the giant wooden board which had been erected at the back of the stage. There were acrylic paints and brushes so I would not need to use my own.

Grandpa pulled up a chair whilst I got to work mixing paints to make a rich midnight blue base layer. 'I'll do the detail later,' I explained. 'I do love rich, colourful night skies.'

Grandpa nodded. 'It reminds me of the paintings in your flat.'

Abi hung around for a while. 'What's it like staying in the manor house?' she asked. 'It looks amazing from the little gap in the bushes near the iron gates. We walk past it on family walks.'

'Far too posh for me,' I chuckled.

Grandpa shook his head with disapproval. 'Frank has more money than sense.'

Before Grandpa took command of the conversation, I distracted Abi. 'How long have you had the bakery and the café?'

'My father was the baker in Harp Brook. When he died, I took over the family business. The café was Darren's idea, but I don't think we can keep it going for much longer. The trouble with Harp Brook is that being so small it needs something to draw visitors to the village. Local businesses like ours are struggling because there's not enough footfall.'

'Not even at weekends?'

Abi shook her head. 'It's so quiet. Even at weekends. The Harp Brook Inn has stopped serving food as Vanessa's chef left and it's only the Nag's Head doing pub lunches and evenings now.'

'Where do people eat out in the evening?'

'There are some great restaurants in the neighbouring towns, and some even go into London as it's not far on the train. It's a shame for Harp Brook.' Abi grabbed her winter coat from the side of the school hall stage and put it on. 'I better get back to Darren and the twins.'

'Well, Grandpa and I like it in your café.'

She smiled. 'Thanks. Make the most of it because in the new year we will close it and stick to being a bakery.'

As she walked away, I felt a pang of sadness for Abi and Darren and their bakery-café.

I decided to let the base layer dry overnight. The caretaker said I come in on Sunday evening and do the detail. Grandpa and I headed back to the Manor House.

'That woman called Denise was so rude,' growled Grandpa. 'I was ready to step in and give her a piece of my mind.'

'Calm down, Grandpa,' I soothed, 'the last thing we need is for you to be dragged into this mess. I think Frank has been rude to Vanessa about her pub and she's taken offence. After hearing the way Frank spoke to Layla and Ben, I think he rubs people up the wrong way. He's used to hiring and firing in his big company and maybe he lets that aggressive side of him spill over into his personal life.'

'He has too much money,' grumbled Grandpa.

CHAPTER TWENTY-THREE

Humphrey and I were stood at the bottom of the hill as Ben and Rosie hurtled down it. Rosie was sat in front of her father shrieking, 'Faster, Daddy,' and Ben was sat behind her looking pensive whilst trying to control their sledge. He safely brought the sledge to a stop at the bottom and Rosie leapt out. 'Did you see me go fast, Humph-Wee?'

'Rachel, I think it's your turn,' Ben said, striding through the fresh snow which had arrived overnight. 'I want to see your sledging speed-demon skills.'

Handing him Humphrey's lead, I grabbed the red plastic sledge he'd found for me. 'Watch and learn.' I gave him a cocky wink and he laughed.

It had been some years since I had been on a sledge. I trudged up the hill and wondered whether I would feel the same levels of crazy excitement as I did when I was a child. On top of the hill, they came rushing back. With a huge grin on my face, I jumped on the sledge and whizzed down the hill. It was fantastic to get a rush of excitement. Ben and Rosie clapped and cheered as I brought the sledge to a dramatic stop in a snow drift. I was laughing so much I didn't care about how much snow I was coated in.

'Wow, that was impressive,' exclaimed Ben. 'You really are a speed demon.'

'You better watch out.'

We took turns to go down the hill. I kept an eye on Rosie and Humphrey whilst Ben showed me what he called his sledging moves. Rosie and I were not impressed and laughed as we turned down our thumbs at his performance. I had another go on my own and Rosie gave me an instant thumbs up. She turned to her father. 'Can I go down with Rachel?'

He nodded and I raced after Rosie who was giggling her way up to the top. She let me put my arms around her and warm tingles shot up my spine. I made sure I took a slower route down the hill, but Rosie still enjoyed herself.

After a few more turns, we were all pink-faced and weary. 'Do you fancy going for a coffee?' Ben asked as we trudged back to his van. 'Mum says I can drop Rosie back at the cottage as they are doing some Christmas baking.'

I smiled at him, and he held my gaze. 'I'd like that.'

Rosie tugged on my coat. 'Can Humph-Wee stay with me and Nana?'

Ben looked to me for approval before agreeing. 'As long as you keep him in the kitchen and make sure he doesn't escape.'

Rosie nodded. 'He will be a good boy.'

Once we'd dropped Rosie and an excited Humphrey off, Ben drove to a farm shop and café a few miles out of Harp Brook. Luckily the main road out of the village had been gritted overnight.

We took our seats as our drinks were being made for us.

'Ben, this morning was a lot of fun. Thanks for inviting me.' Sitting near him over a little table, staring into his eyes and thinking about those large hands of his filled my chest with that familiar fluttering sensation.

A cheeky boyish smile swept across his face, and I had to stop myself from reaching out to skim his cheeks with my fingers. He said, 'I think the next time we go sledging, it should just be me and you.'

I grinned. 'You want a race?'

He nodded. 'Sure do. I want to race the speed demon.'

A waitress brought our coffees. Ben stirred in a cube of sugar. He lifted his face to mine. 'I want to know more about you, Rachel.'

'There's not a lot to tell,' I said, with a chuckle. 'I was made redundant earlier this year and have struggled to get another job, so I have been busy collecting interview rejection emails. My flat ceiling is leaking so when I have not been reading an email which starts with, "Thanks for applying for this role..." and ends with "but no thanks", I have also been collecting buckets of water.'

He smiled at my sarcasm. 'Your life is going well then?'

I laughed. 'Amazing.'

After taking a sip of his coffee, he put his hands flat on the table. 'Look, I have a confession to make.'

'A confession?' My voice crackled.

His eyes held mine for far longer than necessary. 'I think we've met before.'

'Ben, I don't think we've met before.'

He took a deep breath. 'Perhaps the word, *met,* is misleading.' His fingers nervously tapped the table. 'Earlier this year an old friend of mine tried to set me up...'

I knew what he was going to say. Oh God, he was Olivia's friend from uni. It was Ben. 'You're Olivia's friend – aren't you?'

He nodded and I noticed his eyes had become watery. 'She... ummm...'

Instinctively I reached out and touched his hand. 'I know, Ben. Olivia was my flatmate and one of my best mates.' Tears rushed to my eyes and spilt down my cheeks. 'I miss her so much, Ben.'

Within seconds he was up from his seat and pulling me into his strong arms. I pressed my face into his shoulder and sobbed. His hug eased some of the pain inside my chest. When I eventually looked up, I saw that his cheeks and eyes were damp. He let me go and we returned to our seats, looking a little awkward.

He spoke first. 'Olivia sent me a photo of you and her. I didn't recognise you until we were stood on the steps to the house.'

'I didn't see you at her funeral.' I rummaged around for a tissue in my coat pocket.

From his coat he gave me an unopened packet of tissues. 'Rosie broke her arm doing gymnastics. I couldn't leave her.'

I nodded and then gasped. 'You emailed me and I...'

'Ghosted me,' he chuckled.

We both laughed. 'I'm sorry for ghosting you, Ben.'

He shrugged. 'It wasn't my finest dating email. Even Olivia told me it was crap.'

'Now that sounds like Olivia. So, you met her at uni – right?'

'Sophie... ummmm.... who gave birth to Rosie and...'

'Ben, I know about Sophie, Olivia told me.'

Relief swept across his face. 'Well, Sophie and Olivia met in halls at uni, and I dated Sophie. We all became good friends. Olivia was there for me when they told us Sophie's tumour had spread and she was with me and Sophie at the end. Rosie was a baby, and I was a mess.'

'I'm sorry, Ben.'

'Sonia called me to tell me about Olivia. It was an awful

day.' He rubbed his neck. 'I miss her messages, her flying visits to see us and her friendship.' He smiled. 'I do know that heaven will have got a lot louder with both Sophie and Olivia up there. How are you doing?'

'Me? Well, coming here has made me see how much of a mess I have been since she left us. What I do know is that life must go on, but I will never forget her.'

He smiled at me, and I found myself wanting to be in his arms again. 'How do you fancy coming out for dinner with me on Sunday, Rachel?'

I wanted to say yes but then I remembered the nativity scenery. Sunday evening would be spent adding the finishing touches. 'I've agreed to paint the scenery for the primary school nativity play and on Sunday evening I'll be finishing it off.'

Ben leaned back in his chair. 'I'll bring dinner to you in the school hall on Sunday evening then.' He smiled and held my gaze.

CHAPTER TWENTY-FOUR

After collecting Humphrey from Ben's house and hearing at length from Rosie what a good boy he'd been, I walked back with him up to the manor house. It was a chance to process Ben's revelation – he was the Ben whom Olivia had tried to set me up with. Knowing that he knew Olivia, made me want to get to know him more.

As I trudged, I took out my phone and updated Connor and Kate on our WhatsApp chat.

Connor was the first to respond with a row of shocked-faced emojis:

> Wow – this is a bit freaky. So, he's the widower then. Olivia loved to organise everyone, so I am not surprised she's doing that from heaven. She will be jumping up and down with excitement up there. I do hope God has his earplugs in because she will be making a racket.

Kate was next:

> Didn't you ghost him – the widower?

Connor's response made me smile.

Kate, all the best romances start after a bit of casual ghosting.

Fluffy snowflakes started to twirl and dance before me. Humphrey dived into a patch of snow, his tail wagging like crazy.

Gazing towards the manor house I saw the heavy slate grey sky above it. More snow was on the way. It was fun to sledge in; however more snow would put the nativity play at risk as the school might have to close.

As I approached the manor house, I saw Layla waving her arms at me. Humphrey and I picked up speed. Something was wrong. My first thought was Grandpa. Had he been ill? Before I left early this morning, he had seemed fine, bright, and bubbly.

'It's Eric!' gasped Layla, running to meet me. With all the talk with Ben about death I immediately assumed something was terribly wrong. Had he fallen ill? Emotion rose up inside me. 'Oh God, is he sick?'

She stared at me oddly, then held up a piece of paper. 'He's not ill. Your grandfather has gone on an adventure.'

'What?' I gasped, staring at the paper. In his messy handwriting, it said, *'I've gone on an adventure to find Dorothy. Tell Rachel not to worry about me. Eric.'*

I gazed up at the sky and the mass of swirling snowflakes and then down to the snow-covered ground. Grandpa was out walking in this weather. He had no idea where Dorothy lived and nor did I for that matter. At eighty years of age, he was unsteady on his feet. Suddenly gripped with panic, I turned to Layla. 'I need to find Dorothy.'

Layla nodded. 'I know her daughter Kay, but not Dorothy.'

'I need to find Grandpa. Hold Humphrey and take him inside. I'll get my car.'

After handing over Humphrey I trudged towards my car. Luckily my keys were in my back pocket. As I was wiping the snow off my windscreen I heard Layla shout. Turning around I saw Humphrey race away from her, his lead dragging along behind him. 'Humphrey!' I wailed at the dog who was bounding through the snow.

'I'm sorry, Rachel,' groaned Layla.

'It's fine, he's a little nightmare. Get inside. I'll be back with Grandpa and the dog.'

The second I started my car, the petrol light flashed. 'Aghhh,' I shouted, hitting the steering wheel. 'Why do you have to do this now, car? Well, I am sure there will be enough fumes to get around town.'

After crawling down the winding driveway at a cautious snail's pace I wondered whether Ben and his mum knew Dorothy. I parked up and he must have seen me getting out, as he came to his front door. 'You okay?'

I shook my head. 'Grandpa has gone off by himself to find Dorothy and I have no idea where she lives or where he is. Plus, Humphrey has run off.'

Ben grabbed his keys, and I heard the doors to his van unlock. 'Jump in. We'll take my van as the weather is going to get bad.'

'I'm sorry to call on you, Ben.'

He smiled. 'It's nice to see you again.'

We climbed in beside each other. 'Do you know Kay's mother, Dorothy?'

'Yes, and I know where her cottage is too. I did some work for her last year.'

I would never have found Dorothy's cottage as it was down a tiny country lane. It hadn't been gritted, even Ben's van struggled.

He parked up and I leapt out. There was no answer at

Dorothy's which made me panic. In my head, I could see Mum shaking her head with disapproval at me from her sunbed and Aunty Karen pointing her to list of dos and don'ts when caring for Grandpa Eric on her phone. One of which was: *Don't let him out of your sight!*

'Oh God, where is he?' I began to tremble. 'What if Dorothy found him collapsed in her doorway and has taken him to hospital? My family didn't trust me to look after him and this will have proved that they are right. I don't know why they asked me...'

Ben placed a warm hand on my shoulder. 'Calm down. Let's not assume anything about Eric. We'll find him. Let's get in the van and head into town.'

He parked near the church, and it reminded me of the first day Grandpa and I ventured into Harp Brook to search for Humphrey. He'd been engrossed with reading the church's social noticeboard and going over to the Nag's Head for a drink. Kay's shop caught my eye. I could ask Kay whether she'd seen her mother and Grandpa. It was then Ben called out to me and pointed at the window in the pub. There was a familiar face waving at me.

'Grandpa,' I snapped before marching across the road and into the pub.

As I entered Grandpa raised his pint glass to me and nudged Dorothy, who was sitting next to him. 'My taxi home has arrived,' he called out. 'Hurray!'

'Grandpa, I have been worried sick,' I snapped. 'Where have you been?'

He cast me a tipsy grin. 'I went to find Dorothy but finding her cottage felt like too much hard work, so I came to the pub instead. Guess who was coming out of her daughter's shop as I was about to enter.' Leaning over he placed his arm around Dorothy. 'My sweetheart.'

Ben came over and Grandpa put down his pint to shake his hand. 'Nice to see you, Ben.'

'Right, I think you've had enough to drink, Grandpa, let's get you home.'

To my amazement, he nodded and rose from his seat. I helped him into his coat as he was unsteady on his feet. Dorothy planted a kiss on his cheek. 'I'll see you soon, Eric. Thanks for a lovely time this morning, I haven't laughed so much in a long time.'

'We will meet again, my love,' Grandpa said. 'Now I need to go home for forty winks.'

Ben helped Grandpa into the middle passenger seat in his van. I sat by the door and blocked him in. 'Humphrey has gone missing again, Grandpa.'

Grandpa raised his hand. 'I wouldn't worry. That dog is like me, we know how to have a good time.'

I didn't reply but pressed my face against the window and muttered to myself about troublesome dogs and grandfathers.

CHAPTER TWENTY-FIVE

Once we got home, Ben helped me get a tipsy grandpa inside the house and into the chair in his bedroom. He kept saying he wanted to have a nap. Grandpa's eyes closed the second we gently rested his head against the chair. I placed a blanket from the bed over his legs in case he got cold.

We both crept out and tiptoed away.

'I better get back and taste Rosie's cakes,' Ben said, with a smile. 'You can leave your car outside mine for now as the snow is coming down.'

'Thank you for helping me, Ben. I appreciate it.'

He nodded and, for a few seconds, we gazed at each other. Ben was no longer the handsome builder who made smartass comments. He was someone who knew Olivia and he was someone who made me melt inside. His pink lips looked soft and kissable, and I longed for his strong arms to pull me into another hug. We heard Layla coming down the stairs carrying Zac and the moment between us disappeared. Ben left with a smile.

'Have you found Eric?' she asked with a look of concern. Zac was busy sucking on his toy lion.

'Grandpa was in the pub with Dorothy and is now sleeping it off.'

Layla nodded. 'Why was Ben here?'

'He helped me with Grandpa. Earlier he and I went sledging with his daughter, Rosie. He's lovely.'

Layla cast me a puzzled look. 'You're looking dreamy. Do you *like* him?'

I felt my cheeks getting warm.

She didn't let me answer. 'A word of advice. Be careful with him. I've heard he's a heartbreaker.'

'Really?' I gasped. 'Ben?'

'Have you met Denise – Vanessa's sister?'

The tall woman with straight brown hair from the school hall appeared in my mind. 'If this is the Denise who I met at the primary school the other evening, who had an issue with me painting the nativity stage scenery because of my family then yes, we have had a run-in.'

Layla nodded. 'That's her.'

'She's Vanessa's sister?'

'Yeah,' said Layla. 'Denise went on a few dates with Ben a few months ago. I'm not sure what happened but she told everyone in the pub he wasn't nice to her and broke her heart. She tells everyone to avoid him.'

I scratched my head and tried to visualise Ben with bolshy Denise. They seemed an unlikely couple. The thought of those two together left me uncomfortable. Surely Olivia would have told me if Ben had red flags?

'Be careful, Rachel, that's all I am saying.'

I went into the kitchen and made myself a cup of tea. Layla followed. 'Have I upset you?'

'No,' I said with a heavy sigh. 'I do like Ben, but I think I am getting carried away. We took his daughter sledging, went for one coffee, had a "moment" and then he helped me search for

Grandpa. My initial impressions of him were that he's a decent guy. Do you want a cup of tea?'

She nodded and studied my face. 'What was this "moment" you had?'

I flicked on the kettle. 'I discovered that Ben and I have a connection. We both knew my best mate, Olivia, who died a few months ago.'

Layla placed her hand on my arm. 'Sorry, Rachel, to hear about your friend.'

'Thanks. In the café, I got upset over Olivia. Ben and I ended up hugging. What's weird about Ben is that before Olivia died, she was arranging for us to go on a blind date. It never happened as he emailed me and then... I ghosted him.'

Layla raised her eyebrows. 'Wow, that's a bit mad.' She let Zac crawl about with his toy lion.

I thought some more about what she'd said. 'I'm glad you've told me though about Ben.' Sam's face appeared in my mind. 'My ex-boyfriend dumped me on Christmas Eve last year. He'd been cheating on me. Eight months we were together. My friends kept warning me about his ex-girlfriend, but I didn't listen, and I ignored the red flags. I need to learn not to go at a hundred miles an hour.'

Layla nodded. 'I always thought Ben was a good guy, but Denise tells a different story. She said he was seeing several women at the same time as her.'

'Several women?'

'Just be careful.'

As I made the tea, I wondered whether Olivia had been wrong about Ben. Maybe after his partner, Sophie, died he decided to play the field. Grief can make people do strange things. I had one nagging doubt though, – if he was a player why did he ask Olivia to be his dating consultant? Those were the words she'd used that day when she came up with the idea of a blind date.

Layla took out her phone and groaned. 'Another customer of mine has told me they no longer want me to do cleaning for them.'

I carried our mugs to the table. 'Oh, I am sorry. Have they given a reason?'

Layla bowed her head. 'Vanessa is behind this. She has made my life unbearable.'

'Vanessa?'

She lifted her face to mine. 'Ryan, my ex-boyfriend... He's Vanessa's son. When I found those photos on his phone from those women, I made the mistake of telling Vanessa. She accused me of lying. I even showed her the abusive texts he used to send me.'

'He sent you abusive texts?'

Layla nodded. 'He said some horrible things to me, Rachel. The next day after I told Vanessa, Ryan threw me and Zac out. Since then, my cleaning jobs in the village have started getting cancelled. By the time Mr Baxter comes back I will be fired from this one and then I really will be in trouble.'

'Layla, I will do everything in my power to stop you from getting fired from this job. I will talk to my sister. We do need to think about how we can deal with Vanessa.'

'What happened with your brother-in-law and Vanessa made her worse...' She stopped abruptly, her eyes widening dramatically.

'What happened with Frank?' I asked.

Fear flashed across Layla's face. 'I meant... I... ummm.' She was mumbling.

'Layla, tell me what happened.'

My phone began to ring. It was Mum calling me from

Tenerife. As I answered it, Layla scooped up Zac and raced upstairs.

Mum appeared on the screen. She was sat inside her villa against the white wall. Her tan looked amazing. 'Where are the daily updates, Rachel?'

I clamped my hand over my forehead. 'Sorry, I have been busy.'

Mum shook her head with disapproval. 'It's been hard to enjoy ourselves out here not knowing Dad is okay. Your aunty Karen has been worried about Dad. As his carer she's missing him.'

I bit my tongue when Mum referred to Aunty Karen as Grandpa's carer. From what Grandpa had told me, her visits lasted all of two minutes and were done on his doorstep. Aunty Karen was trying to impress Mum.

'Rachel, put Dad on the phone please so we can all see him.'

'Grandpa's asleep and you all saw him the other day.'

Mum glanced at someone sitting behind her phone. 'Rachel says Dad's asleep.'

'Tell her to wake him, Janice,' Aunty Karen hissed. 'I won't sleep tonight until I know he's okay.'

I let out a heavy sigh. 'Mum, tell Aunty Karen that Grandpa is fine.'

Mum turned her attention back to the phone screen and to me. 'Rachel, please do what Aunty Karen says because she'll have one of her tension headaches and you know I struggle when she has one of those.'

Grandpa was still asleep when I crept went into the annexe bedroom. 'Grandpa, wake up, Aunty Karen is on the phone.'

With a jolt, he woke up. 'Dorothy?' He called out looking confused. 'Is that Dorothy?'

'Show me him,' barked Mum. I put the phone screen in

front of Grandpa. She peered down the camera at him. 'Dad, it's me, Janice. You look groggy. Are you unwell?'

'I went to the pub,' he said, 'think I had a few too many.'

Mum shrieked. '*What?* Rachel let you get drunk. What the hell is she doing?'

I snatched the phone back. 'Grandpa disappeared and I didn't know where he was. It was stressful but luckily, I found him in the pub.'

In the background Aunty Karen was saying to Uncle Robert, 'Rachel let Dad go on a drinking bender down the pub.' Uncle Robert replied, 'What was Rachel doing whilst your father was on a bender? Was she with a fella?'

'Janice, ask Rachel what she was doing whilst letting Dad go on a drinking bender,' Aunty Karen ordered.

Grandpa held my gaze. 'Rachel, ignore them. I had the best time with Dorothy earlier. Your mother and Karen would never have let me do that.'

Mum overheard Grandpa. 'Dad, you're right there, Karen and I would not let you get drunk at your age. I honestly don't know what Rachel is doing.'

Through gritted teeth I said, 'I had no idea you were going to do a disappearing act on me, Grandpa. I came home and you'd left a note to say you'd gone on an adventure.'

He grinned. 'I told you that was what I came here to do – go on an adventure.'

'Where's Maddie's dog?' barked Mum, making me groan. I'd forgotten all about Humphrey. Oh God, he was still missing and out in the snow. 'I bet you've lost him as well.'

'No,' I lied, thinking on my feet. 'Layla, the cleaner, is out walking him.'

'The *cleaner* is walking Maddie's beloved dog,' Mum gasped. 'Have you lost your mind, Rachel?'

'Mum, please will you listen to me about what really

happened with Grandpa,' I pleaded. 'I did not know he would be in the pub.'

'Rachel, you've let us all down,' snapped my mother. 'You agreed to look after your elderly grandfather over Christmas and abide by our rules. We have had no regular updates and today you dropped him off at the pub to drink himself silly whilst you enjoyed yourself. We are all disappointed with you, Rachel. Maddie would not have behaved like this.'

I could feel anger at my family bubbling up inside of me. Mixed in with this was my frustration over finding out Ben was a walking red flag and an ongoing worry about who Maddie had married.

'You should be ashamed of yourself,' barked Mum.

'Will you listen to me?'

'I don't need to listen to you, Rachel,' snapped Mum. 'This is serious. Gary was taking us out tonight to his favourite restaurant and now after hearing this, we won't be able to enjoy our food.'

Something inside me snapped. My family were great at controlling at each other and manipulating situations. I was tired of their rules and my mother's rants about how I had disappointed them all. For thirty-two years of my life, she'd been telling me this. In a moment of madness, I hung up on my mother. My hands were trembling as I stared at my phone. No one did that to Mum. If she was not going to listen to me then I wasn't prepared to be shouted at. Once the call had gone, I turned off my phone.

Grandpa cheered and shook his fist. 'Yeah, a family rebellion. This is great. Way to go, Rachel.'

CHAPTER TWENTY-SIX

Grabbing my coat and my wellies, I ordered Grandpa to stay in the house. 'I need to go find Humphrey. Please don't do one of your disappearing acts.'

He nodded and gave me a thumbs up. 'I have done enough adventuring today, Rachel.'

I pulled up my hood and stepped out into a blizzard. As I trudged down the driveway and struggled to see a few yards in front of me due to the snow, I panicked at the thought of poor little Humphrey being out in this. Maddie would kill me if she knew.

I made my way into the village, passing my car which was covered in snow outside Ben's cottage. Seeing his van in the driveway made my heart flutter, which was annoying. My heart was clearly not aligned with my brain. It had taken me months to recover from Sam's cheating confession and the way we ended. The last thing I needed was a Christmas romance with Ben which would take another six months to get over. I wasn't sure my heart could withstand more pain. Especially from someone like Ben who had been close to Olivia and already had somehow taken control of my heart in a few hours. I had to keep Ben as a friend and work on suppressing my feelings.

'Humphrey!' I shouted as I got further along the lane and nearer the village. There were no sounds of barking.

I trudged through the little high street shouting for Humphrey. It was deserted. Everyone was at home in the warmth, probably wrapping presents and deciding not to venture outside.

Little lanes led off from the high street which filled me with panic. Humphrey could be down any of them. He could have been run over or injured. My stomach began a nauseating slow spin cycle. I was the worst dog sitter ever. In my head I could hear Mum telling me how disappointed everyone was with me.

After shouting his name repeatedly, I decided to turn back, clear the snow off my car and drive around. Even though my petrol light was on I could probably do a wider search than on foot. I walked past one little lane and took one final yell. 'Humphrey!' A distant bark made me look down the lane. The barking continued and it was getting louder. I jogged down the winding lane which was hemmed in with bushes on either side. As I came around the corner, Humphrey raced towards me, his red lead trailing behind him in the snow.

'Humphrey,' I cried, as a wave of emotion hit me. With open arms I ran to him and to my horror the little rascal turned and began to trot back the way he had come.

'Get here now, Humphrey,' I hissed, racing after him. The closer I got, the faster he ran. No matter how fast I went I couldn't grab him or his lead.

'This is not playtime, Humphrey,' I said, cursing him, and my sister for not training him.

He ran into the garden of a little cottage and then scooted around the side. 'Where the hell are you going, Humphrey?' I yelled, staggering after him in the snow. I entered the cottage's garden by climbing over the little wall and trudging through deep fresh snow. Once I got around the side of the house I heard a pet door flap. The cheeky dog had gone into someone's house.

Wiping snow from the window at the top of the door, I peered in and spotted Humphrey looking up at me. He began to bark from inside the house. 'This is someone's home, Humphrey.'

It was then something moved in the background behind Humphrey. I gasped. It was the arm of someone who was lying on the floor. 'Help me, please,' the person called out.

'Oh God,' I gasped, rummaging in my pocket for my phone. I needed to call for help. Upon taking it out and switching it on, I saw that it only had 1% battery left. Before my eyes it died. 'Damn it.'

The handle to the back door was no use as it was locked. I surveyed the downstairs windows in case one was open, but they were all closed.

Humphrey dived out of the pet flap and started barking again. I wanted to vent my frustration at him but that would waste time. 'Help me, Humphrey. How do I get inside?'

He ran to the opposite side of the cottage where there was a small garage with a flat roof. I gazed up past the roof. There was an upstairs window open. If I could get on the roof I could get to the window. It was big enough to climb through. My first challenge would be to get up on the roof.

I surveyed the side of the garage and scanned the garden. In the corner was a shed. After racing over to it, I yanked open the door. Inside it was a large wooden crate holding tools. I emptied it and took the crate to the side of the garage. Standing on the crate I was able to haul myself onto the garage roof. I shuffled across praying it would take my weight.

Climbing in through the window was tricky. At one point, I did get stuck. After a lot of wriggling, pulling and telling myself

I wasn't a disappointment, I fell through the window and face-planted a bed. The snow had been blowing inside the window and had made the covers damp, but I was grateful to have got in.

I raced downstairs and into the kitchen to find Humphrey sitting by an old lady who was sprawled on the floor.

'I was losing hope,' she mumbled, trying to get up. 'Your little dog kept going to get help and coming back to sit by me. I should have trusted him.'

'It's okay, I'm here now. Are you in pain?'

She moved her head slightly. 'I can't move my leg.'

'Stay where you are. Let me call an ambulance. What's the address?'

'White Cottage, Boar Lane.'

I grabbed the handheld phone on the coffee table in the living room and dialled 999.

Once the operator had all the information and we'd established the lady was called Mrs Hall and she was eighty-one, they informed me an ambulance was on its way. They advised me to make sure Mrs Hall didn't move. I said I would stay with her and make her as comfortable as I could.

I grabbed a woollen throw from the settee and placed it over Mrs Hall. Sitting beside her I held her hand in mine. 'We're going to get you sorted, Mrs Hall.'

'You and your dog are angels,' she croaked.

I chuckled. 'Not sure about Humphrey.' He was lying with his head on my lap gazing at Mrs Hall.

'He appeared after I'd fallen this morning,' she explained. 'He shot through the pet flap and began barking at me.'

'Really?'

'It was like he knew I needed help.'

I stared at Humphrey. 'Maybe you're an angel, Humphrey.'

'I had a horrible argument with my daughter last night,'

croaked Mrs Hall. 'It was on my mind when I came down this morning.'

I covered her hand with my own.

'We both said some terrible things.' She let out a little sob and Humphrey whimpered.

'We all say things we don't mean in the heat of an argument.' I thought about the conversation with my mother earlier.

Mrs Hall looked up at me. 'Do you think she'll forgive me?'

I stroked her hair. 'Definitely.'

'It's Christmas and I don't want to argue with her.'

'It's going to be okay, Mrs Hall.' I thought about my argument with the family on WhatsApp.

'Everything is so fraught at this time of year. I don't know why Christmas does this to us all.'

'You're right. Everything is so stressful at Christmas.'

The phone began to ring at my side. 'It could be the ambulance. Shall I answer it?'

Mrs Hall moved her head. 'Yes please, dear.'

'Hello.'

'Who is this? Where's my mother?'

'Oh, your mum's had an accident, my name is Rachel, and I am sat with her waiting for an ambulance.'

The female voice gasped. 'Oh God, I'll be over now.'

It wasn't long before a lady pulled up in a black car and let herself in through the front door. I rose up from the floor so she could see her mother.

'Mum – what's happened?' The woman crouched down beside her mother.

'I fell over. I can't feel my body on this side. Listen to me, this woman and her dog are angels. If it wasn't for her dog, I don't know what would have happened to me.'

The woman beamed at me. She was in her forties and once

she'd removed her hood, I could see she had bushy blonde hair. 'I can't thank you enough.'

'I told the lady how we argued last night,' said Mrs Hall.

'Mum, it's over now,' soothed the lady, 'let's concentrate on getting you better.' She looked up at me. 'I will stay with Mum. You can go.'

I grabbed Humphrey's lead. 'Nice to meet you, Mrs Hall. I did use the crate from your shed to climb onto the garage and get up to the bedroom window. I'm sorry about that.'

The woman smiled. 'Don't worry, thank you so much.'

Once Humphrey and I got outside, the snowfall had eased. Humphrey pulled on the lead which made me smile. 'Oh, I see, you now want to rush home.' A wave of happiness crashed over me. Humphrey wasn't the little rascal we all thought him to be. He'd barked for help when Derek had his car accident, he'd stayed with Mrs Hall when she'd fallen, encouraged Dorothy to go to the Tea Dance and he'd found Rosie when she'd gone exploring.

I bent down and stroked his brown head. 'You are my hero, Humphrey. Let's go home.'

CHAPTER TWENTY-SEVEN

The following morning, I woke up feeling like I'd run a marathon in my sleep. My body ached and my limbs felt like they were made of lead. On the bedside table was my phone which had been charging overnight.

Once I'd returned from rescuing Mrs Hall, I'd made butternut squash and bacon soup for tea to warm us all up. I was also hoping Layla would join us for tea so I could ask her about my brother-in-law – but she stayed upstairs with Zac.

While I made the soup, Grandpa, and I sang along to Christmas songs and at one point we had a little dance together in the kitchen. We polished off the soup and after I'd washed up, I decided to plug in my phone to get it charged and turn it on. There were ten unread WhatsApp messages, two missed calls plus a voicemail from my mother waiting for me.

Remembering what Mrs Hall had said about everything being fraught at Christmas I went onto the family chat and wrote, *'Grandpa and Humphrey are fine.'* Feeling exhausted I went to bed early with my phone and left it to charge by my bed.

Reaching over I grabbed the phone and saw that there had

been no new WhatsApp notifications overnight. This was strange as I assumed the whole family would have piled in with their comments into the early hours. Opening WhatsApp I saw that Mum had sent me a message this morning to say:

> Aunty Bev has agreed to come and sort you out. She'll arrive this afternoon.

Sitting up in bed I stared at Mum's message. Blimey, things must be bad if they were sending Aunty Bev to bring me into line. Also, had Mum not seen the weather reports? The snow in the south was bad and it would be a treacherous drive for Aunty Bev once she left the motorway.

I messaged Aunty Bev.

> I hear you are coming to Harp Brook – the snow is bad, take care x.

She responded almost immediately with:

> Looking forward to seeing you and Dad. Ignore your mother and my sisters on WhatsApp. I can't believe they have asked ME to come and sort you out – ha ha!

I placed my phone back on the bedside table and stared out across the bedroom. The events from yesterday pinged into my head one by one and before I knew it my mind was flooded with thoughts about whether Ben would be another Sam and break my heart; whether Maddie was happy in her marriage to Frank; what had gone on between Frank and this Vanessa woman who I'd yet to meet; whether Layla would get herself back on her feet; would I get the nativity scenery finished later; and whether Mrs Hall was okay.

Overwhelmed, I lay back down and wished Olivia was still alive. She'd been a calming influence in chaotic times. We'd stay up late talking, sharing piles of buttered toast and in the morning my world would not have felt so scary.

I grabbed her pink notebook and began reading the next chapter in her guide to surviving the loss of a wonderful friend.

It was titled, *Make your friend proud.*

I read how Olivia had been encouraged to start writing romance books by her friend, Sophie.

I started writing in secret. I don't know why I hid my new hobby from my friends, but I did.

One day I plucked up the courage to show Sophie my entry for a short story competition in a women's magazine. I thought she would laugh at what I had written but she loved it. She couldn't believe I had written it during my lunch break at work.

My entry was a funny story about a woman who found herself falling in love with a male time traveller who kept whisking her away in his time machine for hot dates.

Things didn't go to plan as his love for her made him miscalculate the timing of their dates and they ended up having a not-so-romantic picnic in an air raid shelter during the middle of the Second World War, losing each other at the Woodstock music and art festival in 1969 and realising… quite quickly… that 1665 was not the best time to go sightseeing around historical London, especially when there was a plague outbreak.

I came 2nd in the competition and with encouragement from Sophie I began writing short romance stories. Sophie willed me on to write something longer like a book, but I didn't have the confidence.

When Sophie died, I put writing on hold. Grief took hold of me and sitting by a typewriter was the last thing I wanted to do.

> However, it was Sophie's boyfriend, Ben. He said, 'Make Sophie proud and become a novelist.'
>
> Making Sophie proud was the best I ever did. Writing and self-publishing my romance novels gave me a purpose in life and so much enjoyment. You would not believe how the act of writing books has transformed my life. I know that Sophie would be proud of my Amazon author page. Each book has been dedicated to her.

I couldn't take my eyes off his words *He said, 'Make Sophie proud.'* That had been such a thoughtful thing to do. Ben must have known how much Sophie believed in Olivia, how happy Sophie would have been knowing Olivia was writing novels and he must have known how much Olivia loved writing. My heart performed a series of flips. I thought about what Layla had told me about Ben seeing multiple women as well as Denise and my heart stopped flipping and sunk.

At the end of the chapter, Olivia asked her reader to think about what they would do to make someone, who they had lost, proud. My stomach began to gurgle and I sat up in bed. What could I do to make Olivia proud? The answer came to me in seconds – food. Olivia would not want me to carry on creating complicated spreadsheets, writing dull project updates, and trying to save over-budget projects which were always doomed to fail. She'd been telling me for two years to change my life and do something with food. Maybe it was time to return to catering?

Mum's face appeared in my head. She wouldn't be happy, and I would get nothing but hassle and nagging for not doing what she called a 'proper job.'

As I hauled myself out of bed, I found myself questioning my life decision years ago to shut my catering business to please my mother. What had my years of working as a project manager for an IT firm brought me? A rented flat filled with buckets of water, tall office buildings outside my window which made me feel like they were edging closer and imprisoning me, a redundancy package, and a lot of painful memories.

In contrast my mother was now living the life she'd always dreamed of – basking in a luxury villa in Tenerife with Gary. No one in the family had dared question where Mum and Gary got the money to live in such luxury with four bedrooms and their own pool. Mum had been living in Tenerife for years after getting a job as a holiday rep out there. That was where she'd met Gary, an expat like her, who ran a small tour company and kept bumping into her on airport drop-offs.

Before her luxury villa, Mum had owned a small apartment in a complex with a shared pool. I have always assumed one of them had a win on the lottery or Gary's love of casinos paid off.

Aunty Bev arrived after lunch in her battered old Fiesta. Grandpa and I stood waving as she pulled up. I had Humphrey on a tight lead as I'd learnt too many painful lessons with him.

Aunty Bev's long brown hair was in giant pink curlers, and she was wearing one false eyelash. 'The other fell off on the M25,' she chuckled, as she hugged us both.

Her travel outfit consisted of a fancy leopard print coat, skintight cerise leather leggings and gold boots. She dragged the world's biggest suitcase plus an array of plastic bags from her car. 'Did your mum tell you about me coming for Christmas?'

I let out a silent groan. Aunty Bev was staying for Christmas as well? Why had my mother done this to me? All my plans for a quiet and relaxing Christmas were well and truly gone. I loved Aunty Bev, but she gravitated towards chaos, wild parties, and trouble.

Grandpa leaned in close as Aunty Bev locked up her car and whispered, 'Trouble is here.'

I nodded and he shook his head with a grin. 'Let's go large.'

'All the problem relatives have been sent here to Harp Brook,' said Aunty Bev, dragging her belongings after her. 'Janice had a plan to keep us all here.'

After helping Aunty Bev with her luggage, we left it in the hall and went to the kitchen.

'Dad, you look well,' observed Aunty Bev, studying him under the bright lights. 'Rachel has clearly been looking after you.'

Grandpa placed his arm around me. 'She's been brilliant.'

Aunty Bev turned and pulled me into a hug. 'I love the shorter hair and I never doubted your ability to look after Dad.' She surveyed the hallway, the kitchen and poked her head through the construction sheet. 'Wow – Frank is getting the world's biggest kitchen built.'

She came over to the kitchen table and sat down, adopting a serious expression. 'Who else here is worried about Maddie?'

I stared at her in shock. Aunty Bev was worried about Maddie as well?

Grandpa raised his hand.

Aunty Bev glanced at me. 'Rachel – what about you?'

'Yes, I have been for a while. I thought I was the only one.'

'There's something not right with Maddie,' explained Aunty Bev. 'She's not the same anymore. I made her tell me why she came home from California too. There's something not right about her and Frank. This is the reason why I am here in Harp Brook. Sadly, it's not to look after you two.'

Grandpa started clapping.

Aunty Bev grinned. 'The rest of the family think we...' She paused to point at the three of us. '...we are the problems, but we know what's really going on. We know that my sister's new villa in Tenerife was paid for by Frank...'

I gasped. 'What? Frank paid for that?'

Aunty Bev nodded. 'Oh yes, he did. That's why my sister is ignoring what's going on with Maddie. She's scared her dream life will be taken away from her.'

Grandpa scratched his chin. 'I have always said Janice was blinded by Frank's money.'

Aunty Bev nodded. 'I also think Maddie knows and this is keeping her from telling all of us what life is really like with Frank.'

An uncomfortable feeling passed over me as I thought about Frank using money to get Mum on his side, the secret of the west wing and the secret about Frank and Vanessa.

However, there were more pressing matters. I checked the time on my phone. The nativity scenery needed to be painted. 'I need to go and help out at the primary school,' I said. 'Grandpa, you can stay here with Aunty Bev and introduce her to Layla.'

CHAPTER TWENTY-EIGHT

It was nearly seven in the evening, and I'd been painting on the school stage for a few hours. Painting the scenery had proved therapeutic as it had given me time away from the unfolding family drama. My painting brief was to make the sky come to life, create a stable background but leave it empty inside as the school has a crib and lots of eager children to play all the characters. Abi said that competition had been fierce for the animal roles which made me smile.

There was a knock at the hall doors. It was Ben. My heartbeat quickened despite my cautious mind replaying what Layla had told me about him. As I made my way across the hall I silently repeated, *I don't want to get my heart broken again and he's a player.*

I opened the doors, and he held up a plastic bag. 'Blame Olivia if my food choices are wrong.'

He came inside, brushing past me with a smile. 'I recall her telling me you love interesting sandwiches. She said that you would make the world's best sandwiches, I think steak and onion were her favourites. Apparently, you used to say you were changing the world one sandwich at a time.'

I stared at him. Wow, he'd remembered what Olivia had told him about me. My heart went berserk. 'Well, that's true.'

He gestured at the stage scenery. 'That's great, the kids will love it.'

'I hope so,' I gushed, 'I've not had much time.'

He grinned. 'Well, I think you need a break from your artistic work. I have made us something which I am hoping will come up to your high sandwich standards.' He laid out a picnic blanket on the edge of the stage. Out of the plastic bag he brought some tin foil wrapped packages. Whatever he'd made smelt amazing.

'This is Ben's Christmas club sandwich, which has turkey, maple bacon, cranberry chutney and spiced red cabbage in it. Plus, home-made potato wedges and a variety of dips. I also have an array of soft drinks as I didn't know whether you'd want a drink.' He arranged two plates and laid out his stacked sandwiches.

'You made all this.'

He nodded. 'I'm a foodie when I am not a builder.'

'Really?' *Why had Olivia kept this from me?*

His eyes held my gaze. 'I hope you enjoy my Christmas club sandwich, and I will be nervous as hell as you eat it. Not sure what I will do if you don't enjoy what I have cooked.'

'Ben, I am sure it will be wonderful.'

His meal was delicious. It was so good neither of us talked, we just ate. I didn't feel nervous about not talking and concentrating on enjoying his food. With Sam I always felt like I had to fill empty spaces between conversations.

After we'd both finished, he tidied everything away. Was this guy a heartbreaker? Because from what I had just seen he was thoughtful and considerate. He could have gone to a takeaway and bought us a chow mein or a pizza. Instead, he'd remembered everything Olivia had told him about me and spent the afternoon cooking something which would be meaningful to me.

He smiled. 'So, what's the verdict on my Christmas club sandwich?'

'Ben, it was a taste sensation, and I am very impressed.'

A cute boyish grin spread across his face. He reached into his pocket and brought out his phone. 'I'm still in touch with Sonia and I hope you don't mind but I told her I'd finally met you.'

'Ah, that's nice. I messaged her on Olivia's birthday. Is she okay?'

He nodded. 'She and Ray, you know, Olivia's dad, are back together.'

I gasped at his news. Olivia's mum and dad had split up ten years ago. She always used to say that one day she hoped a miracle would happen and they would get back together.

Ben passed me his phone. 'Read what she said. Losing Olivia brought them back together.'

As I tried to read the texts, tears pricked my eyes. Ben offered me a napkin. Sonia spoke about her love for Ray and how together they would learn to live again without their daughter. She knew Olivia would have wanted them to reunite and she hoped Olivia was looking down on them from heaven. I smiled at Ben once I'd got control of my emotions. 'Anything Olivia-related and I'm a mess.'

He nodded. 'Yeah, I know how that feels. Rachel,' he said, holding my gaze. 'I know we have the link to Olivia which is great. I want you to know that I am...' His words faded away as we stared at each other.

'You're what?' I whispered as our heads travelled towards each other.

Our lips were almost touching.

'I'm very attracted to you,' he whispered. 'You were pretty

in the photo Olivia sent me but in real life you're gorgeous. That shorter haircut is so sexy and don't get me started on those reindeer pyjamas.'

We both smiled.

'To be honest I'm struggling...' He paused and reclaimed his serious look. 'You're making me want to spend hours cooking delicious things for you. I see you in the kitchen and I must refrain from pulling you close. It is getting harder to...'

'To stay away?' I murmured, tilting my head so our lips could meet.

'Mmmm...' he murmured. 'All I want to do is kiss you.'

I closed my eyes and he pressed his soft lips against mine, and we kissed. It was a beautiful and tender kiss until my mind began replaying Sam telling me that he and Chantelle had been seeing each other. I broke away abruptly. My defences rose at lightning speed. I couldn't allow myself to get hurt again. 'I'm sorry, Ben. I can't...'

'It's okay,' he said interrupting me, 'we're probably moving at a hundred miles per hour.' He packed up his stuff. 'I better get home. Rosie will probably be expecting a bedtime story.'

I tried to catch his attention, but he wouldn't lift his eyes to mine.

'I better go, see you around, Rachel.' He headed towards the door.

Panic set in as he hurried away. 'Thanks for the lovely food,' I called out.

He didn't look back. 'No worries, good luck with the painting.'

I returned to my painting feeling uncomfortable. It had felt right to pull away, but I now felt like I'd hurt him.

Picking up my phone I facetimed the WhatsApp group I had with Connor and Kate. At the same time, I prayed they were both able to talk.

Connor appeared first. He was grinning and holding aloft a tall flute of fizzy Prosecco. 'Don't tell me,' he chuckled, 'Grandpa Eric and the dog have gone AWOL again.'

Kate appeared and laughed as she caught the tail end of what Connor had said. She was holding a gin glass.

'I need advice,' I said. 'Ben and I kissed tonight.'

Connor gasped. 'Wow – Olivia will be chuffed in heaven tonight.'

Kate nodded. 'So, what's the issue? Is he a naff kisser?'

'Washing machine kiss?' Connor enquired. 'Or was it a cold clamp kiss?'

I shook my head. 'It was a great kiss. His technique is brilliant, but...'

Connor peered at the nativity scenery behind me. 'Did you paint that?'

I nodded.

'Did you not want to make out with him in front of the nativity scene?' Connor asked, arching his eyebrows at me.

'Stop it,' I snapped, getting frustrated with Connor's quips. 'Someone told me that Ben is a heartbreaker and a player.'

Kate took a sip from her gin glass. 'Olivia wouldn't have set you up with a love rat.'

Connor nodded. 'She had a red flag radar. One of the best. Remember when I was dating that hygienist guy. Olivia told me after one look at him that she sensed he had a lot of red flags. I ignored her and on the fifth date the guy told me he was bankrupt and on bail for an assault charge. To this day I still don't know how she knew all that in one glance.'

'Olivia knew you were fragile,' Kate explained.

'I don't want to get hurt again,' I said, rubbing my chest. 'Also, I will be gone after Christmas.'

'And?' Connor asked. 'Surrey and London are not hundreds

of miles away. Relationships have survived across longer distances.'

'How have you left it with Ben?' Kate asked.

'He left looking embarrassed.' I wiped a layer of sweat from my forehead. 'I feel bad because he's a foodie and he made us these delicious Christmas stacked sandwiches. He'd remembered what Olivia had told him about me and my love for a good sandwich.'

Connor drained his flute of fizzy wine. 'I hate to say this, but heartbreakers don't do stuff like that. They turn up with a bag of chips, a battered sausage, a cheap bottle of wine and a cheeky smile. They certainly don't do embarrassment. Trust me, I have dated quite a few.'

Kate nodded. 'I agree. Also, Olivia will be managing this situation from heaven, and she won't let anything mess up her good work.'

I smiled. 'You're right.'

'Talk to Ben,' urged Kate.

CHAPTER TWENTY-NINE

I finished the scenery, took several shots on my phone, and sent them to Abi. She rang me and squealed down the phone. 'Oh, my goodness, Rachel, that's amazing. That sky is so dramatic and I love the stable.'

'I'm glad you like it.'

Abi laughed. 'Like it? I love it. Seriously, you have some talent there.'

'Thanks, that means a lot.'

I packed everything up and made my way home. On the way I thought about Ben, our kiss, and the rumours of him being a player. Inside me, a war was raging. Half of me wanted to run away from him and protect my wounded heart. However, the other half of me wanted to kiss him again and ignore the rumours.

The manor house was silent when I entered. I assumed everyone was asleep but I was wrong as Aunty Bev was sitting at the kitchen table. She'd taken out her curlers and her long brown hair extensions were full of bouncy curls. Her pearl-coloured silk shirt offset her dark, tanned skin. At her feet was a snoozing Humphrey.

'You still up?' I said, as she lifted her head and grinned. She gestured for me to grab a glass and join her in a bottle of red. Once she'd poured me a glass, she leaned back with a mischievous glint in her eyes.

My heart began to thump. Aunty Bev was making me nervous. Over the years we'd all been witness to one of Aunty Bev's impish looks. They usually preceded trouble like when she announced one family Christmas that she was going on a cruise with a ninety-year-old millionaire who had paid for her ticket and had agreed to cover all costs. That announcement had started with the same look of mischief. My mother nearly dropped the roast turkey in shock as she carried it to the table.

There was also the time when Aunty Bev announced to the family on WhatsApp she was getting back into singing. She'd sent us all a photo of her grinning with a microphone in her hand. Two nights later she sent us a clip of her getting on stage at a rock concert and doing a duet with the lead singer.

A sense of unease passed over me.

'I have the keys to the west wing,' she grinned. 'I might have *borrowed* them from the cleaner's handbag in the hallway. I am going into the west wing.'

I gasped. 'You can't do that.'

Aunty Bev shrugged. 'Layla won't miss them now. She made the mistake of telling me she cleans both sides of the house and that Frank has banned her from showing the west wing to anyone. It was like showing a red flag to a bull. Rachel, you know how I have spent my life struggling with the word, "no". You'd think I would have understood it in my fifties, but it's getting worse. I've been waiting for you to get home as I hate being naughty by myself.'

The thought of betraying Layla made me shake my head. 'Aunty Bev, I can't get Layla in trouble.'

Aunty Bev rolled her eyes before leaning across the table. 'Aren't you curious?'

'About what's in there? Yes, I am.'

Aunty Bev drained her glass. 'I smell a rat in this manor house. Something is not right, and I am going to get to the bottom of it.'

'But what happens if Frank has cameras set up and he sees you entering the west wing?'

She laughed. 'He's too busy doing deals in Malibu and anyway you've had Layla stay with you. If he'd been paying attention to his cameras, he would have sent you instructions to have her removed. She told me how vile he has been to her and how she must leave her employment come the first of January.'

I felt uncomfortable. 'This feels like we are invading their privacy but...'

'What?' Aunty Bev frowned.

'I can't talk. I am sleeping in a bedroom in the west wing. I took Grandpa into Frank and Maddie's master bedroom and I let him borrow one of Frank's suits.'

Aunty Bev poured herself another glass of wine. 'I know you're worried about your sister, Rachel. Now, I don't like my sisters much, but if one of them was in a weird marriage to someone like Frank I would be doing what I could to find out what was going on behind locked doors. You're different to me in that you and Maddie have always been close.'

I hang my head. 'It's been on my mind for ages, Aunty Bev.'

'Great,' said Aunty Bev, 'let's stop stewing over this. I am feeling naughty.' She rose from the table and dangled the keys. 'Let's go exploring.'

'But Layla...' I tried to stop Aunty Bev but she turned around.

'Maddie is your sister. Your loyalties are to her.'

Nausea ate away at me as we headed for the reception hall.

Aunty Bev rubbed my arm. 'Don't look so scared, Rachel. Frank won't know and even if he did – what exactly is he going to do from Malibu?'

'I know but what if...'

Aunty Bev slotted a key into the door adjacent to the east wing living room. It wasn't the right key, so she tried another until she had success. 'Bingo,' she said, with a cackle of laughter. She turned the handle and opened the door.

We stepped inside and Aunty Bev flicked on the lights. We both gasped in awe. It was a living room the same size as the one in the east wing. However, it was nothing like the east wing. It was funky and cool with raspberry-coloured walls, a white ceiling, a white fireplace, purple sofas and several distressed brown wooden cabinets, shelves, and bookcases.

'Why are they hiding this from us?' Aunty Bev gushed, running her hand over the purple fabric sofa. 'This is much better than Frank's lifeless living area.'

'This must be Maddie's living room,' I said, surveying the furniture. 'The bedroom I am staying in upstairs has a similar bold, colourful vibe.'

In one corner of the room was a collection of photos. My eyes were drawn to the familiar tall guy with black curly hair who was waving from a tractor in one photo and standing next to a horse in another. It was Josh. He was older now but still had that boyish smile.

I remember him from when I used to go visit Maddie at Oxford University and they'd both take me out for milkshakes. When he went to collect our drinks orders Maddie would gush about how cute his smile was. Had Frank seen these photos? I walked over to a desk which was tucked away at the back of the room. It was clear apart from an orange leather journal.

Aunty Bev came to stand beside me. She peered over my shoulder. 'Look inside.'

Reading Maddie's journal felt like a step too far. 'I can't do that.'

Aunty Bev shrugged and led the way through a door opposite the desk. After she turned on the light, we both gasped once more. We were in a kitchen-diner, painted in duck egg blue, with cream units. 'So, Maddie has her own kitchen?' Aunty Bev said, surveying the little jars of herbal tea.

'Why would she need her own kitchen?'

Aunty Bev folded her arms across her chest and surveyed the room. 'They're living separate lives.'

'What?'

She nodded. 'He lives in the east wing, and she lives in this wing.'

'But they're newlyweds and...' I thought back to their wedding, the way Frank tenderly kissed her once they were man and wife, the way she gazed at him adoringly outside during the wedding photos and the way they giggled like lovestruck teenagers at their reception.

Aunty Bev shrugged. 'I don't get it. If they were living separate lives, why would they go to such lengths to keep it a secret and tell everyone they only live in one part of the house because the other is too expensive.'

'Maybe living separately works for them?' I suggested. 'They live inside this house 24/7 so this is how they stay sane?'

Aunty Bev let out a heavy sigh. 'That's another thing I don't like. Why does he confine them to this house?'

'He's not liked in Harp Brook,' I explained.

We walked back into the living room. I went to study the framed photo containing the front cover of the *Hello* magazine which featured their wedding.

'Who the hell is Vanessa?' Aunty Bev cried out. I whirled around to see Aunty Bev reading from Maddie's journal.

'Maddie has written – "Frank and Vanessa" and circled it in red pen. Do you think she suspects them of... having an affair?'

The blood drained from my face and my heart ground to a halt. Was that the secret Layla was referring to? On jellied legs I staggered over to the desk where Aunty Bev was stood. Aunty Bev lifted her gaze up from the journal. 'Who is Vanessa?'

'She owns the pub in town. Everyone fears her, and she's been horrible to Layla. Her son was the guy who made Layla homeless. Layla did say there were rumours about Vanessa and Frank. I thought he'd argued with her or something as she said something about how Frank had made things worse.'

'I want to read more,' said Aunty Bev, closing the journal and placing it under her arm. My heartbeat quickened. Instinctively I snatched it back. 'No, we've read enough. I think we should put it back. Those are Maddie's inner and private thoughts.'

Aunty Bev shrugged and placed the journal back on the desk. 'I have a feeling we will regret not reading more. Do you know when me and my sisters were younger, I read all their diaries in secret? Did you know Karen thought Robert had a wandering eye at sixteen? Some things never change. Jackie has always liked weird men and Polly had a fling with a woman before she met Kevin.'

I ignored her family gossip. 'Let's get out of here. I need a drink.'

Once we'd locked up Aunty Bev placed the keys back where she'd found them, and we went to sit in the kitchen.

'Frank's having an affair and he's bank-rolling my sister,' groaned Aunty Bev, pouring herself a glass of wine.

'We don't know for sure,' I said, trying to think calmly. 'We don't know why she circled their names.'

Aunty Bev continued. 'I have done some stupid things in

my time, but they don't come close to letting a man like Frank buy me a villa in Tenerife.'

'What shall we do?'

Aunty Bev shook her head. 'We need to sleep on it. Maybe the affair is why they are leading separate lives?'

I ran my hands through my hair. 'She and Frank seemed happy.'

Aunty Bev drained her glass. 'Appearances can be deceiving.'

It was Ben's face that flashed up inside my head. Was I being deceived by his outwardly nice-guy appearance?

CHAPTER THIRTY

Sleep wasn't my friend. By two in the morning, I was still wide awake and thinking about Maddie, Frank, Vanessa, the secretive side of the house and betraying Layla. My head was full of questions. Were Frank and Maddie living separate lives? Had she caught Frank cheating on her? When I came to bed, I did think about texting Maddie to ask about Frank and Vanessa, but I stopped myself. Aunty Bev and I had assumed the worst. There could be a plausible explanation for why Maddie had circled their names. There had to be another way of bringing this situation out into the open. Aunty Bev and I needed proof.

At the edge of my mind sat my thoughts about Ben which were also trying to attract my attention. Reaching over I grabbed Olivia's pink notebook. I needed to read her words and feel like she was with me. Flipping over the first page I felt instantly soothed at seeing her swirly handwriting – *How I Got Over Losing a Wonderful Friend, by Olivia Lunn.*

I opened it to the next chapter I was on. The title made me skip a breath. *Don't Make Stupid Mistakes.*

Propping up pillows behind me I started to read.

Grief makes you do stupid things. It takes hold of your mind and body and instructs you to do things which on a normal day would make you freak out. Grief leaves you untethered and alone. It turns off the lights and makes you reach out for support. The trouble is, when you do try to cling to something and the lights go on, you realise you made a dreadful mistake.

She'd been gone for a month, and I was helping my friend look after his baby daughter. His daughter was sleeping upstairs. We were sat on the sofa together.

My heart had started to beat so loud I could hear it thumping inside my chest. All the saliva in my throat had evaporated. Ben was the friend whom Olivia was with. I clamped my hand over my forehead. Did I want to read what sort of mistake Olivia made with Ben?

Nausea swirled around my tummy. What the hell had Olivia done?

Through the gaps between my fingers, I read on.

I wanted someone to hold me. I was bereft. I was emotional and I wanted physical touch.

I slammed the book shut. Oh God, Olivia had slept with Ben in a grief-fuelled state. I didn't want to read it. Closing my eyes I massaged my temples. I took some deep breaths and remembered what Connor had said. Maybe Olivia was managing this thing with Ben from heaven and maybe she trying to show me something. With a trembling hand I opened the notebook again and gasped.

I threw myself at my friend. I kissed him on the lips, pressed my body against his and I ran my hands through his hair.

Shutting my eyes I let out a wail of frustration. 'Oh, Olivia, what are you doing to me? I can't read this.' An uncomfortable feeling passed over me. Olivia had slept with Ben. This was her stupid mistake. She was stunning with an hourglass figure, raven silky locks and a sexy smile. Ben would not have resisted her advances. I placed the notebook under my pillow. This situation with Ben now felt awkward and messy. I decided to lock my feelings for Ben away at the back of my mind.

Sleep found me soon after and teleported me to the perfume counter in Boots where Olivia was trying to persuade me to buy Angel by Mugler. She was frantically waving the little white tester card under my nose and saying, 'Isn't this divine?'

As I got showered and changed after waking, I thought about the old me who sat in her flat day in, day out, swapping over buckets and finding more things to stick in my Olivia shrine.

I now wanted to do things like cook, paint and help the local community. Throwing back the bedroom curtains I surveyed the snow-coated countryside. It was a much better view than that of those claustrophobic office buildings which always felt like they were hemming me in. Harp Brook was growing on me, despite the Frank situation. I liked being away from the city and I wanted to be close to people like Maddie, Layla and Abi. I could feel Olivia here too, in Harp Brook, and that was something which wasn't scary, it was giving me a lot of comfort.

Tom arrived first the next morning. 'Ben's going to be late,' he explained as I handed him a mug of tea. Relief swept over me at not having to see Ben after what I'd read.

Layla and Zac came into the kitchen. 'Morning, Rachel and Tom,' Layla said with a smile. 'Did you get the scenery finished?'

I nodded. 'Yes, and I am going tonight to watch the nativity.

Abi just texted to say Grandpa and I have two tickets. Any news on Derek?'

She beamed. 'He comes out tomorrow. We have talked every day since I saw him in hospital.'

Aunty Bev appeared. 'Morning, all. Can you believe it – this morning I woke up and tried to blow out my phone alarm like it was a candle. I think living in this huge house is giving me delusions of grandeur. Bring on the extra strong coffee.'

Layla grinned. 'That's funny, Bev. Has anyone seen Humphrey?'

'Humphrey?' I searched for him under the table. He wasn't in his basket. 'Oh no,' I groaned, 'Has he gone missing again?'

Grandpa appeared behind me. 'That dog is off enjoying the start of his Christmas week. Leave him alone.' He turned on the radio and soon the kitchen was filled with East 17's Christmas pop hit.

Layla surveyed the kitchen as Grandpa urged me to dance with him. She poked her head through the construction sheet. 'Tom, you seen Humphrey?'

Pulling away from Grandpa I ran my hand through my hair. 'That dog is a rascal!'

Grandpa placed a hand on my shoulder. 'Relax, he's probably saving someone's life again or finding a lost child. That dog is a little hero. When he disappears, we shouldn't panic. Who wants a cuppa?'

I made us all a cup of tea and some fried sandwiches as it was the start of our Christmas week. Aunty Bev went into the hallway. She returned as I carried the sandwiches to the table and glanced around the kitchen. 'Can you hear a dog barking?'

Leaping up I turned off the radio. She was right. There was the sound of a muffled dog bark. 'Humphrey?' I called out, walking into the reception hall.

Layla followed with Zac on her hip. 'Humphrey?'

I gulped as I realised the barking was coming from inside the west wing. Layla noticed as well and walked towards the locked doors. 'He's in the west wing. How the hell did he get in there?'

Without thinking I ran to Layla's bag in the hallway, grabbed the keys and ran to the door. She stared at me. 'How do you know they're the keys? Did you just go in my bag?'

Blood rushed past my ears and my heart thumped against my ribcage. 'Layla, I just guessed...'

I handed her the keys, and she opened the door to let an excited Humphrey out. 'I know you've been in here, Rachel.' Swiftly she shut the door and locked it. 'You've let me down, Rachel, after everything we have been through. I trusted you.' Before I could say another word, she ran away upstairs.

Aunty Bev appeared and made a fuss of Humphrey.

'Layla knows we have been in the west wing,' I mumbled with a heavy chest. 'She knows we found the keys in her handbag. I have betrayed her.'

'Don't worry,' soothed Aunty Bev, 'I'll speak to her.'

'I didn't want to put her in a difficult position. She's been through a lot.'

'Relax,' assured Aunty Bev, 'it will be fine. We had to find out what was going on.'

As I walked back into the kitchen, Grandpa was holding up my phone. I groaned as I saw that Mum was facetiming me. We hadn't spoken since I'd hung up on her.

'Hello, Mum,' I said, after pressing accept.

My mother's face appeared on the screen. Once again, she was on her sunbed. Today she was wearing a bright red halterneck bikini. Her hair was pinned up at the back and in her ears were gigantic golden hoops. 'Hello, Rachel. It's good to see you've calmed down.'

I bit my lip at her dig. 'How are you?'

She frowned. 'Where's Bev?'

'Janice, I'm here,' shouted Aunty Bev, peering over my shoulder and waving.

Relief passed over Mum's face. 'Thank God you're there, Bev. We've all been so worried.'

Aunty Bev cackled with laughter. 'As well as drinking and partying, Janice?'

'Bev, this is no time for jokes. How is our father?' In the background the sounds of heels clopping towards the phone could be heard, followed by Aunty Karen's voice. 'Janice, prepare yourself, Bev has walked into utter chaos.'

'He's fine,' shouted Grandpa, holding aloft his cup of tea.

Aunty Bev smiled. 'Janice and Karen, I haven't seen Dad this happy in a long time. He told me that living here is a hundred times better than back at his home with Karen popping in every day.'

There was the sound of hissing and mumbling in Tenerife. Mum must have passed her phone to Aunty Karen as she appeared on the screen. Her pink sunburnt face made me gasp. 'Beverly, that's a hurtful thing to say. I do such a lot for Dad.'

'Like what, Karen?' Aunty Bev shouted. 'From what I've heard – you do bugger all!'

Aunty Karen yelped with shock. 'How dare you say that, Beverly! You never come up here as you're too busy cavorting with that ninety-year-old millionaire, the one who pays for you to go on luxury holidays with him every time you flash a bit of leg.'

'At least I enjoy myself,' roared Aunty Bev. 'I'd rather be on holiday with Harold and his millions than sitting watching Robert gawp at my hairdresser.'

Irritation at my family prickled away at me. I didn't need another facetime argument and there were more pressing matters at hand like my sister's husband having an affair and me betraying Layla's trust. 'We're not having another row on this phone; we have enough stress going on here as it is.'

My mother snatched the phone back from Aunty Karen as I let out an inner groan. Why did I say the last bit of that sentence?'

'What do you mean, Rachel? I knew you were not telling us everything.'

I had to act fast. 'Mum, Christmas Day is on Friday, and I must cook for us all. There is more snow forecast and it's hard work here keeping everyone fed and watered.'

Mum eyed me suspiciously. 'You're making me worry and I want a cocktail. It's still early here and Gary has said no booze until after lunch.'

'Please can I have one, Janice,' sobbed Aunty Karen in the background. 'Beverly has hurt my feelings.'

I'd had enough of my family. 'Look, it's Christmas, can we all be nice?'

'I don't want to speak to Beverly,' wailed Aunty Karen.

'Merry Christmas,' shouted Aunty Beverly and I hung up.

CHAPTER THIRTY-ONE

'I want to go check out Vanessa.' Aunty Bev had calmed herself down after the family call. 'I want to send out a message that if she wants to fight, I am ready for her.' She pulled on her leopard-skin coat. 'Do you know where this pub of hers is?'

'You can't just walk into her pub,' I said. 'Anyway, she hates this family. I have had quite a few locals warn me to not go anywhere near her pub.'

Aunty Bev shook her head. 'Why does she hate the family? If she's having an affair with Frank – why would she be stirring up trouble? Unless she and Frank have broken up and it's not been amicable. That would tie in with what Layla told you, how what happened between Frank and Vanessa made everything worse.'

'We're running away with this.' I took a deep breath. 'We don't know the full facts.'

'Vanessa doesn't know me, and I will lie when they ask me who I am,' explained Aunty Bev.

I felt uncomfortable at the thought of Aunty Bev going off on her own to meet Vanessa. Aunty Bev was a loose cannon at the best of times and one stray comment could result in a screaming match. Also, we still didn't know for sure if Maddie suspected Frank and Vanessa of having an affair. Layla was still upstairs, and I wasn't even sure she would speak to me again after the key incident.

Grandpa rose from the table. 'I'm coming too.'

'No, Grandpa,' I snapped, feeling on edge. 'You stay here.'

He placed his hand on my shoulder. 'I'm coming. I am still on the lookout for an adventure. Beverly has filled me in on everything.'

I glanced at Aunty Bev, who nodded. 'Dad needed to know, Rachel. Right, let's take my Fiesta.'

'You do know the snow is still bad?'

Aunty Bev laughed. 'My old Fiesta can handle a bit of snow. She loves off-roading.'

As I climbed into the back of Aunty Bev's car, I had a worrying feeling about this situation. 'Can we not mention who we are? I don't want to cause trouble.'

Aunty Bev nodded. 'Don't worry, I will say that we're on our way to see family and wanted a pitstop in Harp Brook.'

To my amazement Aunty Bev's Fiesta got down the snow-coated drive and onto the main road. The Harp Brook Inn was at the far end of the high street. It was a quaint historic coaching inn, and a sign outside informed us everyone was welcome, and the Harp Brook Inn had been in the Good Pub Guide in 2010 and 2015.

'Do we know what she looks like?' Aunty Bev asked as she parked in the pub car park.

'I've only had the pleasure of meeting her sister, Denise.'

'We can check out the staff whilst we have a drink,' Grandpa said rubbing his gloved hands together. 'I'm in need of a decent pint.'

'Grandpa, it's still early. If they're open, we'll have coffees or a pot of tea.'

He muttered something under his breath as we all trooped inside.

There was a young woman behind the bar. 'Can I help you?'

'Are you serving coffee?' Aunty Bev asked.

She nodded. 'Sit down and I'll come and take your order.'

'Is Vanessa working today?' Aunty Bev asked, making me flinch.

To my relief the young woman shook her head. 'No, she's not. Do you need to talk to her?'

I decided to speak for Aunty Bev. 'No, we're fine, thanks.'

'Are you local?' The woman beamed before pointing to a table in front of the window.

Aunty Bev shook her head. 'No, I'm Maddie Baxter's aunt and I'm from Brighton. This is Maddie's sister and Maddie's grandfather.'

My entire body froze. She had promised not to reveal who we were.

The young woman's smile evaporated. 'Oh, I see. Have a seat.'

Once we were seated, I leaned over and hissed at Aunty Bev. 'Why did you tell her who we were?'

Aunty Bev shrugged. 'I was feeling naughty again. Did you see her face change when I told her who I was? She knows something.'

'This is putting Maddie in a difficult position, Aunty Bev.'

The woman came over to take our coffee order and there was a definite tone change in her voice. As she was leaving to head back to the counter and make our coffees, Aunty Bev stuck her hand up. 'Excuse me. Can you tell us why several locals have been warning my niece and father about Vanessa and telling them to stay away from this pub?'

My heart ground to a halt and Grandpa gleefully rubbed his hands. 'That's my girl, Beverly. You go get 'em!'

The young woman fiddled with her notepad. 'I don't know why you have been told that.' She bowed her head and hurried away.

'Aunty Bev,' I hissed. 'What the hell is wrong with you?'

Aunty Bev grinned. 'Sorry, Rachel, but I gravitate towards trouble.'

Grandpa fist-pumped the air. 'Go large, Beverly.'

The woman brought over our coffees. She didn't say a word and scurried away soon after. Aunty Bev let out a heavy sigh. 'It's a shame Vanessa isn't here.'

'I think it's for the best,' I muttered.

We drank our coffees and left. To my relief there were no more outbursts from Aunty Bev.

Layla was in the kitchen when we returned. Grandpa and Aunty Bev went to sit in the lounge. I decided to talk to Layla and apologise.

Zac clung to her hip and was chewing on his teddy. She turned away as she saw me entering the kitchen. 'I'm sorry, Layla. I never wanted to hurt you or get you in trouble.'

She handed Zac his milk beaker. 'You went in the west wing – didn't you?'

'Yes. We did go inside the west wing – more to figure out what's going on with Maddie than anything else. We shouldn't have taken the keys out of your bag without asking.'

The sounds of Zac glugging his milk filled the air. Layla bowed her head. Guilt consumed me. I had let her down. 'Layla, say something. I am sorry, and we did it because we were worried about Maddie.'

She nodded before walking over to the kitchen table. After pulling out a chair she sat down. 'People rarely apologise to me. This is a first.'

My heart was thumping inside my chest.

'Rachel, it's okay, you're a good person. I know that.'

Relief flooded through me as I walked over to the coffee machine. 'The trouble is, we don't know all the facts. It's like a jigsaw puzzle where some of the pieces are missing.' I turned to the coffee machine. 'You want a coffee?'

She smiled and nodded. 'That would be great.'

Once I'd made us two cappuccinos, I carried them over to the kitchen table. 'I'm glad we're talking,' I gushed, 'I didn't like us falling out.'

She grinned. 'Me too.' Taking out her phone she showed me her latest text conversation with Derek. 'His GIFs makes me laugh. That's us. Talking non-stop.'

I smiled at the GIFs of two little dogs chattering away.

'Have you thought anymore about getting in touch with your dad?'

'The thought is there. I don't know what to say.'

She gave me a knowing nod. 'I get it. With me I had to start with, "I think you used to date my mum and I am your kid."'

'That must have been hard.'

'I drunk a lot of beer before I pressed send. Sometimes a simple "Hello" works well. He knows who you are. Trish, my friend, stopped talking to her best friend from years ago. She tracked her down and sent her an email that said, "Hello – love Trish." That friend replied and came back into her life. She supported Trish through her messy divorce and did a bit of match-making. Trish is now dating her friend's neighbour who is the nicest bloke in the world.'

I smiled at my new young friend. 'I might try Trish's approach.'

CHAPTER THIRTY-TWO

As I made lunch for everyone I couldn't stop thinking about Olivia's notebook and Ben. Even though I didn't want to read about Olivia sleeping with Ben, I needed to know. As they all tucked into an array of sandwiches I ran upstairs and grabbed Olivia's notebook. With a trembling hand I flicked to the page I was on.

My friend Ben is a true gentleman. He could have taken me to bed and had his way but instead he pulled away and said, 'This is wrong. I like you, Olivia, but not in that way.'

After a lengthy awkward silence, he made us a cup of tea. Once I'd apologised profusely and told him I wanted the ground to open and swallow me whole, he laughed and offered me some of his home-made cookies.

'Oh God, Ben isn't a player,' I muttered staring at the words. 'You're showing me the truth – aren't you?'

I will always be grateful to my friend. He was brilliant and we still laugh about it today.

Shutting the notebook, I hugged the book and closed my eyes. 'Thank you for showing me this, Olivia,' I whispered.

'Hello, Ben,' I said, as he strode into the kitchen. It was after mid-afternoon. His presence made me melt. I thought about Olivia saying in her notebook that he was a 'true gentleman'. The urge to run to him and tell him everything that was on my mind was strong, but I resisted. Casting me a weak smile, he ran himself a glass of water.

'How are you?'

He nodded before drinking the water and began to walk back towards the construction sheet. Something was wrong. He seemed distant. I reached out and caught his arm. 'Are we okay, Ben?'

Turning towards me he smiled. 'I'm sorry about last night. I sensed it's time for me to back off and give you some space.'

'About that...'

He raised his hands in a surrender like pose. 'Rachel, you don't have to explain. Look, I'm busy out there so I better get back.'

He pulled the sheet up and I felt a deep longing to be in his arms again. I wanted him to kiss me like he had done in the school hall. I wanted him to hug me again like he'd done in the café. 'Ben, can we talk later?'

'You don't need to...'

Today he was more handsome than ever in his grubby black cargo trousers, black fleece, and woollen hat. 'Ben, are you going to the nativity play later?'

His green eyes held mine. His face softened and he smiled. 'Yes, are you?'

I nodded. 'Do you fancy talking this evening?'

'I'll have to put Rosie to bed.'

'It would be good to talk.'

A grin stretched across his face. 'My bedtime stories take a long time.'

'I can wait.'

We stood and stared at each other like two lovestruck teenagers before he pointed out into the hallway. 'I have fixed the front door. It will be easier to close now and it might help with Humphrey.'

'Thank you, Ben. That's from me and Humphrey.'

He smiled. 'See you later.'

The nativity play was brilliant, and Grandpa shouted, 'BRAVO' at the end when all the children and teachers were busy taking a bow. I even got a mention from the headmaster who thanked me for my fabulous scenery. Everyone gave me a round of applause. Two of the mums even reached over and said thanks. The feeling that I'd helped the school community after their stage artist had been taken to hospital filled me with warm, tingling feelings.

Rosie was one of the narrators and it was great to see her reading out part of the story. Ben was sat in front of Grandpa and me. Whenever Rosie talked, I noticed his face reddened. Seeing her made him emotional and I loved this.

After the play Grandpa and I walked back to the car. As I opened the door for Grandpa, I heard someone say, 'Why can't the Baxters leave Harp Brook?'

I looked up and saw Denise surrounded by a group of women. She was staring at me. 'Now that you painted your little nativity scenery, can you all just pack up and go?'

The women around her giggled.

'Your family has given Harp Brook a bad name. Your brother-in-law hurt my sister.'

I have never been one for quick-witted responses in tense situations. Afterwards, I will always come up with a hundred imaginary responses and wish I had thought of them at the time. Words jostled around on my tongue, but nothing came out.

Denise made a scoffing sound and walked off with her crowd.

'What did she say?' Grandpa asked as I pulled out of the car park.

'Our family has given Harp Brook a bad name.' I missed out the part about Frank hurting Vanessa.

Grandpa shook his head. 'Frank has caused this. What has he been up to?'

An uncomfortable feeling passed over me.

I dropped Grandpa back to the manor house and made him promise to not tell Aunty Bev about our encounter with Denise. The last thing I needed was Aunty Bev to get in her car and go look for a fight with Denise. Grandpa gave me his word and I walked to Ben's cottage.

Ben and Rosie were doing a Christmas jigsaw on the table. Rosie patted the seat next to her and grinned. 'Where's Humph-Wee?'

'He's being a good boy.' I smiled, finding a missing piece from Santa's hat in the jigsaw.

'I miss him,' sighed Rosie. 'When I am sad again, he will show up.'

'Humphrey misses you too, Rosie. He told me you are the best person on a sledge he's ever seen.'

'Better than Daddy?' she asked.

I nodded. 'Humphrey says you were much better than your daddy at sledging.'

She smiled and giggled at her father who was trying to squeeze the wrong jigsaw piece into a gap. Once Ben had read her a bedtime story he came back downstairs and made us both a cup of hot chocolate. He came to sit next to me on the dark red sofa. His living room was small and cosy. Low imposing dark beams stretched across the ceiling and the cream walls on either side of the stone fireplace were adorned with Rosie's paintings from school, her swimming certificates and framed photos. My eyes were drawn to the photos directly opposite of Ben and a heavily pregnant blonde-haired woman. I assumed that was Sophie. She had a beautiful smile and the camera loved her. Lifting my gaze, I caught sight of Olivia standing alongside the blonde woman. They both looked young and happy.

Ben jolted me back to the present. 'So, what did you want to talk about?'

His arm brushed against mine as he stirred his hot chocolate. My whole body became engulfed in tingles.

'I like you... a lot. The other day I heard something about you, and it made me act the way I did last night...'

He interrupted me. 'This sounds interesting.'

I took a deep breath. 'I believed the rumour for a bit and...' My words tailed off as he held my gaze.

'You have to tell me the rumour.'

I fiddled with a loose thread on my jumper. 'You're a bit of a ladies' man.'

I lifted my face to his. His eyebrows were arching in surprise. 'Me – a ladies' man? Wow – that's quite a rumour.' He scratched his stubble-clad chin. 'That's the sort of rumour I would have loved to have heard in my youth.' After a heavy sigh he turned to me. 'Look, I know where this has come from. I have been on one date in six years, it was a total disaster, and that person has been saying nasty things about me.'

'Denise?'

He nodded. 'I didn't fancy her and at the end of the evening I told her I wanted to be friends. Well, she took it badly. She told me that no one turns her down and started spreading these rumours about me. One of her boys at school has also been giving Rosie a hard time.'

'That's not nice.'

He shook his head. 'It's not nice. I'm sorry you had to hear that. I'm the last person to be a heartbreaker and a player. Believe me.'

'About that kiss?'

'Oh yes, about that. I meant what I said. If you want me to back off...'

I twirled a piece of my hair around my finger. 'That's the last thing I want you to do.' With a suggestive smile I leaned forward and pressed my lips against his. Our kiss was even better than the one in the school hall. It was warm, sensual and when we broke for air my head was swimming.

He stroked my hand. 'Wow, that was a proper kiss. Can I ask what changed your mind about me?'

I took a deep breath. 'Olivia.'

He looked surprised. 'Olivia?'

'Before I left my flat in London I found this notebook in her bedroom. It was an advice book she'd written about how to get over losing a friend.'

'Sophie,' Ben whispered, hanging his head. 'She wrote it about losing Sophie.'

I reached out and placed my hand on top of his. He leaned towards me, and I wrapped my arms around him. We didn't say anything. I simply held him close.

He pulled away and smiled. 'Thank you for that. Sophie

was a huge part of my life, and I will always have a hole in my heart.'

I stroked his hair. 'I understand.'

'Why did Olivia mention me?'

'She talked about how you told her to make Sophie proud by writing romance novels.'

'Sophie would have loved to know that Olivia was following her dream. Was that the only thing it said about me?'

I cast him an awkward look. 'She also talked about how she... ummm...'

'Kissed me?'

I nodded and he smiled. 'We laughed about that for ages afterwards. It sounds horrid of me to say that, but I didn't want her to feel embarrassed or guilty. Olivia, Sophie and I were always taking the mickey out of each other. When Olivia surprised me by planting her lips on mine, I knew it was grief.'

'She said you were a true gent.'

'She was a good friend to me, and I respected her a lot. Wow – I can't believe she's written about that.'

'Her book has really helped me over the past few weeks, Ben. When I came to Harp Brook, I was a mess.'

He held my gaze with his beautiful green eyes.

'I've spent the last few months sat in a lonely flat with a leaky ceiling, surrounded by some of Olivia's belongings and feeling lost. I was applying for jobs I didn't want, and I wasn't getting, I was haunted by my ex-boyfriend dumping me on Christmas Eve, plus I was basing my life on what my mother wanted me to do. Olivia's advice has helped me in so many ways. Without it I wouldn't have cut my hair, got involved with the nativity scenery painting or decided that I wanted to change my career and do something with food instead of project management. I also wouldn't have allowed myself to come here tonight and... kiss you again.'

His fingers wrapped around mine.

'Do you know something, Ben? I feel closer to Olivia here in Harp Brook than I have done in my flat since she died. It feels like she's with me.'

'Have you finished her book?'

'I am part way through.' I ran my hands over my jeans. 'I want you to know I am on a journey right now. My life needs to change. I know that now and I must work out how.'

He smiled. 'So, where do we go from here?'

'I am going to carry on reading her book and see what happens.'

'Rachel, I'm here and whatever you decide I will support you.'

I leaned against his shoulder, and he pulled me close. 'Does that mean I can't kiss you again until you've finished her book?'

'That would be torturous,' I said with a mischievous smile. 'Why don't you carry on kissing me and I'll figure out my life over Christmas.'

'Deal.'

CHAPTER THIRTY-THREE

Later I returned to my bedroom at the manor house, feeling warm and gooey inside after my hot chocolate chat with Ben. The worrying incident with Denise had left my mind and all I could think about was how gorgeous Ben was.

The smell of vanilla greeted me as I stepped inside the room, and it made me smile. It could have been from one of Maddie's perfumes and creams on the dressing table, but I chose to see it as a sign Olivia was with me.

She entered my dreams again after I fell asleep. We were still in Boots and had moved away from the perfume counter. She was leading me down the expensive haircare aisle telling me that she was in a serious relationship with her hair, and it was making her spend a lot of money. I woke up smiling.

Before getting out of bed, I read the next chapter titled, *Make a Big Life Change.* Olivia talked about her decision to leave Surrey and head for London. She applied for several jobs and secured a marketing position. After selling her car, she bought a bicycle and applied for a vacancy in a flat-share with three other girls. This was her big life change.

When someone special dies your entire world is flipped upside down. Once your world corrects itself and flips back over, life isn't the same again. Living in Surrey wasn't for me anymore. That part of my life died with Sophie. Making such a life change was what I needed to do.

The flat-share arrangement with the three girls would slowly drive me insane as I would keep bumping into half-naked men on the landing in the middle of the night, but it would eventually lead me to my soul sister, Rachel Reid.

I stared at Olivia's words and my name. Tears pricked my eyes, and her swirly writing went blurry. After getting showered and dressed I went downstairs.

Layla was at the table with Zac on her knee. He was squealing at Humphrey who was sat wagging his tail and staring up at him.

'Coffee, Layla?'

She grinned. 'Yes, please.'

I carried the mugs over to the table. 'Last night I had a run-in with Denise.'

Layla cast me a worried look. 'What did she say?'

'My family have given Harp Brook a bad name.'

'That's not true. I have heard people around town singing your praises about helping the school out.'

'Will you tell me what you know?'

She tried to smooth down some of Zac's unruly curls. 'Maddie lives in the west wing. Whenever I come to clean and there are no guests, Maddie is in the west wing and he's in the east wing. It's like they're neighbours.'

I took a sip of my coffee. 'Do you think they're living separate lives?'

Layla shrugged. 'I'm just their cleaner. It's always felt strange to me.'

'My aunty Bev peeked at Maddie's journal.'

Layla's thick eyebrows shot up her forehead. 'Really?'

I nodded. 'She only read one page. Maddie had circled in red pen the names Frank and Vanessa.'

Layla bowed her head. 'All I know is that...' she paused. 'Frank and Vanessa had an affair.'

Tears pricked my eyes. It was true. Frank was a scumbag and a cheat. My poor sister.

Layla continued. 'It was the worst kept secret. Everyone knew what they were up to.'

'Is it over now?'

'He dumped her. Apparently, he drove her to a local picnic area and told her he had to end their affair.' Layla took a drink of her coffee. 'He had asked her to sign a legal document at a dinner date a few days before he ended it with her. She didn't know what was coming next and signed it. Ryan told me she'd had far too much champagne. The signed document meant she couldn't go to the press.'

'Oh no.'

'Vanessa went mad at the picnic site. The rumour is that she took out his pink fluffy handcuffs and locked his hands to his steering wheel. She then phoned Ryan to come and collect her. Frank went berserk. I don't know who rescued him.'

'I can see why Vanessa doesn't like Frank. It also explains the handcuffs being in the suit Grandpa wore to the Tea Dance.'

Layla nodded. 'Vanessa was upset. Ryan told me she could see herself becoming the next Mrs Baxter.'

'Maddie must have found out somehow.'

'That's the odd bit. Maddie spends all her time in the house. She's never seen in the town.'

'Weird. If you knew my sister before Frank, you'd know she was the life and soul of her old community.'

Layla fiddled with her gold chain. 'Please can you keep me

out of this? I don't have a job after Christmas, and I know Frank can make people's lives a misery.'

'I promise you, Layla, I will make it clear that you were not a part of this.' I reached across and gently squeezed her hand. 'We are going to get you sorted. I promise.'

Layla smiled. 'Thanks. I am still grateful to you for everything you have done for me. What will you do?'

'I think we will get Christmas out of the way on Friday and then when Maddie and Frank return after, I will speak to Maddie.'

'About Christmas...' Layla said, squirming in her seat. 'Zac's still young and he doesn't understand what's going on, so I am not getting him any presents. I know it sounds cruel, but I don't have much money and...'

'I understand. Don't worry. Grandpa, and I would like to get little Zac a gift. Is there a toy he wants?'

Layla's face brightened. 'There is a toy car garage in the charity shop which I know Zac would love. It's ten pounds and is in great condition.'

'I'll go into town in a bit and go buy it. Do you fancy coming with me?'

'I'd love to, but I also need to drop some keys off at a cottage I have been cleaning. The owner is putting it up for rent after Christmas.'

After, I made breakfast sandwiches for everyone, including Ben and Tom, who were both full of festive cheer. When everyone was talking in the kitchen about their favourite Christmas song, Ben pulled me through the construction sheet for a quick kiss. 'Hello,' he whispered. 'I like your breakfast sandwich although I think mine is going to be better.'

'Fighting talk,' I said, with a cheeky wink.

'One day you will have to stay over and try one.' He arched his eyebrows suggestively and we both laughed.

After ordering Aunty Bev to keep a close eye on Grandpa, Humphrey, and little Zac, I took Layla into town.

The little Fisher Price garage was perfect for Zac. It was colourful, had lights which flashed, music, a car wash, a huge ramp to a car park on the roof and a few little cars. I also bought some wrapping paper and tags.

While Layla went into the pharmacy, I popped into Kay's gift shop. Kay wasn't working. I was served by a teenage girl who helped me pick out some earrings for Layla. She deserved a little Christmas gift.

Back in the car, Layla gave me directions to the little cottage which was coming up for rent. It was called 'The Duck House' and was on the grounds of a farm. I parked the car on the road, and we trudged up to the main farmhouse.

'Do you not fancy renting somewhere like this, Layla?'

She shook her head. 'Living on a farm is not for me. What about you? I can see you living here. Wait till you see The Duck House.'

As the old farmer came out to meet us, Layla pointed to the tiny blue cottage sat apart from the rest of the farm. It was like someone had taken it out of a toy box and placed it in a field. My heartbeat quickened.

'In the summer I let it out,' explained the farmer, 'but in the winter I struggle to find someone to rent it. The Duck House has one bedroom, a shower room, a galley kitchen, and a small living area downstairs.'

'When would you need it for the summer?' I asked the farmer.

He scratched his head. 'Start of May.'

Layla gave me a nudge. 'It's better than a London flat with a leaky roof.'

The thought of returning to London made my heart sink. I didn't want to leave Harp Brook and now that I knew Maddie's marriage was in trouble, the urge to stay closer was even stronger. My landlord had sent me several apologetic emails about the leaking roof, and it still wasn't fixed. I could rent The Duck House for a few months to get myself on my feet and see what happened. I saw Olivia's notebook in my mind. Maybe this was the big life change I needed? Maybe my life in London had died when Olivia passed away?

Mum's face appeared in my mind. There would undoubtedly be a new family WhatsApp chat created about me.

We walked over to The Duck House. It was tiny inside, but it was perfect.

'I'll rent it,' I said, without hesitation. The farmer grinned. He reached out to shake my hand. 'Well, that's made my Christmas.' He caught sight of one of his farm hands trudging towards us. 'Josh, I've found someone to rent The Duck House.'

My mouth dropped open as my sister's ex-boyfriend, Josh, walked towards us. He saw me and smiled. 'Rachel, is that you?'

'Josh – how are you doing? I didn't realise you lived near here?'

He grinned. 'I have always wanted to own a farm, so I am working with Bob to learn the ropes and one day buy my own farm.'

'That's great,' I said, 'I will tell my sister...'

His smile disappeared and I sensed something was wrong. Wanting to change the conversation quickly, I turned to Bob. 'Can I come over after Christmas, next week sometime, to sort everything out?'

He nodded. 'Layla has my number. Send me a text and you can come over for a pot of tea and some of my wife's Christmas fruit cake.'

'Thank you and merry Christmas.'

❄

Ben accompanied me on a dog walk around the snowy grounds of the manor house when I returned. Once we were away from the rest of the house I told him my news about the cottage. 'I'm going to be renting The Duck House here in Harp Brook.'

'The Duck House? On Harp Brook Farm?' He queried as if he had misheard me.

'Yes – why? Do you know something about it?'

He fiddled with his woollen hat. 'How did you know it was up for rent?'

'Layla had to drop the keys off. Why? Ben – you're acting strange.'

He laughed. 'Sorry, I don't mean to act strange. That is great news,' he pulled me close. 'Have you finished Olivia's book?'

'No – why?'

After kissing me he said, 'I think you should hurry up and finish it. Tell me when you have, because then I will tell you why I acted a bit odd just then.'

I looked at him. 'I don't like secrets.'

'When you move into The Duck House, can I date you properly?'

'Yes, and I promise I won't ghost you this time.'

We laughed and I remembered my encounter with Josh. 'I bumped into a guy who Maddie used to date years ago on the farm.'

'Really?'

'He's called Josh. It was weird seeing him at the farm as the last time I saw him he was working in Oxford where Maddie went to university.'

Ben took hold of my hand. 'Will you invite me for dinner at The Duck House?'

'I might do,' I said, with a cheeky smile. 'You can't stay over though as there's only one bedroom.'

He grinned. 'I bet I can make you change your mind about that.'

CHAPTER THIRTY-FOUR

It was late. Grandpa, Layla, and Zac had all gone to bed. Aunty Bev and I were in the east wing living room enjoying a bottle of wine and discussing the way forward with the Maddie situation. She wasn't shocked when I told her what Layla had revealed earlier.

'I knew someone like Frank Baxter couldn't stay faithful,' exclaimed Aunty Bev. 'Have you seen the stuff on Reddit about him in his acting days?'

I nodded and tried to steer away from the subject of Frank's wild past. 'So, what should we do?'

Aunty Bev took her phone out and, with her reading glasses perched on the end of her nose, tapped something into her phone. 'Frank Baxter was known as a Hollywood sex symbol. His early acting career was filled with intense love affairs. Rumours were rife upon the release of his action blockbuster – *Running Out of Time* – that Baxter and his married co-star, Roxy Fisher, were enjoying a secret romance.' She looked up from her phone. 'I never liked Roxy Fisher in that film. She was so wooden when it came to acting.'

'Aunty Bev, let's discuss what I need to do when Maddie comes back.'

To my annoyance, Aunty Bev went back to her phone. 'On the set of Baxter's action film, *Danger Ahead,* actress Suzie Wood claimed she and Baxter couldn't keep their hands off each other, which was difficult as her long-time partner at the time was directing the film. The co-stars enjoyed a raunchy two-month affair.' Aunty Bev let out a heavy sigh. 'Frank, you dirty dog.'

'I don't want to hear any more about my brother-in-law,' I said, raising my voice slightly. 'This is not a great situation to be in and to make matters worse, he bought my mother a villa in Tenerife.'

'Janice has always had a soft spot for Frank,' said Aunty Bev, making me let out a yelp of frustration. 'I do hope she kept her hands off...'

'Aunty Bev,' I shouted. 'Please stop this. We need to talk.'

She cast me a worried look and peered over her glasses at me. 'Are you feeling all right, Rachel? I saw you with that handsome builder earlier. I was thinking of making a pass at him myself, but you beat me to it.' With a flick of her long curly hair, she put down her phone and took a sip of her wine.

I was losing patience. 'Okay, let's get through Christmas and I will speak to Maddie when she returns.'

Aunty Bev nodded. 'At least the affair between Frank and Vanessa is over as well. Maybe he's trying to change his ways. I mean, look at your uncle Robert – it can be done.'

'Uncle Robert had a midlife crisis.'

Aunty Bev shook her head. 'Rachel, he had a twenty-something crisis, a thirty-something crisis and a forty-something crisis. This is a well-trodden path for your aunty Karen. He does have a thing for hairdressers though. Did I ever tell you the time she came back from a week's break in Benidorm to find him naked and having his hair cut by a hairdresser (who was also naked) called Heidi?'

I stood up. 'I'm off to bed. This is all too much.'

Aunty Bev nodded. 'Pass me the bottle. I'll finish up and carry on reading about Frank's early acting career.'

I gave her the bottle which was three-quarters full. Aunty Bev had found the key to Frank's cellar whilst I was walking the dog and had picked us out a bottle. I had told her that he had left out cheaper bottles in the wine rack, but she'd laughed and said, 'He's having an affair, Rachel, it's time to enjoy ourselves.'

'What did you think about that guy Josh working at the farm?'

'Maddie is an angel, she'd never do anything to rock the boat,' said Aunty Bev. 'She'd also have your mother to answer to. Knowing Maddie, she's probably in an unhappy marriage and suffering in silence.'

'I'm done. See you in the morning.'

'The reappearance of Josh is interesting though,' said Aunty Bev. 'It could be coincidence. On my last cruise I found myself sitting at the bar next to an old ex-boyfriend of mine. It was a shock to turn round and see him smiling at me. Luckily my ninety-year-old millionaire friend had gone to bed early.'

'Wasn't the ninety-year-old millionaire friend the one who had paid for your cruise?'

She nodded. 'Yes, but he knows that I am not exclusive these days. Tell me about Josh?'

'He and Maddie were close. They went through a lot of stuff together. The one thing that stands out from that time is when she and Josh used to roll around laughing at each other's jokes.'

'That's a sign,' said Aunty Bev. 'Oh, before you go. You've done a cracking job with Dad. He tells me he has had a fantastic time.'

'Thanks, Aunty Bev, that means a lot.'

'He wants Dorothy and her daughter Kay to come for Christmas lunch. Can you add them to the catering list?'

'What? Has Dorothy – and more importantly her daughter – agreed to this? The last time we saw Kay, she dragged her mother away from Grandpa telling her not to associate herself with the Baxter family.'

Aunty Bev nodded. 'Janice and Karen will have kittens when they hear his news.'

'News?' I felt uncomfortable. Grandpa had news.

'He proposed to Dorothy over the phone earlier and she said yes.'

'*What?*'

Aunty Bev giggled. 'You were out with Layla, and he was going on about marrying this Dorothy woman, so I let him call her. They're engaged. Oh God, it was sweet.'

'Does her daughter know this?'

Aunty Bev shrugged.

I stared at my aunt. 'Mum is going to kill me.'

Aunty Bev cackled with laughter. 'I am itching to tell them on WhatsApp. It will be sweet revenge for all the times they have bitched about me on there.'

'Where's he going to live?'

'Oh, he's moving in with Dorothy after Christmas.' She drained her glass and poured herself a new one. 'Good luck, Dorothy. Cheers to the happy couple.'

'He can't do this,' I muttered, imagining my mum and Aunty Karen's faces when I break the news to them.

Aunty Bev shrugged. 'Let him get on with it. He's eighty and lonely up there. Good grief if I was being cared for by Karen and Rob, I would be asking the first person I met to marry me just to get away from them.'

'Mum will kill me.'

'Life's too short to worry about what your mother thinks. Anyway, she's hardly living a perfect life.'

'I have given my landlord notice on my flat and I am also going to have to explain to Mum why I am moving here with no job.'

Aunty Bev looked at me. 'Rachel, your life is not your mother's business.'

I grabbed my empty wine glass. 'Fill me up, Aunty Bev, I need a drink.'

CHAPTER THIRTY-FIVE

'Grandpa, we need to talk,' I said the next morning, as he came into the kitchen. His white hair was sticking out on one side but on top it looked like he'd been using gel as it was almost spiked at the front.

'Aunty Bev told me you're now engaged.'

A huge grin broke out across his face, and he fist-pumped the air. 'Isn't it the best news? Can you put it on that What's-it called thing?'

'WhatsApp?' I shook my head. 'No, Grandpa, I am not sticking it on there. You hardly know Dorothy, Grandpa. How are Mum and the family going to react?'

'They might throw me and Dorothy an engagement party?'

'Grandpa, I am being serious. You can't get engaged to Dorothy.'

He sat down at the kitchen table. 'Why not, Rachel? I am a lonely eighty-year-old man who doesn't want to spend the last years of his life wasting away in his shed and with Robert and Karen caring for him.'

'What I am saying is, why can't you date Dorothy first and then get engaged?'

He shook his head. 'I might drop down dead next week, Rachel. I don't have time to date. This is what I want to do with my life. Now, I need you to get your mother on the phone.'

Blood drained from my face. Mum would go berserk. Even though it had been on Aunty Bev's watch when the proposal had been made, I would be the one who got blamed. 'Grandpa, it's Christmas Eve tomorrow. Let's get Christmas out of the way. We can tell Mum once Christmas is over.'

To my dismay he shook his head. 'I want to tell her my good news.'

'Does Dorothy's daughter know about this?'

'Dorothy said yes so that's the important bit.'

I groaned as Aunty Bev staggered into the kitchen. Her hair was matted, her eye make-up from last night was halfway down her cheeks and she was still in her clothes. 'I shouldn't have gone down to Frank's cellar and got myself a second bottle of wine. I have a new theory – the dustier the bottle, the worse the hangover.' She slumped down at the kitchen table next to Grandpa. 'Morning. What's going on?'

'I was telling Rachel about my engagement and how I am keen to let Janice and Karen know the good news.'

This would not end well. My mother would probably fall off her sunbed in shock and horror whilst Aunty Karen would probably have a full breakdown. I couldn't cope with this along with everything else. It was supposed to be Christmas. 'You can't do that, Grandpa,' I pleaded. 'Mum will blame me. This will be my fault. I will never hear the end of this.'

Aunty Bev looked at me. 'Rachel, you need to stop letting your mother have so much control over you.'

'Huh?'

Grandpa nodded.

'You can't be responsible for everyone's actions, and I hate to say this, but you live your life in fear of going against her wishes.'

'I was supposed to be caring for Grandpa. Getting engaged was not on Aunty Karen's list.'

Aunty Bev shook her head. 'If your mother and Karen were so concerned about Dad they should have stayed in the UK and looked after him themselves. Instead, Karen buggered off to Tenerife to be with Janice and party Christmas away. Do you know something? Karen had a bloody cheek sending you that list of dos and don'ts. After talking to Dad, it's very clear Karen doesn't do any of that back home.'

I placed my head into my hands.

Aunty Bev gave my arm a rub. 'Rachel, you have so much talent. You do things to food which I can't recreate at home. The dishes you cook are amazing and don't get me started on your sandwich-making abilities.'

Grandpa beamed at me. 'Rachel is changing the world one sandwich at a time.'

I smiled at him. 'You remembered my little phrase, Grandpa.'

Aunty Bev continued. 'It was upsetting for me when I heard Janice tell me all those years ago you were jacking in your catering company to work in an office.'

'She's right,' said Grandpa.

'Stop living your life for your mother, Rachel. Start living it for you. Move out of that awful flat, come here and start a new life. Block your mother on WhatsApp while you are at it, too.'

I rose from my chair and began to cook breakfast. Aunty Bev made everyone coffee before looking at the weather on her phone. 'Oh God, there is a snowstorm coming on Christmas Eve.'

Grandpa fist pumped the air. 'Adventure time.'

'It's going to be bad,' explained Aunty Bev. 'Have we got enough food?'

'Have you seen the cupboards, the fridges, and the freezers? Frank has bought so much food we could stay here for weeks and eat comfortably.'

As I walked over to give Grandpa and Aunty Bev their food, my phone began to vibrate. I checked it and saw it was Maddie.

'Hey, how's Malibu?'

'Rachel, I can't talk but I need to tell you something.' Her voice sounded shaky and emotional. It reminded me of the calls Maddie used to make when she was in California and not coping.

'Maddie – are you okay?'

The phone began to crackle, and I couldn't hear what she was saying. 'Maddie, I can't hear you. What's wrong?'

'I'm okay, don't worry,' said Maddie. 'Speak soon.'

Aunty Bev and Grandpa had worried looks on their faces. 'Is she okay?' Aunty Bev asked.

'I don't know, she didn't sound all right.'

Grandpa shook his head with disapproval. 'Why is she so far away? She needs us.'

My phone vibrated. It was a message from Maddie.

I am fine. Please don't worry. Bad line. Hope you are having a lovely time. Give my love to Grandpa and Humphrey x.

I showed Aunty Bev my phone. She was about to reply when there was a knock at the front door. Humphrey leapt out of his basket. 'Oh no you don't,' I said, grabbing the lead and attaching it to his collar. 'I've learnt my lesson.'

After opening the door I saw that it was Kay from the gift shop. Judging by her narrowing eyes and pinched mouth, she wasn't pleased with the engagement news. 'My mother is *not* getting engaged to your grandfather,' she snapped. 'I will not allow her to marry into *your terrible* family.'

Frustration and anger at Frank which had been simmering inside my belly after Maddie's call now came to the boil. 'Can everyone stop assuming we're all like Frank Baxter? We're *nothing* like him. Nor is my sister who made the unfortunate mistake of marrying him. If you all took the time to get to know my grandfather, my sister, and me, you would know that we are the opposite of Frank Baxter. Instead, you all have assumed we love the fact an arsehole called Frank Baxter married into our family and brought us all a lot of pain and misery. Have I made myself clear?'

Before she could say another word, I turned and somehow managed to shut the heavy front door on her.

'Who was that?' Aunty Bev asked as I strode back into the kitchen.

'A door-to-door salesperson,' I said and went to lose myself in stacking the dishwasher.

'Dad has decided to leave his big announcement until after Christmas,' Aunty Bev announced. 'I think it's for the best.'

'Let's get through Christmas,' I mumbled.

CHAPTER THIRTY-SIX

The snowstorm barrelled in at ten thirty on the evening of Christmas Eve. I felt like I had been given some much-needed respite, as Christmas Eve turned out to be lovely.

As Ben and Tom were not working, I invited them both for drinks and nibbles in the afternoon. I also invited Rosie, and Ben's mum.

Grandpa tried to invite Dorothy, but she declined telling him that her daughter, Kay, was upset over the engagement news. I hadn't told him about Kay turning up on the doorstep the previous day as I believed it would have upset him. To my surprise I heard him telling Dorothy to stay strong and that they would be together soon. He told her they were the eighty-something versions of Romeo and Juliet.

My proudest moment was paying for Derek to arrive by taxi and Layla rushing down the steps to hug him. It made tears spring to my eyes. We all helped Derek and his crutches into the house. I'd agreed with Layla he could stay until Boxing Day.

I made an array of nibbles from marmalade glazed pork bites, sausage rolls, chicken wings and a variety of my finest stacked turkey sandwiches to my own mince pies and Chocolate Yule log.

Layla and I set up a buffet table in the east wing and covered it with Christmas decorations. Rosie agreed to be my little helper and she served everyone a mince pie.

Aunty Bev oversaw the drinks and created her own version of a Christmas punch which didn't look appetising as it had a gloopy consistency and was the colour of volcanic lava. When questioned Aunty Bev said she had got carried away with making a sugar syrup. She reckoned it tasted amazing and claimed she'd used a full bottle of Grand Marnier, a bottle of vodka and some ginger ale to give it what she referred to as a 'festive thump.'

I told Grandpa not to touch a drop.

After nibbles we all played charades. Ben and I sat together, and I liked the way he draped his arm across my shoulders. We sang Christmas songs and Rosie performed a solo by the Christmas tree whilst holding little Zac's hand.

It was one of the nicest Christmas Eves. I got so much pleasure from seeing Grandpa in fits of laughter with Tom over a sherry, Layla giggling at Zac giving Derek a squashed handful of Yule log, Ben's mum dabbing a tear at Rosie being a grown-up waitress, Aunty Bev knocking back her Christmas punch, and Ben kissing me under the mistletoe.

For a short time, I forgot about Maddie's unhappiness, Frank's actions, their marriage, Grandpa's engagement and my mother and Aunty Karen in Tenerife. Aunty Bev had made me promise that I would put fictional updates on the family WhatsApp. 'Tell them what they want to hear,' said Aunty Bev. 'Say Grandpa is in a chair with a blanket over his legs and hasn't touched a drop of booze.' She grinned. 'Also say I have been quiet all day and it's been boring.'

I followed her advice and we both giggled at the number of likes. Aunty Karen replied to my update on Grandpa with:

> Glad to see things have calmed down and Dad
> is being cared for properly.

If only she knew the truth, I thought looking up at a drunken grandfather, wearing a flashing reindeer hat, doing the hokey-cokey with a tipsy Tom and an excited Rosie.

Everyone loved the fact Aunty Bev had been quiet. Petra, Aunty Bev's snake-breeding daughter was the only one to question why her mother was unusually quiet. Her comment was dismissed as my mother replied saying:

> Petra, it's a blessing when your mother is quiet.

If only she knew the truth, I thought looking up and seeing Layla and Ben help a drunken Aunty Bev, who was giggling to herself, back to her room.

There had been many photos shared on WhatsApp of Christmas Eve in Tenerife. Aunty Karen kept adding comments that my mother was spending most of her day in the hot tub and next to Gary's best friend Max, along with several shocked face emojis. Aunty Bev told me she secretly fancied him.

Aunty Karen had decided to wear a pink bikini which clashed with her sunburn. She'd updated everyone to say she was not speaking to Uncle Robert, who had been more interested in Max's twenty-something daughter, once she revealed she was a hairdresser.

Fay was clearly not doing any nursing work as she kept sending heart emojis to all my mother's photos.

At teatime everyone left for their own Christmas Eve celebrations. I think I will always remember Ben helping a drunken Tom down the snowy drive.

Before he'd left, Ben and I had shared a kiss in the new kitchen which looked amazing. 'Will I see you tomorrow?' Ben asked, as we came up for air.

'Yes, I would love to see you tomorrow.'

We had another passionate embrace, and I sent a silent prayer of thanks to Olivia for matchmaking me with such a fantastic kisser.

Grandpa retired early to his annex which was sensible given he had drunk far too much sherry with Tom.

Layla put Zac down and we both cleared away. She then went to bed, leaving me to prepare the food for Christmas Day. As I was peeling a mountain of potatoes, I noticed that it had started to snow again. Giant snowflakes were tapping the French windows and trying to get my attention. It was going to be a proper white Christmas. The wind started at about ten in the evening and raced around the manor house whistling and howling.

I finished the veg prep at eleven and as I cleared away the power went, plunging the house into darkness. 'Bugger,' I said, turning on my phone light. I had no idea whether Frank and Maddie had candles. After doing a grid-by-grid search of every cupboard, I found a box of candles and matches. If the power hadn't come on by the morning, we still had candles.

With the aid of my phone light I took out a selection of meats from the freezers as they would need to defrost overnight. There was an old stone larder next to the fridges. It would be perfect for the dairy stuff if the power didn't come back on in the night. After I went through all the freezers to see what could be salvaged and stored in the larder. Sadly, a lot of the frozen food was going to be wasted if the power didn't return.

❄

To my dismay the power had not come back when my alarm woke me at six.

I pulled on a sweatshirt and found my slippers. I crept downstairs using my phone light to guide the way. Humphrey leapt out of his basket and danced at my feet with excitement. This dog loves chaos. 'Merry Christmas, Humphrey. If you trip me over, no one will eat today.'

I checked my phone. The wifi was down, and I had one lonely bar of phone signal. Maybe it was just the power to the Manor House that had gone down? I wondered whether anyone else was without power. In a cupboard I found a kettle which could be heated up on the gas hob. At least I could have a cuppa before everyone got up. I lit the Agas, made sure they had enough wood and checked my timings.

Layla appeared first. She shone her phone light at me huddled in the kitchen. 'Happy Christmas, Rachel. What a day for the power to go!'

I got up and hugged her. 'Merry Christmas, Layla. Cuppa?'

She nodded. 'Zac's still sleeping. I leant over to switch on my bedside lamp and there was nothing.'

'I wonder whether it's just the manor house. Anyway, we have candles and two wood burning Agas so we should be okay. I just hope they can get the power on soon.'

Layla checked her phone. 'It's still early, but give it an hour and I will walk into town to see whether anyone else is affected.'

'Let me put the meat in first and I'll join you.'

She turned to me. 'I haven't bought anyone presents.'

'Layla, don't worry. No one is expecting presents.' I went to my bag in the corner. 'I did get you a little something as I think you've had a hard year, and you deserved a little treat. Also, I still feel bad for the west wing situation.'

'Rachel, you shouldn't have,' she gushed staring at the little wrapped box.

I placed my hand on her shoulder. 'I'm going to make sure you will not be homeless again, Layla. We're going to get you sorted.'

She threw her arms around me. 'Thanks, Rachel.'

'Don't worry about anything today, Layla. Even though we don't have any power, we are going to have a fabulous Christmas Day.'

She tore away the paper and opened the little black box. 'Oh, Rachel.'

'I hope you like them.'

She grinned. 'They are gorgeous.' Lifting the little dangly gold earrings she held them to her ear. 'I am going to look so fancy... in the dark.'

We both laughed and I gave her a hug. 'I am so glad we met this Christmas, Layla. I know we're going to be friends.'

She nodded. 'I have had such a lovely time. You and your grandpa are so funny and kind. I am glad you didn't take any notice of me about the Denise and Ben thing. You and Ben make a great couple.'

'I have put my trust into my best friend who tried to set us up initially.'

Layla smiled. 'Good for you.' She leaned in and whispered, 'Beverly is a bit of a handful, though.'

'You're not alone with that thought,' I quipped.

It was then Grandpa appeared in a bright red Santa outfit and a wonky stick-on beard. 'Merry Christmas,' he bellowed, making Layla and me laugh.

As he got closer, we could see he hadn't done up his tunic or belt. 'There's no power so I had to do some guesswork in the dark,' he explained.

CHAPTER THIRTY-SEVEN

Ben and Rosie met us halfway down the driveway. They had been trudging up to the house as Layla and I were making our way into town. 'Merry Christmas,' Ben cried out, planting a kiss on my cheek. 'We've got no power and Mum is having a small breakdown as my oven is electric.'

'We've not got any power either,' I said, before wishing Rosie a Merry Christmas and high-fiving her. 'Come to ours for Christmas lunch.'

Ben looked at me. 'We can't do that: we put you to enough trouble yesterday.'

I arched my eyebrows. 'Ben, I love cooking. We have two giant wood-burning Agas and a gas hob. You can be my cooking assistant.'

His face lit up. 'Really?'

I nodded. 'Get your mum and come up. Bring candles.'

Rosie cheered. 'I can give Humph-Wee my present for him.'

'Okay,' said Ben, 'I'll go get Mum and candles. Are you going to see who else has no power?'

'Yes, will be back in a bit.'

Layla and I made our way into the village. The snow was

deep in places and driving was going to be difficult as the roads had not been cleared. As we walked, we looked out for lights on in houses. To our dismay everywhere looked dark and gloomy.

As we reached the bakery, I saw Darren coming out of the shop door. He looked harassed and was holding the hand of his two emotional twins.

'Power has gone,' he snapped. 'We live above the bakery. Abi is in hospital as the baby came early yesterday and she's being kept in until tomorrow. The twins are having a meltdown because there is no Christmas TV and at this rate there will be no dinner.'

I staggered towards him and gave him a hug. 'Come to the manor house. Bring the kids. Rosie is coming so they can all play together. I am cooking. We have more than enough food.'

Frank could stick his wish to keep the locals away from his manor house where the sun doesn't shine. It was Christmas and people needed us.

Darren's eyes widened. 'Seriously?'

I nodded. 'Definitely. Ben is going up now so he will be there when you arrive.'

Kneeling in the snow I smiled at his two tear-stained twins. 'Fancy playing hide and seek in a big house today?'

They both cheered. 'Can we go to Narnia?'

We all laughed, and I stood up. 'Get yourselves over there.'

Darren smiled. 'Thanks, Rachel, this means a lot to me.'

Layla and I made our way along the high street. It was eerily quiet. As we were about to turn back, I noticed the blonde woman who was the daughter of Mrs Hall, the lady I had rescued. She was coming along the road. 'Bloody power cut,' she snapped. 'Mum's home from hospital and we have no bloody power.'

Out of the corner of my eye I noticed Layla flicking her eyes

246

to the floor. The woman stared at me. 'You're the woman who rescued Mum – aren't you?'

I nodded. 'She's okay then?'

The woman nodded. 'Broke her arm but she's okay. I can't thank you enough.' She outstretched her hand and smiled. 'I'm Vanessa.'

Every part of me clenched. So, this was the infamous Vanessa. She was attractive with bushy blonde hair, a golden tan and sparkling blue eyes. There was no contest on beauty between her and Maddie though: my sister was far superior in terms of looks.

Layla was still looking at the ground and I recalled what Layla had told me about Vanessa and her son Ryan. I thought about Denise, the lies she had spread about Ben, and how her son had made Rosie sad.

'Rachel,' I said, 'I'm Maddie Baxter's sister.' My old voice had returned. The tough voice I once used to stop a gang of girls from bullying Maddie at school. The stern voice I used to tell drunken blokes to stop being rude to me when I was serving them hot food at festivals. The powerful voice I used when I told Mum I was going to turn an old van into a mobile kitchen.

The strong and assertive voice that I lost when I started listening to Mum.

An uncomfortable silence descended. Vanessa's eyes flicked to the snow. She cleared her throat and lifted her gaze to mine. 'Oh, so you're her sister. I have been hearing a lot about you. You and an older woman came into my pub looking for trouble.'

'I have heard a lot about you, Vanessa,' I said, shifting my weight and leaning on one hip. 'I know *everything* so there's nothing you can say that will shock me.'

Vanessa looked taken aback. 'Do you?'

I nodded. 'Yes, I do. Look, I need to get back as I am cooking for quite a few people in the town. Luckily my sister made

Frank keep the old Agas.' With a fake smile I said, 'It's been good to finally meet you and give my love to your mother.'

Vanessa turned her attention to Layla. 'Aren't you going to say hello?'

Layla looked terrified and that made me cross. I stepped in front of her and stared at Vanessa. 'I know about how horrible you have been to her. She works for me now.'

'Have you told your new boss about all the lies you told me about my Ryan, Layla?'

'They were not lies,' Layla mumbled.

I looked Vanessa in the eyes and the old me stepped up. 'Why are you and your family making her life a misery? She's twenty-one, she has a baby son and when I arrived here, she was homeless. I also heard you'd been urging her cleaning clients to cancel her jobs. You are a grown woman. You should be ashamed of yourself.'

Vanessa took a step back in shock. Her mouth hung open. It was clear no one had ever stood up to her.

'Why is your sister spreading lies about Ben and getting her son to pick on his daughter?' I took a step forward and she took a step back. 'Why did you have an affair with my sister's husband?'

She raised her hands. 'Can we talk about that?'

I scowled at her. 'I don't talk to bullies. Goodbye, Vanessa. Come on, Layla, we are leaving.'

I strode away and Layla trudged after me. 'Oh God, Rachel, you were amazing,' she squealed. 'I have never seen Vanessa back down like that.'

Once we were out of sight from Vanessa I turned to Layla. 'Hug me. I am trembling.'

She laughed and threw her arms around me. 'You were the best.'

As we trudged back, we saw a few people gathered outside

their houses. Fuelled by my bravery against Vanessa, I found myself saying, 'If you need Christmas lunch – come to the manor house. We have so much food and I would love to see you there.'

'Really?' A woman cast me a shocked look.

I nodded. 'My name's Rachel. I would love to see you all there. Merry Christmas.'

'But there's four hungry people in my family and...'

'Bring everyone who needs feeding and is without power.' I laughed. 'It's on Frank Baxter so let's have a good Christmas. I'll be serving up at 2pm.'

To my amazement they all cheered.

Layla and I made our way back to the Manor House. 'I can't believe you've invited all those people,' she exclaimed. 'Where will we put them all?'

'Okay, I want to open up the west wing,' I explained. Her eyebrows rocketed up her forehead in shock. 'Do you think that's wise?'

'We can tidy up afterwards and it will look like no one will have been in there. I will do a buffet style dinner and people can go sit with their families.'

'Frank and Maddie won't be happy,' said Layla.

'They are away in Malibu and will never know,' I said with an air of confidence.

CHAPTER THIRTY-EIGHT

'How many are we catering for?' Ben asked as I walked back into the kitchen. He was wearing a blue apron, a white fitted shirt, and black jeans. His hair was gently tousled, and he'd even tidied up his beard.

'A lot.' I giggled with nervous hysteria. 'I invited quite a few people in the town, and I told them to spread the word.'

Ben scratched his head and cast me a worried look. 'You know what you're doing so I will be your glamorous assistant chef.'

'I am thinking a buffet-style Christmas lunch. We can use the back work surfaces. People can walk along and fill up their plates like you would do in a carvery. They can then go into the house and eat their food.'

Ben stared at me. 'Wow, you do know what you're doing.'

I nodded. 'I still have a lot of nibbles left over from yesterday so we can add those; plus there's things we can make in the next few hours.'

'What do you want me to do?'

'Are you any good at Yorkshire puddings?'

He grinned and said confidently. 'The best.'

'Fighting talk, Ben. They better be good.'

He laughed. 'Right, show me where you want me to set up my Yorkshire pudding factory?'

Once he had got to work, I went into the east wing living room. Aunty Bev, Grandpa, Ben's mum Cath, and Darren were all admiring the photos of Darren and Abi's new addition, a baby boy called Freddie. I hadn't had a chance to have a peek at the photos yet.

'Ah, he looks cute,' I cooed.

Darren cast me the proudest smile. 'He's adorable and my wife is amazing.'

'Where are the kids?' I said, looking around for Rosie and the twins.

Cath smiled. 'Playing hide and seek with the dog upstairs. You don't mind – do you?'

I grinned. 'It's Christmas Day. I hope they're enjoying themselves.'

Aunty Bev leaned in and whispered, 'I hope you know what you're doing. Letting little kids run wild never turned out well for me.'

I smiled. 'It's Christmas. Relax.'

Cath gestured for the door. 'I am going to go check on the little rascals.'

Layla came into the lounge. 'Do you want to open up the west wing, Rachel?'

I nodded. 'Let's do it.'

To my surprise Aunty Bev gasped. 'Is that necessary?'

I turned around. 'We have a lot of people to accommodate?'

Aunty Bev rubbed her forehead. 'I don't think that's a good idea.'

I dismissed her. 'It's only one day, Aunty Bev. Once everyone goes home, I will clean up every room.'

Grandpa placed his hand on my shoulder. 'Listen to your aunty Bev.'

I shook his hand away. 'Grandpa, it will be fine.'

Layla opened the west wing lounge and whilst she was talking to Aunty Bev, I hid Maddie's journal and the photos of Josh in a desk drawer.

'Rachel,' Layla said, 'Cath is shouting for you upstairs.'

I raced up the stairs to find Cath outside the master bedroom and three naughty looking children. 'Rachel, I should have been watching them.'

My heart ground to a halt. 'What have they done?'

She let out a heavy sigh and pushed open the door. I gasped as there were pink lipstick drawings all over one of the cream walls. 'They've also spilt a can of Coke inside the wardrobe, and I think Humphrey weed on the bed.'

My eyes flicked to the huge damp stain on the bedding and my nose picked up the aroma of dog urine. 'Okay,' I squeaked. 'Cath, can you take the kids downstairs while I clean up.'

Once they'd left, I closed my eyes and let out the biggest groan. They had caused havoc. After a deep breath I surveyed the damage. I raced into the en-suite and grabbed a few wet wipes and used them on the lipstick. To my relief it came off easily and I wiped away a picture of a pink snowman, four stick people and what looked like a baby stick person, a dodgy looking dog, and the word 'DAD' in big letters.

The bedding would have to be dry cleaned but that could be done as Maddie and Frank were not due back for another week. I stripped the bedding and peered into the wardrobe. Frank's shoes were swimming in cola. Shit.

The clean-up operation took longer than I had hoped. Layla came to give me a hand with the wardrobe, and she carefully wiped down Frank's expensive leather shoes.

'This is going to be okay,' I muttered, 'all this is fixable.'

Layla cast me a worried look. 'It still stinks of dog piss in here.'

I bit my lip. 'Okay, let's open the windows and get as many air fresheners as possible on.'

She nodded and hurried away as Aunty Bev peered inside. 'You need to get rid of that smell, Rachel. Frank dislikes the dog at the best of times so he won't appreciate bed reeking of Humphrey's piss.'

'I know, Aunty Bev,' I snapped.

By the time I returned downstairs I was exhausted. More people had turned up early and were sat in both the east and west wings. As I passed a few reached out and thanked me.

'You have saved the day,' said one lady, 'my son is over from Australia, and he would have been so upset without his Christmas dinner.'

I nodded as she pointed to a large family stood by Maddie's bookcase. 'That's him, his wife and his three children.'

To my horror one of their children was fiddling with one of Maddie's books and the other was drawing in one. There wasn't time to sort that out. I would replace damaged books.

A young man waved at me as I was about to head for the kitchen. 'The wifi isn't working. Can you sort it out?'

'There's a power cut,' I said, trying to remain calm.

'Oh,' he said looking bewildered. 'Is that why we are all here? I thought it was free food?'

I had to hurry away to save my sanity.

Ben, Layla, Aunty Bev, and I spent three hours preparing the lunch. We did a great job despite the circumstances and the Christmas buffet looked amazing.

I made sure Layla, Grandpa, Cath, and Rosie were at the front of the queue, which snaked out of the kitchen and into the reception hall.

Everyone loved the food, and it was a wonderful sight to see them all shovelling plates of my Christmas buffet food into their mouths. The queue had reduced dramatically when Aunty Bev came running from the front door. 'Kay and Dorothy are here,' she hissed.

'What?'

I walked into the hallway to find Kay and Dorothy standing with pink noses, damp hair and rosy cheeks. Kay smiled at me, and I knew she'd forgiven me for my outburst the previous day. 'Mum and I have no power and I can't cook anything on my electric oven,' Kay explained. 'I am sorry about yesterday; it was a bit of a shock hearing Mum was engaged.'

'I can understand,' I said, with a smile. 'Come in and join the buffet queue. Shall I tell my grandfather you're here?'

Dorothy's face lit up. 'Please can you go fetch Eric? I have been thinking a lot about him.'

As she took off her coat I went to get Grandpa. I don't think I have ever seen him move so fast. I had to run to catch up with him as he rushed to see Dorothy.

'My darling,' he cried, on seeing her. 'Oh, how I have missed you.'

As they cuddled and hugged Kay led me away by the arm. 'Do you think we could encourage them to date first rather than rush into an engagement?'

'You have my backing. I have been trying to persuade my grandfather to date Dorothy first, but he's so headstrong.'

Kay nodded. 'Overnight Mum has lost all her common sense. She claims Eric makes her feel like a love-struck teenager again.'

'Let's take a joined-up approach.'

She rolled her eyes at her mother and Grandpa engaging in a kiss under a sprig of mistletoe. 'To think my mother was against me marrying a boy at eighteen all those years ago. He'd proposed after a month of dating. She went mad at me. Now – look at her.'

'At least you had a month of dating under your belt,' I said with a chuckle. 'Those two have met three times.'

Kay laughed and I showed her to the queue for the food. She looked around the hallway and at the dramatic staircase. 'This house is so beautiful.'

'Thanks.'

'It would make a great restaurant,' she said. 'People would love to eat amongst all this splendour and they'd love this buffet style of dining.'

I looked around. Kay did have a point. There were two sides to the house, which could transform into two different dining experiences. 'That's a good idea, Kay.'

She nodded. 'Harp Brook needs somewhere fancy. Plus, you have the grounds so that would work in the summer.'

My heartbeat quickened as I envisioned the east wing serving traditional food and the west wing Mediterranean cuisine with dishes like fish, smoky lamb, vegetable tagine and meatballs. It was a few seconds before my mind reminded me this was Frank and Maddie's home.

The downstairs was packed. People were milling in the hall, in both living rooms and on the stairs. Grandpa had turned on the Christmas music and Rosie and the twins were handing out crackers.

Humphrey was being stroked by a group of ladies, Kay was talking to a friend and Darren was showing everyone photos of his new baby son.

Ben tapped me on the arm as I headed for the kitchen. 'You need to see who is at the front door.'

'Who?'

I raced to the hallway to find Vanessa, Denise, her children, and a young man who must be Ryan. Vanessa handed me a bottle of wine. 'Peace offering. Mum says we should all be friends after what you did for her.'

I took it from her, and she nudged Denise. 'Sorry. I have told Denise's boy to be nice to Rosie.'

Vanessa looked at me. 'Say no if you like, but is there any Christmas food left? The energy company are struggling to get the power back on.'

It was Christmas Day, and I didn't want to see them go hungry. Maybe this would go some way to repairing the rift between our two families. With a half-smile I steered them into the hallway.

As they joined the queue, I saw several people with open mouths and wide eyes fixed on Vanessa and her family at the Baxter Manor House eating Christmas lunch.

Ben came up to join me and I felt his arm circle my waist. 'Wow, you've achieved the unthinkable.'

As I leaned in for a kiss, I caught Denise staring at us.

CHAPTER THIRTY-NINE

We'd finally reached the pudding course. My leftover Yule log and mince pies from the previous day came in useful. I had managed to make a bowl of Eton Mess and little chocolate mousses. Aunty Bev had also found a ready-made cheesecake and trifle in one of the fridges. The pudding queue was getting shorter, and I was looking forward to everyone going home. Every part of me ached and I was struggling to suppress a yawn. Once they all left, I would start the clean-up operation and then sink into a hot foam bath. Ben was helping Rosie lift a piece of Yule log onto her plate.

A hand tapped me on the shoulder. I whirled around to see Denise's icy stare. 'I see you've nicked my man.'

I stepped back in shock. 'Your man?'

'Everyone knows I have had a thing for Ben,' she hissed. 'I might have known a bloody Baxter would step in and take him away from me.'

'He's not your property, Denise.'

She looked away and muttered something under her breath.

'Please eat your food and go, Denise,' I said, cursing myself for feeling charitable.

She leaned in. 'A mother at school has also been messaging him, plus there's another woman he's in contact with.'

'Go away, Denise.'

She laughed. 'See you around, Rachel.'

Ben looked up at me and I averted my eyes to the floor. In my head I could hear Sam's voice. It was happening again. Why had I let my guard down? Hot and emotional I raced out of the kitchen

It was then I heard someone shout, 'Frank Baxter is here.'

Blood drained from my face and my bowels loosened. Oh God, was this true? It couldn't be true. Maybe there was someone in Harp Brook who was a convincing lookalike?

'Frank Baxter,' said someone else. 'He looks angry.'

I felt sick. The room began to sway. Was Frank back from Malibu? His house was full of people, the west wing was open, his bedroom stunk of dog wee and the trouser leg on one of his suits was ripped, plus one pair of his expensive leather shoes had not survived being submerged in cola.

The urge to run and throw up was strong. 'It can't be true,' I said and raced through throngs of people.

In the reception hallway I came face to face with Frank. 'Oh God,' I muttered as he stared at me with cold, narrowing eyes. Behind him was his chauffeur who had a sweaty pink face.

'We had to ditch the Merc because of the snow and walk up the driveway,' puffed the chauffeur. 'I had to carry the bags through all the snow.'

Frank turned to his chauffeur. 'Have you quite finished?' He turned back to me. 'Why is my house full of locals, Rachel?'

I looked behind him and the chauffeur. 'Where's Maddie?'

He let out an angry snort. 'Why are you asking a stupid question when you know full well that she's with you? Where is she?'

'What?'

He let out a sarcastic laugh. 'She came home two days ago. You know this.'

'Two days ago?'

He ran a tanned hand through his grey hair. 'We had some problems in the States. Where is she? And why has she agreed to this... circus?'

'Frank, I haven't seen Maddie,' I cried. 'Where the hell is she?'

He studied my face. 'She called me saying she was home.'

'You must believe me. Maddie is not here.'

He took out a phone from inside his ski jacket. He pressed it to his ear. There was no answer. 'She's not picking up.'

'Look at what the cat has dragged in,' said a familiar voice from behind me. I spun around to see Vanessa glaring at Frank.

'What the hell is she doing here?' he cried. 'Have you lost your mind, Rachel?'

'There was a power cut and I made everyone Christmas lunch,' I said, quietly.

Vanessa barrelled past me. 'Why are you here, Frank?'

'Not now, Vanessa,' he pleaded, scrolling through his phone. 'I need to find my wife.' He pushed past us, strode into the centre of the reception hall and began clapping his hands. Everyone's attention turned to him and within a few seconds the sea of festive smiles was washed away by a tide of scowls and dirty looks. The atmosphere inside the manor house became charged. 'Please can you all leave my house! Thank you.'

The young man who had complained about the wifi shouted, 'I haven't had my pudding yet, mate.'

Frank shook his head and pointed at the young man. 'Get out. The party is over.'

People began filing out. As they passed me everyone said, 'Lovely food, thanks,' and, 'You saved Christmas Day, Rachel.' Some hugged and kissed me on the cheek.

An old lady in the west wing living room was struggling to stand as her walking stick had fallen by the side of the sofa. I expected Frank to rush and help her. Instead, he stood at the doorway and clapped his hands. 'Get out or I am calling the police.'

Instinctively I barged past him and ran to help her. She gave me a warm smile and squeezed by hand. 'Thank you, my dear.' I guided her past Frank and to the door.

To my surprise Vanessa took hold of the lady's other arm and smiled at me. 'I'll help Joan back through the snow.'

Frank scowled and looked away.

I smiled at Vanessa. 'Thank you.'

On his way out Darren gave me a huge hug. 'I can't thank you enough, Rachel. I was struggling this morning. Did my two cause much havoc upstairs?'

I shook my head. 'It was all sorted. Give my love to Abi.'

He nodded. 'She called me to say she never got to taste your wonderful food.'

I steered Darren and his twins to one side. 'Wait there.'

Racing over to the buffet food, I grabbed a plastic box and filled it up with sausage rolls, a few sandwiches, and some nibbles. Darren grinned as I returned. 'You are too kind. I will give her these when she comes home tomorrow.'

Ben, Layla, and Aunty Bev were tidying up in the kitchen and were unaware of the drama unfolding with Frank. The kitchen was in a state. One side had the remnants of the buffet and the other side plus the island were covered in empty plates and glasses. If Frank saw the kitchen he would explode. I tried to beat him to the kitchen, but I was too late.

'What a bloody mess. Time to go home,' Frank shouted.

Layla cast me a worried look and I mouthed, 'It will be okay.'

Grandpa turned around and saw Frank. 'What the hell are you doing here?'

Frank shook his head. 'Sorting out this circus, Eric.'

'Where's Maddie?' Aunty Bev asked, sticking her head up from the dishwasher.

'She came home two days ago,' I said, beating Frank to it.

Aunty Bev shook her head. 'Well, we've not seen her.'

Frank stared at Aunty Bev. 'Who invited you, Beverly? I bet this was all your doing. You love chaos. If Maddie had told me you were coming I would have said no.'

Aunty Bev scowled at him. 'Merry Christmas to you too, Frank. It was Janice's idea if you must know. Why don't you go crawl under the stone you came from.'

He muttered something under his breath and turned his attention to Layla. 'You're fired now I am back. I will be getting a new cleaner.'

She nodded and carried on clearing plates.

I turned to Frank. 'Layla is staying here until she finds a new place to live.'

Frank turned to me, incredulous. 'I am not a charity, Rachel. She leaves. Today.'

I could feel the anger rising inside of me. 'You can't throw a woman out with a child on Christmas Day, Frank.'

'I can do what I want, Rachel. I hate to remind you, but this is my house you've—'

Humphrey began to bark and a voice from behind us made him stop. 'Back off, Frank.'

We all turned to see Maddie and behind her was Josh.

'Frank, we need to sort things out.'

I couldn't help but notice Maddie was holding Josh's hand. Aunty Bev, who is the most observant relative I have, must have seen the hand holding too. 'Well, I'll be damned...' she muttered as Frank turned around to see Maddie.

CHAPTER FORTY

Everyone left the kitchen, until it was just me, Maddie, and Frank at the table. Aunty Bev had wanted to stay but Maddie urged her to look after an emotional Grandpa.

Maddie, with Humphrey at her feet, was sat next to me, and we both faced Frank's stoney expression.

The power had come back on in a twist of fate shortly after Maddie appeared. We had the lights on in the kitchen as it was almost dark outside.

Underneath the table Maddie held my hand and every so often gave it a little squeeze.

'Your sister invited Vanessa to this circus of hers,' snapped Frank. 'Of all the people she could have invited.' He massaged his tanned forehead. 'I can't believe what I walked in on earlier. You swore to me your sister would be "good as gold."'

'Leave it, Frank,' Maddie said.

'Seeing Vanessa again after everything that's happened was too much,' he said, running a hand through his grey hair.

It was time to put my cards on the table and tell Maddie about Frank's affair. 'Maddie,' I said, 'I know about him and her...'

She shook her head and looked at me. I noticed she didn't have those sad, glassy blue eyes anymore. They were shining. 'No, you don't know everything, Rachel.' She smiled at me. 'You did something amazing today by cooking everyone Christmas lunch. I overheard some of the locals as I came in and they were all raving about what you'd done. I would have done the same.'

'She put on a bloody circus,' raged Frank. 'My beautiful house has been ruined.'

Maddie stared at him. 'You've hated this house ever since we moved in, Frank. Don't make out it's something precious to you.'

He muttered something under his breath and loosened his shirt collar. 'Not only did she invite Vanessa, but she also had your whacky aunt staying here. I am surprised I came home to the house still standing. Beverly is a liability.'

Maddie turned to me. 'Rachel, you need to know that Frank and I broke up back when we were in California last year.'

My eyes widened and my jaws dropped in shock. I stared at her. 'What?'

She took out a hair clip from her pocket and pinned up her blonde curls. 'I wanted to come home when we were in California. I'd realised I didn't love Frank and that I had made a terrible mistake. Josh was the man I loved and wanted to spend my life with. However, Frank had this big film company deal on the horizon and he's worked hard to turn around his image. He's no longer seen as the ex-actor with the tumultuous past but as the family-orientated CEO of a successful media company.'

Judging from what I'd seen of Frank earlier when he first arrived back home, I felt like he had more to do on his image clean up.

Maddie continued. 'Frank and I came to an arrangement.'

'An arrangement – what do you mean?' Underneath mine, my sister's hand was trembling.

'Do we have to go through all this?' Frank snapped whilst tapping something into his phone.

Maddie ignored him and took a deep breath. 'I would pretend to still be married to him and he would do the same. We would show the world that Frank Baxter had changed. He was married and ready to start a family.'

Frank rubbed his face. 'This is excruciating to listen to Maddie. I need a whisky.' He turned around. 'Where's the cleaner? She could pour me a drink. Layla – come here please.'

Maddie tapped him on the arm. 'Frank, go and get yourself a drink. Layla is a cleaner not your waitress.'

He glared at Maddie. 'She's an employee and I need a drink.'

'She's my employee now, Frank.' My sister's tone was assertive and steel-like. Frank growled and shook his head.

Layla appeared at the door. 'Yes, Mr Baxter – you called?'

Frank opened his mouth, but Maddie beat him to it. 'We don't need anything, Layla, thank you.'

Maddie carried on. 'Once he bought this film company, he would be the face of these heart-warming films with good family values. We came to an agreement.' She paused. I could tell this was hard for her to share with me. 'I would give him a child and once they were born, we would quietly separate. We would co-parent and split the child's homes between the UK and America.'

'You mean – all this has been fake?'

'Your sister couldn't go through with her part of the bargain,' snapped Frank, causing Maddie to glare at him.

I looked at Maddie. 'Tell me.'

She hung her head. 'Frank was not the only one seeing someone else.'

'You were seeing Josh?'

She nodded. 'It was part of the arrangement. To the public

Frank and I were husband and wife who were madly in love with each other. In private we led separate lives. I know it's a shock, but Frank tells me this is common. Frank and I agreed our side affairs wouldn't become an issue. They wouldn't threaten our public image.'

I looked at Frank who was scrolling on his phone. 'Vanessa became an issue – didn't she, Frank?'

He nodded. 'That woman threatened to destroy everything at a key time with this film company deal. We were days away from closing the deal and Vanessa started playing dirty. She realised I was never going to commit to her or stay with her. I had to take action.'

Maddie squeezed my hand to get my attention back. 'I couldn't give Frank a baby because...' My eyes flicked to her other hand which was rubbing her tummy. 'I was already carrying Josh's baby.'

'What?'

She nodded. 'I'm pregnant.'

Frank muttered something under his breath before looking away.

My mouth hit the floor and my heart ground to an abrupt halt. 'Does Josh know?'

Maddie smiled. 'He knew I was pregnant before I did a test.' She rested her head on my shoulder. 'I'm sorry to tell you this today.'

'When did you find out?'

'The day before you arrived in Harp Brook.'

'And I flew her to Malibu,' snapped Frank. 'What a waste of time and money.'

I stared at her. 'I knew something was wrong, but you wouldn't tell me.'

Frank was staring at me. 'She told me when we were in

Malibu. I was ready to conceive a child. A clinic was lined up, and this happened.'

Maddie laid her hand on the table to get his attention. 'I don't think I could have gone through with it, Frank. The thought of having a baby as part of a business transaction felt wrong. I'd been thinking it through for weeks.'

He let out a heavy sigh. 'My PA has got me a hotel in London. I'll be back tomorrow.' He rose and walked towards his driver who was busy cramming in a mouthful of buffet food. 'We're leaving.'

I turned to Maddie and pulled her into my arms. 'Oh, Maddie, my lovely, sweet sister.'

She began to sob. 'It's a mess, Rachel. I have caused Frank so much heartbreak and I am so sorry to break the news to you like this. I wanted to tell you before I went but I was an emotional mess.'

'So, when did Josh come back into your life?'

She lifted her face and wiped her cheeks. 'You know I had multiple hen-dos – right?'

I nodded.

'Well, one was back in Oxford. In the day, me and all my uni friends went horse riding. Josh was working on the farm where the stables were. It was fate. Nothing happened between Josh and me on that day. We swapped email addresses and phone numbers. There was something between us. I ended up emailing him from a bar later that evening. My uni friends got so drunk they didn't see me sneak out and meet Josh.' My sister had a dreamy smile on her face. 'It was like old times. He took me to a night café, and we talked for hours. A week later, on my wedding day, I realised I had made a terrible mistake. I didn't love Frank. He dazzled me with a lot of money, and he made Mum happy by letting her live in one of his villas in Tenerife.'

'Aunty Bev said he bought her a villa.'

Maddie shook her head. 'Frank has many properties. That's one of them. She rents it at a very good rate.'

Maddie sighed. 'I thought California would change me. I stopped emailing Josh and I tried to make myself love Frank. I went to therapy. Frank paid for the best therapist in California. Deep down I knew I had made the wrong decision. Josh flew to California, and I slept with him. I was the one who destroyed my marriage.'

I gulped in shock.

'I came clean and told Frank I wanted to separate. He suggested this agreement. We bought this house and Josh moved down to Harp Brook Farm. Frank started seeing Vanessa soon after he'd been introduced to her.'

Maddie laughed. 'It didn't take Frank long at all. For the first few months it worked. We both stayed in the house in the day and at night we would go see our respective partners.' She fiddled with a strand of her golden hair. 'It was okay until Vanessa wanted him to divorce me. She put pressure on him and then said she would do a "kiss and tell" to a tabloid newspaper. Frank had this deal going through, so he had to find a way to end it.'

I said, 'He tricked her into signing the NDA.'

Maddie nodded. 'I didn't know about all that until afterwards. That's when Vanessa started a war against us.'

'Tell me about Josh.'

Maddie's whole face lit up in a way that made tears rush to my eyes. I had not seen her this happy in a long time.

'Josh is amazing, and I love him, Rachel. He's going to make a wonderful dad.' She smiled. 'He's not a millionaire like Frank, he doesn't have a villa in Tenerife for Mum to rent and he doesn't have eye-watering investments, a chauffeur, and a beautiful lifestyle. Josh is kind, he makes me laugh and he's normal. You don't know how long I have craved normality. Frank's world is not for me. Mum will have a breakdown when she hears all this, but I don't care. All I have ever wanted is to be free and live my life the way I want to live it.'

I pulled her into a hug. 'I love you, Maddie, and I can't wait to meet my niece or nephew.'

'You will need to teach them to cook as both Josh and I are dreadful.' We both laughed.

'So, you came home two days early?'

She nodded. 'I rang you, but I was too emotional to say everything. I have been with Josh on the farm. Bob and his wife Marjorie are adorable. Josh told me about The Duck House. I didn't want to make an appearance as I wanted some time with Josh to make sense of everything. Malibu was awful. Not the place, I mean. It's stunning but everything with Frank fell apart. He was so angry at me when I told him I was pregnant. I was alone and scared in a strange place. In the end I managed to buy a plane ticket and I ran away.'

'You ran away from Frank?'

She nodded. 'He's got a lot of issues.'

'I would never have guessed,' I said, with a wry smile.

Maddie stroked Humphrey underneath the table. 'His mother didn't show him any affection when he was growing up. He had a negative image of himself when he was a child and that's why he has always wanted to feel superior and special as an adult. He's not proud of his past when he was an actor and is desperate to show everyone he's different.'

We both went silent. My brain was frantically trying to process everything. For years our mother had painted Maddie in an angelic, almost perfect light. Maddie would have the idyllic life with her ex-film star and business tycoon husband while the rest of us mere mortals spent our time squabbling on

WhatsApp, gossiping about Aunty Bev, and doing whatever the family wanted us to do.

She turned to me. 'I love the short hair, Rachel. It suits you. I know this is a huge shock, but I was with Frank for all the wrong reasons. It's weird to say but with Josh I feel more like myself than I have ever done.'

CHAPTER FORTY-ONE

Ben was waiting for me outside the kitchen as I told Grandpa and Aunty Bev to go into the kitchen. I remembered what Denise had said. 'Please leave me alone, Ben.'

'What did she say?'

I batted his hand away. 'Nothing, I need to be on my own.'

'Rachel,' Ben said softly, 'talk to me.'

'I believed Olivia,' I said, with a voice thick with emotion. 'Why did Denise tell me a mum from school is messaging you? And she's not the only one apparently.' Tears rolled down my face. 'I should have stayed away.'

He placed his arms around me and took out his phone. 'Okay, look at this. One of the year six mothers – Zoe – texted me to ask which child grief counsellor I used with Rosie when she was struggling a year ago. Do you want to see her text? I also text Sonia about Olivia because I want to stay in touch, and she keeps asking how we are doing. The other texts I have are from my mother and Tom. Rachel, I am not a woman magnet. I told Denise I didn't want to date her because Olivia had introduced me to her amazing and beautiful friend and even though this friend had ghosted me I had this strange feeling I would one day meet her again.'

'Really?'

He smiled. 'Before she died Olivia texted me to say to not give up hope on Rachel. I wished I'd kept that text.'

I looked up into his eyes and he cupped my cheeks with his warm hands. 'Rachel, I only have eyes for you.'

He held me close and pressed his lips against mine. I ran my hands through his hair as our kiss got more passionate. We both broke away after we heard voices in the kitchen. Grandpa let out a cheer and Aunty Bev exclaimed, 'You're pregnant and Frank's not the father? Oh God, I need a stiff drink.'

Ben smiled. 'I'll see you tomorrow. It sounds like you're needed in there.'

'See you tomorrow, Ben.'

As I sat down next to Grandpa, Aunty Bev put her hands together in a prayer-like pose and prayed out loud. 'Thanks, God, for this wonderful news. I am looking forward to seeing the faces of my sisters when they hear this, especially Janice. If only Maddie could record the moment she tells Janice. I would treasure that recording for years to come.'

We all smiled. Grandpa was sat next to Maddie holding her hand. 'I am delighted for you, my lovely girl.'

I grabbed four glasses, a bottle of wine from the rack and an elderflower soft drink for Maddie.

Aunty Bev took her glass, threw her head back and drained it. 'I needed that. Pour me another one.' Then, after taking a mouthful from her second glass, she said, 'So, when do we meet Josh?'

Maddie grinned. 'Josh? Are you still there?'

We heard footsteps and there was Josh beaming at us from the doorway. 'Hi, all.' He smiled and came to sit next to me. 'We met the other day at the farm, didn't we?'

I grinned. 'I thought you acted suspicious.'

Maddie squeezed his hand. 'This is the man I love and want to spend the rest of my life with, everyone.' She wiped a tear from her cheek. 'I'm not going to create any more mess.'

Grandpa gave her a cuddle. 'Hey, you're amongst fellow mess creators – me, Beverly and Rachel.'

We all giggled. Aunty Bev pointed at me with her wine glass. 'Rachel has broken every rule given to her.'

'You were the one who snuck into the west wing, Aunty Beverly.'

She grinned. 'So I was. Maddie – sorry about that. I struggle with the concept of "no" at my age.'

My phone began to vibrate. As I took it out of my pocket, I saw that it was Mum facetiming me from Tenerife. 'Oh God,' I croaked, showing Maddie.

She gave a silent nod and took the phone from me. 'Stand well back,' she whispered. 'I am about to cause an explosion.'

'Hello, Mum,' she said, as Mum appeared on the screen. I peered over Maddie's shoulder and saw total shock take hold of Mum's face. 'Maddie,' she gasped. 'Why are you back? Has Rachel burnt your house down?'

'I'm pregnant, Mum,' said Maddie.

Mum squealed with delight. She turned to the room behind her. 'Everyone – Maddie is pregnant.'

An almighty cheer could be heard, and Aunty Karen came over to hug Mum. 'Oh, Janice, this is great news,' she gushed. 'You're going to be a grandmother to a celebrity baby.'

Mum grinned from ear to ear as Uncle Robert shouted, 'Is it Frank's baby?'

Mum scowled at Uncle Robert and Aunty Karen shouted at him, 'Robert, don't say stupid things.'

'Maddie, this is the best news and what a Christmas present,' gushed Mum. 'I bet Frank is over the moon.'

'It's not Frank's baby,' said Maddie.

Mum's face froze and her eyes glazed over.

'Mum – are you okay?'

We were all distracted by Aunty Bev who threw back her head and guffawed with laughter. Aunty Karen took the phone from Mum, who looked like she had seen a ghost.

'Maddie, can you repeat what you just said,' gushed Aunty Karen. 'Bad line.' She let out a nervous laugh. 'Say it again and slowly please.'

'The-baby-is-NOT-Frank's, Aunty Karen,' said Maddie, slowly, clearly and emphasising the key words. 'I-had-an AFFAIR-with-JOSH-from-uni. The guy Mum never liked. Frank and I are SEPARATING.'

Aunty Karen's eyes started to roll around inside her sockets and her face went chalk white. We gasped as she fainted, and Uncle Robert had to catch her crumpled body. 'For God's sake, Karen, this is not a good time to pass out.' Uncle Robert laid her down. 'She'll be fine in a sec,' he said as Gary came rushing over.

Aunty Bev chuckled away to herself. 'Thank God Robert never entered the medical profession.'

Robert turned to Mum who was in a trance. 'Janice, do you need a drink?'

She remained silent. Uncle Robert turned to us on the phone. 'Congratulations, Maddie, I never liked Frank. Good on you.'

We could hear Aunty Karen groaning on the floor beneath the screen, Gary popped his arm around Uncle Robert's shoulder and grinned at us. 'Rob and I going to nip to the beach bar. These two can sort themselves out.'

As they waved us goodbye, I heard Aunty Karen croak, 'Get Janice an emergency ciggie ASAP.'

Aunty Bev burst out laughing. 'Karen, Janice needs more than that.'

Once the call had ended, I caught sight of Josh looking shell-shocked. 'This is normal for us, Josh,' I quipped. 'Welcome to the family.'

Maddie placed her face in her hands. 'Wow, that was surreal.'

I rubbed Maddie's shoulder. 'You have now got what you always wanted – a secret family WhatsApp family group chat titled, *Maddie needs our help ASAP!*'

Once we'd stopped laughing, and we gathered our thoughts, I turned to Maddie. 'So, what happens now?'

She smiled. 'That's what we need to talk about.'

'What do you mean?'

'Frank and I signed a prenup. I get this place in the event of a separation. This place was always going to be mine. Frank didn't want me getting my hands on his empire. I did worry about that as I was the one who had the affair and ended the marriage, but Frank has confirmed via his lawyer this place is mine.'

'Wow, Maddie, what are you going to do with it?'

Her eyes sparkled. 'How about we make our business idea happen? Let's turn part of this place into a café or restaurant. You and me, Rachel. Like we discussed in Greece all those years ago. Your amazing culinary skills and my business management brain. What do you think?'

CHAPTER FORTY-TWO

Mum facetimed me late in the evening. I was in bed reading the final chapter in Olivia's notebook. Mum had been drinking as she was swaying on a stool and her golden Christmas hat looked wonky.

'What the hell has happened to Maddie?' Mum said, shaking her head with disapproval. 'I think she's having a crisis or some sort of mental breakdown. Who in their right mind would cheat on Frank Baxter and get pregnant to some–'

'You mean have a baby with someone who she truly loves?'

My mother scowled down the phone. 'Don't be so ridiculous, Rachel. I would have expected that sort of silly behaviour from you but not from Maddie. She was my perfect child.'

Something snapped inside of me. I'd spent years allowing Mum to talk to me in this way. It was time to cut myself free. 'Mum, I'm leaving London next week and I am moving down here. I have also met someone.'

'Oh, I see.' She looked surprised. 'I take it you have got a new job.'

'I'm starting my new career. I am going to be setting up a new café.'

Mum let out a groan. 'Rachel, we've talked about this.'

I cleared my throat and found my old voice. 'Mum, I am tired of you talking to me like you have zero respect for me and thinking you have some say on the direction of my life. I am thirty-two years of age, and I am taking back control. Goodbye, Mum.' I hung up and opened WhatsApp. On the family group chats I went into each one and did something I should have done a long time ago.

Rachel Reid has left the group.

I then video called Connor and Kate who I knew would still be awake at their respective Christmas gatherings. Connor was wearing the Christmas jumper his nana knitted him years ago, which she forced him to wear every year, even though it was now a few sizes too small. The one with the words – 'I am Santa's Little Helper' emblazoned across the front.

Kate's gold Christmas cracker hat was wonky, and she flashed us a tipsy smile.

'Happy Christmas,' we all chorused.

After Connor had told us about his family Christmas and Kate had showed us all the knitting related gifts her family had bought her, they listened to me tell them about everything that had happened here in Harp Brook.

'Wow,' exclaimed Connor, 'you have been naughty in Harp Brook. Olivia would be proud of you.'

Kate rubbed her eyes with shock. 'It was all fake then. Your sister and Frank?'

I nodded. 'It was all an arrangement. I was gobsmacked.'

'So, you're leaving us?' Connor asked, referring to my move to Harp Brook.

'I am but we're not far away at all.'

He grinned. 'That's the best news. You deserve some happiness.'

Kate nodded. 'I agree. Are we invited down for New Year's Eve?'

I smiled. 'Of course. You can meet Ben.'

Connor raised his glass aloft. 'Olivia, your matchmaking skills from heaven are amazing.'

Once we'd said our goodbyes and they promised to drive down on New Year's Eve, I took swig of cold tea as I tapped out, 'Hello' onto an email to Dad. He always added his address to the bottom of his Christmas and birthday cards. I added, 'Love Rachel', and pressed send.

The next morning, Grandpa and I explained to Maddie the situation with Layla. We all were drinking tea at the table and talking about the drama of Christmas Day. I'd got up early and cleared up a lot of the mess.

My sister's eyes grew wide in shock as I told her about everything Layla had been dealing with. 'I didn't know she was homeless. Frank never told me.'

'Layla needs some security and I hate to see her living with such worry.'

Maddie gave me an approving nod. 'Let me talk to her. I think she should stay here.'

'Really?'

Maddie nodded. 'She can be our housekeeper. I think I might need her when the baby arrives.'

I threw my arms around Maddie's neck. 'Thank you.'

We looked up as a worried Layla and a hobbling Derek entered the kitchen. 'I'm not disturbing anything, am I?' she said.

I led her and Derek to the table. 'Maddie wants to talk to you. Don't worry.'

Layla squealed with joy after Maddie explained about needing her to be a live-in housekeeper. 'Oh God, this is the best Christmas present ever.'

I wiped away a tear of pride as Layla hugged Maddie. Derek beamed as he and Layla jumped up and down. 'I won't let you down, Maddie.'

'I know, Layla. We can discuss pay later this evening.'

Grandpa stood up and gave Layla a hug. 'You are one of the family now.'

I placed my hand on Layla's shoulder. 'This is the start of your new life.'

Layla pointed to me. 'Maddie, your sister is an angel. She rescued me this Christmas.'

Grandpa nodded. 'And me too, Maddie. Rachel has given me a fabulous Christmas and I admit at times I have been a little wild, but she's proved to me that I still have a life to live.' He cleared his throat. 'I have an announcement to make.'

We all looked at him and I braced myself for something shocking. One thing I'd learnt from this holiday was that Grandpa was full of surprises and shocks.

'I have decided that I am not happy living in my bungalow with Aunty Karen and Uncle Robert looking after me. Maddie has kindly agreed for me to move down here. I am going to live at Harp Brook and get to know my great grandchild.'

Layla cheered and hugged Grandpa. 'Eric, that's brilliant news.'

He nodded. 'I am still engaged to Dorothy, but we are going to take things slowly.'

We all broke into a round of applause, and he did a little dance which made us all laugh. Maddie put her arm around him. 'To have my baby with my family, friends and the man I truly love here in Harp Brook is the best Christmas present ever.'

Humphrey began to bark, and I stroked him. 'Can we also give credit to Humphrey, the unsung hero. We have all wrongly assumed he's naughty. He's a little hero.' We all clapped and cheered which made Humphrey race around the kitchen in a dog victory parade.

'I bet you didn't get a chance to finish Olivia's notebook?' Ben asked, while we took Humphrey for a walk in the snow. It had been a good opportunity to tell him about everything that had happened with Maddie, Grandpa's decision, our new business venture and my conversation with Mum.

'If you must know I did finish her notebook late last night.'

'Well?' He pulled us both to a stop.

I smiled. 'She rented The Duck House years ago – didn't she?'

Ben nodded. 'When you told me about The Duck House, I wanted to tell you.'

'I'm glad you let me find out for myself. Her last chapter was about finding somewhere to heal and grow.' I recalled wiping away a tear in bed whilst reading Olivia's account of how she had moved to The Duck House after Sophie had died. She described it as the perfect place to heal all wounds and learn to live again.

He took hold of my hand. 'Are you excited about the future?'

I grinned. 'I don't think "excited" comes close to how I am feeling right now. Last night after Maddie told me about our business venture, I nearly wet myself with joy.'

Ben laughed. 'Do you have a name for this new business?'

'Harpers,' I said. 'Maddie wants us to use the west wing as she says it holds a lot of bad memories for her. I think we will start as a posh café and see what happens. We will also open the grounds to the public. This is like a dream come true for Maddie and me. We're going to speak to Abi and Darren in the bakery to see whether they'd be interested in supplying the bread.'

'I love the name,' he said, draping his arm over my shoulder. 'What about Layla and her housing situation?'

'Maddie is letting her stay at the house until she can find somewhere. She's going to be a live-in housekeeper.'

'That's great to hear. Layla deserves a break.'

'She does and I am so happy for her and Zac. He will have a little playmate once Maddie and Josh's little one arrives.'

Ben wrapped his arms around my waist. 'When do you want me to come to London with my van and help you pack up your flat?'

I leaned into kiss him. 'As soon as possible.'

'What will be my payment?' He arched his eyebrows suggestively.

'An overnight stay in The Duck House with me,' I said, before kissing him with such passion and vigour, we both nearly fell over in the snow.

'Will you be my girlfriend?' Ben asked, once we'd stopped laughing and regained our composure.

'Yes, I would love to be your girlfriend.'

Holding hands like a pair of loved-up teenagers we made our way back to the manor house. As we trudged through the snow I looked up at the sky and silently thanked Olivia, my soul sister.

You did get my smile back, Olivia. He's perfect. Have fun up there with Sophie. We will never forget you both.

ALSO BY LUCY MITCHELL

I'll Miss You This Christmas

Second Chances at the Little Love Café

The Car Share

Instructions for Falling in Love Again

ACKNOWLEDGEMENTS

Dear Reader,

Thank you so much for taking the time to read my book, *The Christmas Dog Sitters*.

A huge thank you to the Bloodhound Books team, Betsy, Clare, Tara, Hannah and Lexi.

Thank you to Huw, Seren, Flick for the love, support and for resolving my book issues in the middle of a field on a dog walk.

Thank you to Sue and Catherine for reading my first drafts and giving me your views on WhatsApp in between travelling to far flung places and juggling your own lives. I appreciate you both and Sue – I hope you take note of the order of names in the dedication.

This book started life in a coffee shop in Newport, South Wales. Thank you to Rachel Hughes for encouraging me to drink more coffee and eat more chocolate twist pastry as the idea took shape.

Thank you to Bettina Hunt for her fabulous writer support in terms of messages and video calls.

Lastly, to my mum, and sister Verity. I have made sure this book contains references to little sisters squabbling over boxes of Smarties, expensive handbags, beautiful houses and ball room dancing. Always thinking of you both back up North.

A NOTE FROM THE PUBLISHER

Thank you for reading this book. If you enjoyed it please do consider leaving a review on Amazon to help others find it too.

We hate typos. All of our books have been rigorously edited and proofread, but sometimes mistakes do slip through. If you have spotted a typo, please do let us know and we can get it amended within hours.

info@bloodhoundbooks.com

Printed in Great Britain
by Amazon